SEVEN GHOSTS

PAUL SHADINGER

A MATT PRESTON NOVEL

DEDICATION

This book is dedicated to the real Snooker, Reverend Tomas Frost. Tom was a wonderful friend who read my novels and was always encouraging. I doubt if I'd have written as many novels had it not been for his kind words, support, and pestering, always asking when I was going to finish my next novel. I'm most grateful for both his positive comments and constant beleaguering.

We lost Reverend Frost in 2021 and I wish we could have had more time to spend together. I miss you, Tom. One of my biggest regrets is that you never got to read this last novel. However, I felt you reading over my shoulder as I worked on it.

In life we meet a lot of people. Some are ships passing in the night and some become a rescue lifeboat. Who can explain why some people we meet never seem to really click, regardless of the amount of time spent together? Others from the first moment we meet it seems like we've known them all our lives. For me, Tom was that kind of person. Even though he was called to the Lord's service, he was one of the most down to Earth people I ever met. Regardless of who you were, Tom accepted you as is and never tried to change you. Perhaps that's the reason people were interested his beliefs. It would be wonderful if more people could accept each other as we are!

My biggest hope is after my time with Tom, I'm half as good a man as he thought I was.

Rest in peace Tom Frost. Matt and I will always miss you.

With love and affection,
Paul Shadinger
June 2022

PLEASE NOTE:

Seven Ghosts is a work of fiction. All names, characters, places, organizations, companies, brands, clubs, businesses, streets, and incidents are the product of the author's imagination, or are used fictitiously. Because this is a work of fiction, timelines and facts don't have to add up. Any resemblance to actual events, locals, entities, or persons, living or dead, is entirely coincidental.

If you still have issues with this novel, I invite you to reread the first line of the first paragraph. Thank you.

Matt and I would like to thank you for your interest in this novel and Matt's other adventures, all of which are available on Amazon.com.

This will be the last novel in the Matt Preston series.

Paul Shadinger
June 2022

ALSO BY PAUL SHADINGER

Fiction

Houseboat (2016)
Code Name: Crescent (2017)
The Gypsy Queen (2017)
Quick, Quick, Slow (2018)
Snooker's Legacy (2019)
347 Million (2021)

For I am the leader, I must catch up.
Our Little Bootsie

LIST OF CHARACTERS

Abigail Davis, Snowflake's neighbor

Adam Johnson, nicknamed Moose, fellow ghost

Albert Bradson, President of the United States, lawyer and old friend of Matt

Brian Polk, Captain, Fort Myers Police Department

Bruce Akioka, nicknamed Kapuna, fellow ghost

Colonel Jacob McNaulty, Matt's former commanding officer

Dominick, pilot, works for Henry and Matt

Henry Walbourn, pilot and Matt's business partner

Jamir Williams, nicknamed Snowflake, fellow ghost

Jeff L. Davenport, Commissioner of Police in Seattle, Matt's childhood friend

Jennifer Rockingham, one of Matt's love interests

John Apple Orchard, Admiral. Friend from Vietnam, now head of a super-secret federal agency

John Mescher, replaced McNaulty

John Cole, Director of the NSB, Mescher's boss

Joseph Spielman, nicknamed Talon, former ghost

Lightning, Matt's new puppy

Lois Tollifson, Matt's love interest, works for John Orchard

Martha, Matt's housekeeper

Matt McLaughlin, Little Matt Walter's Son

Max, Matt's faithful dog

NSB, National Security Bureau

Nestor Charles Bricklin, III, nicknamed Trey, fellow ghost

Salvatore Zampuchini, reputed mob boss, Matt's friend

Steve Fox, Mouse Matt's friend.

Thien McLaughlin, wife of Walter McLaughlin

Thunder, Matt's puppy

Timothy Taylor, nicknamed Bullwinkle, fellow ghost

Tuyet McLaughlin, Walter's Daughter

Val, housekeeper for Jennifer and Matt

Walter McLaughlin, buddy from Nam, fellow ghost

CHAPTER ONE

It was small article located at the bottom of the last page in the local newspaper. A very small article, what's called a filler piece and thus easy to overlook.

Since it was my turn to host our weekly card game, I was frantically cleaning the house to get ready for the guys to play poker tonight. This week Lois was in DC and tidiness had rather gone by the wayside.

I picked up the morning papers to throw them away and one page fell to the floor. I snatched it up since the puppies were still at the stage where paper on the floor must be shredded into as many pieces as possible. The small headline caught my eye: Vietnam Vet Dies Crossing Busy Street. Curious, I read the article.

The name jumped out at me: Nestor Charles Bricklin, III. Nestor had been the victim of a hit and run while crossing Del Prado, a busy boulevard in a neighboring town. The headline was partly right --- it's a busy street, but the article said the accident happened at 3:30 in the morning.

At 3:30 in the morning, that street ain't busy. You can stroll down the center line at that time of night. The last sentence said Nestor was a decorated veteran who had served three tours in Vietnam.

And that was the whole story.

But that isn't the whole story.

Not by a long shot.

Many of you know I was involved in the Southeast Asia fiasco. I was in a unit that specialized in doing weird things, many bordering on slightly illegal. One of the rules of our outfit was no one in the outfit could ever discuss what we did over there. But so much time has passed I can share some details without getting either of us killed.

Our class started with a hundred and forty-two people, but only twenty-three graduated. Unofficially, we were called ghosts. We were trained to go in, do our mission, and get out with no one the wiser. Like ghosts. Nestor was a ghost. Of the original twenty-three, three of us were still living. With Nestor gone, there are two.

I was never told exactly why, though it's easy to figure out, we weren't supposed to know each other's names. I learned Nestor's name accidentally. While we were in training, we all picked out nicknames and they were the only names we used. Disclosing your real name meant immediate dishonorable discharge. I'm not going to bore you with the details of our training except to say, look at the dropout rate. To this day I don't know how I made it.

The last time I was in D.C. with Lois, Admiral Orchard, her boss, told me, "The ghost squad is dwindling fast -- four guys have died just recently."

"How many of us are left?"

"Three," he replied.

"Is Nestor Bricklin still alive?"

"You know you're not supposed to ask questions like that, and you're not supposed to know any names," he snapped at me.

I explained to John how I learned his name.

My orders were to go somewhere our government swears we never were and do something our government swears never happened. Our CO was Colonel Jacob McNaulty. If you've followed my adventures, you've heard the name. As I was leaving on a mission, McNaulty took me aside. "If you're lucky enough to get away, stop by Xâ Pha Khinh. We sent a ghost in, but he hasn't reported back. I want you to find out what happened to him"

"Who is it?"

"Trey."

"What am I looking for? Captive, grave…?"

"Use your imagination." And that was the total information received.

My mission went well, and I escaped undetected. The village McNaulty wanted me to visit was out of the way, just a wide spot in the road. Or, more accurately, it was a wide spot by a river. There was a bend in a river and a small settlement had grown around it.

I got to the village around noon and hid for the rest of the day, watching what went on and watching for Trey. There were no VC to be seen, so I guessed he wasn't being held prisoner. Late afternoon a young woman went to the river, and I slipped up behind her. I'd learned the language well enough for simple communication. In a gentle voice, I told her not to be afraid, that I wasn't going to hurt her. I explained I was looking for somebody and asked her if there had been a stranger around recently. She was trembling with fright and didn't answer.

I asked her again, she nodded yes, she'd seen somebody.

"Do you know where he is?"

Again, she nodded.

"Is he here?" I indicated her village.

She shook her head this time.

"Is he close?"

Another nod.

"Can you take me to him?"

She started away from me, and I let her go. She stopped, and then motioned for me to follow.

We followed the river to a small clearing with a hut. Behind it were several terraced fields of rice, some chickens and a couple of goats wandering around the yard. She took me to the hut and motioned for me to come with her, then called out words I didn't understand. I went on full alert.

Another young woman with an old woman behind her came out of the hut.

The young women started to talk, but they spoke so quickly I couldn't follow. The woman from the hut figured out why I was there, and she beckoned me to follow her inside. I wasn't wild about the idea, but I followed her.

The hut was smoky and dark, but I made out a raised platform with a person laying on it. I crossed the hut and looked down into Trey's pale gaunt face. His eyes were closed, and he appeared to be in a great deal of pain.

Kneeling beside the bed, I gently put my hand on his shoulder. "Trey. Trey, it's Tudor." My nickname came from the car I had in storage back home, a 1932 Ford Tudor Street Rod. On my locker I had a picture of the '32 and when anybody asked why I picked Tudor for my nickname, I'd show them the picture of my car.

Trey opened one eye. His lips moved and he managed to whisper my name.

"What's wrong?" I asked.

He moved his head, but he couldn't talk. I asked the young woman what happened. She carefully lifted his shirt away from his body. Across his lower stomach was a large, filthy, blood-soaked bandage with flies crawling over it. I carefully lifted the bandage. There was a deep gouge running from hip bone to hip bone.

All ghosts carry an emergency first aid kit. I pulled his bandage off and the woman took it away. First, I sprayed the wound with antiseptic, then put two large bandages end to end over it. The kit also carried vials of antibiotic. I removed a syringe and filled it with the contents of one of the vials. I gave Trey a shot of antibiotics along with a couple of high-powered painkillers. The painkiller would put him to sleep for a while.

I located Trey's pack and found some more vials of antibiotics, but the syringe case was missing. I held mine up and asked if anyone knew what happened to the kit. Nobody seemed to know.

Trey was in no condition to be moved and I had no idea how safe we were. Through pantomime and my poor language skill I learned it was rare for Charlies to visit the village, but not unheard of. I wanted to take off, but I had to stick around and try to get Trey well enough to be mobile.

Three days later his fever broke. That morning when I entered the hut, he was sitting up. He was surprised to see me and even more surprised I'd been there three days. He didn't remember a thing.

The afternoon of the fourth day, I saw one of the young women returning to the village. A Charlie stepped out from a behind a tree and grabbed her. He tore off her garment and with one arm wrapped around her, he started to free himself from his pants. He was so busy he never heard me coming up behind him. I wrapped my arms around his head, made a quick twist and broke his neck. He dropped to the ground, dead. Without putting her clothing back on, she grabbed one of Charlie's arms and motioned for me to grab the other and we dragged him into the brush.

We returned to the hut as quickly as we could. When we got there, she started talking to the other young woman. Trey's language skills were much better than mine and he could communicate with them. He immediately started to stand up. "We need to go. Charlies in the village and they'll be coming here. Too many people know about me. Can you give me a hand?"

"One of them tried to rape her. I snapped his neck." I told him.

"Shit! It won't take them long to notice he's missing. Let's go." Trey muttered.

"Make sure the girls know they need to leave too. It's not safe for them to stay." I told Trey. He agreed.

Trey couldn't move very fast. I was positive we were going to get caught, but somehow, we didn't, and we made it back to the DMZ.

Trey's wound was still infected and oozing blood and puss. I got him to a field hospital where he received proper medical attention. I went to see him just before I left. He motioned for me to come close. His voice was barely a whisper. "Thank you for coming for me. I owe you big time." I shook my head.

"Look, I know we're not supposed to use our real names, but I have a fiancé back in the states and I want you to let her know what happened if I don't make it home," Trey told me.

"Trey, you're gonna be home before I am."

"Shut up Tudor. You've done so much for me I hate to ask, but please, will you do this for me?"

"I'll try."

"My name is Nestor Charles Bricklin, III. That's where Trey comes from. I'm from Minneapolis. Call any Bricklin in the phone book and they'll get you to the right people. Please tell Christina, my fiancé what happened to me and how much I love her. Tell her to have a good life. Will you do that for me?"

"Like I said Trey, you'll be home before me. But if something happens to you, I'll take care of it. Okay?"

"Promise?"

"Yes, I promise.:"

"Thanks, Tudor."

I never saw Trey again. When I got back to the states, another ghost wrote me that Trey had been wounded again and I decided to fulfill my promise to Trey. I tracked down his father and told them who I was, and that Trey had wanted me to tell Christina how much he loved her.

"That bitch!" his father growled. "She married someone else while Chuck was on his first tour. When he found out, he re-enlisted."

A lot of guys get "Dear John" letters when they're overseas. The problem is women have no idea how close to the edge men are when they're in combat. For a lot of them, getting a Dear John letter is the last straw and they go off and do something stupid, and too often get killed. Re-enlisting for Nam was a good way to get killed.

Orchard never told me whether Trey was still alive, and until I saw the newspaper article, I had no idea. The article bothered me. I wanted to know more about the hit and run. I called Brian Polk, an old friend and now a police captain in Fort Myers. The accident had taken place in Cape Coral, but Brian could get the file.

"Matt! A pleasure to hear from you. What's up?"

We bullshitted for a while and finally, I asked, "Hey, I served with the guy who was killed in the hit and run the other night over in Cape. Can you tell me anything about it?"

"I'll get the file and call you back."

He called few minutes later. "What a strange deal. They thought it was just a hit and run until they recovered the car. It was a 2004 Chrysler Sebring. An entry level car—they never get stolen. And what makes it weirder is the car hadn't been hotwired. It appears the car was started with some sort of a key machine and before the car was dumped, someone wiped it clean. And I mean, not a speck of anything in, or on the car. They even vacuumed the floor mats. Who does that?" I had no answer.

7

"You're telling me that Cape Coral thinks it was deliberate?"

"This is just between us, but yeah, they do. And all my instincts say it was deliberate. He was killed. It wasn't some hit and run, it was a targeted hit." My imagination ran wild. Why would anybody run Trey down so long after being a ghost, it was a long time ago?

"Thanks Brian. By the way, how's Doris? Are you still enjoying married life?"

His laugh was a bark. "Dude, that woman is after me all the time. I always thought it would be really cool to have a woman who wanted to make love all the time. Like they say, be careful what you wish for."

"Oh, you poor baby. I'll get you a bottle of blue pills for Christmas."

I won't tell you what he said in return, but I was laughing when I hung up.

~ ~ ~ ~ ~

I looked around the house one last time, making sure it was presentable. I'm a pig while Lois is gone. She wouldn't have approved of it tonight, but it was fine for the guys. Truthfully, I was happy to have the house to myself. Things with Lois were okay but being together so much was wearing thin.

Lois was only supposed to be gone for a week, but like all good plans, that changed. And that was the problem. I missed her when she was gone, but I wanted my space when she was with me.

I think there's something missing in my DNA. I enjoy women—no, let me rephrase that. I love women, and I don't mind living with one... for a while.

(Yeah, I know. I'm a pig. But we established that a long time ago. Remember?)

For various reasons, living with a woman gets tiresome. I know it's all on me, and I don't have an excuse. I just can't change. Or maybe it's that I don't want to change. Chalk it up to the missing DNA thing. I honestly thought it would be different with Lois.

I was wrong.

SEVEN GHOSTS

CHAPTER TWO

My poker buddies started showing up and once the game started, I tried to put Trey out of my mind; but I couldn't get into the game. Five ghosts had died in the last couple of months. Something was wrong.

"Matt. Matt." It was Dude. "Are you okay?"

"Yeah, why?"

"You had two aces showing and two wild cards and you just folded. Man, you're a million miles away," he said.

"Sorry. I had some bad news earlier. Go ahead and play without me."

Dude started laughing. "It's past 10, time to quit anyway."

"Sorry guys."

The all agreed everybody had days. They hoped tomorrow would be better and headed off.

~ ~ ~ ~ ~

My house has a doggy door which leads to a small grassy patch, but I like to walk the dogs before I turn in. Lightning pawed at my leg signaling she was ready to go out. I rounded up Thunder and got them both on their leashes. Max can't move very fast, and he tends to stay close now when we go for our walks.

My mind was still on Trey. And me. I was one of two left of the original twenty-three. I needed to warn my friend Walter McLaughlin in Washington State that something strange was going on. He was the second ghost left.

Walter and I were stationed together in Nam, and he'd saved my life. When we got home, things didn't go well for Walter. Long story short, He couldn't adapt and I helped him out of some legal difficulties and gave him some land I own on the Olympic Peninsula to settle on. He lives there with his Vietnamese wife and their two children.

I had no idea if all the deaths were a random occurrence or if something sinister was going on. I needed to warn Walter and then go and visit Admiral John Orchard. For my own peace of mind, I wanted some answers. After everything I've done for John, he owes me.

He owes me big time!

And I could spend some time with Lois. Maybe I could get a handle on what's wrong in our relationship.

~ ~ ~ ~ ~

I own a piece of a plane charter business, actually a rather large piece. I called my partner the next morning. "Henry, anything headed for D.C. soon?"

"Dominick is taking the Challenger 605 tomorrow to pick up a charter. I'll let him know you'll be joining him."

"Thanks Henry."

I called Dominick.

"Matt! How are you?" I understand you'll be joining me tomorrow."

"Yeah. What time you do you wanna leave?"

"Can you make it by nine? Is that too early for you?"

I detected a snarky tone in his voice, and I resisted making a crude comment. "I'll see you at nine."

~ ~ ~ ~ ~

I have two puppies who were rescued from a huge puppy mill by a veterinarian friend. She'd rescued forty-five puppies in varying degrees of health and the first night she had them she'd brought me the two Cocker Spaniels who were in the best condition. She just wanted me to foster them for a while, but I ended up keeping them. Max, the dog I had took to them right away and so far, there hadn't been any problems. (Knock on wood) But with puppy mill dogs, you never know.

I called Martha, my housekeeper, and asked her if she could stay a couple of days and watch the dogs.

"It always joy to watch puppies." She loves them just as much as I do.

I called Lois next and asked her if I could stay for a couple of days. She seemed pleased. I asked her not to tell her boss.

"Why?" she asked.

"I'll explain when I get there."

~ ~ ~ ~ ~ ~

The next morning, Dominick was late, and I made sure to bust his balls. "What's the matter, your friend didn't want to let you go?" I chided him.

Dominick is a handsome man with a permanent tan, dark curly hair and bedroom eyes. "I'd give you the graphic details, but I hate it when your face turns red," he retorted.

I felt my ears burning anyway. I'd asked Henry, who is gay, if Dominick was the same religion as him. Henry's answer was Dominick believed in all kinds of religions. I didn't pursue the conversation any further. I had no idea what sex Dominick's friend was, and I didn't care.

I rode in the right seat on the way up and halfway there Dominick said, "I never have properly thanked you for saving my life."

"Dominick, you owe me nothing. It was my fault you were shot. Besides, pilots who can put up with me are hard to find."

"Hey, you can say I don't I owe you all you want, but I do! Now shut up and live with it."

When I got to D.C., Lois surprised me by meeting me with a limo. As we pulled away from the curb, I noticed the windows were tinted and the window between the driver and us was closed. I realized Lois had something in mind. But at this point in our relationship, my feelings were mixed. I was having a hard time working things out in my head, I didn't need to make it any harder.

If you can't figure out what she'd planned, I'm not going to tell you.

~ ~ ~ ~ ~

We went straight to Admiral Orchard's office and Lois went back to her desk while I went in to see Admiral Johnathan Orchard. His middle name is Apple. (Yes, that's really his middle name. His parents had a sense of humor. But that gene seems to have skipped John. He hates his middle name and lacks a sense of humor.)

John embraced me and motioned for me to take a seat. "I didn't know you were coming. What brings you here?"

John and I are about the same age, but his hair has gone completely white. He wears it very short, almost as short as an army recruit. Today he was wearing a starched white shirt with a striped tie, dark blue vest and pants and polished wing-tip shoes. His jacket was on a hanger.

"I need to talk to you. Button your vest and let's go someplace private," I told John.

"How about a cup of coffee? I need a break anyway." John took his coat off the rack. We got our coffee at the same Starbucks where we'd shared other cups of coffee, then crossed the street to a park where he'd once asked me to go on a mission to Alaska.

We sat on the same bench. "Last time we were here you asked me why we had to come out here and freeze out butts off. I'm asking you the same question today."

"John, you and I go back a long way. A very long way. True?"

"Yeah, and?"

"I'm going to ask you to set aside a lot of rules. I need you to be candid."

"Matt, what are you talking about? Are you getting to the point sometime soon?"

"The last time I saw you, you told me the ghosts were dwindling quickly. Quickly enough you took notice."

"Yeah, so what?"

"Remember when I asked you about Trey? You told me he was still alive."

"Yeah, what's your point?"

"Trey died a couple of days ago down in Cape Coral. It was a hit and run."

"That's too bad. Was he crossing against the light? You tell me all the time to be careful crossing any street in Florida."

"It happened at 3:30 in the morning."

John stared at me. "How do you know?"

"An article in the local paper. If I hadn't known his real name, I'd never have noticed it. I called a friend at the Fort Myers police department. He was able to get the information. The police don't believe it was a random hit and run. And that's another ghost, gone."

Orchard whispered, "Just two left…"

"Yeah, Walter and me. I want to see all the ghosts service jackets. I want to see if there's anything strange about the way they died, like with Trey."

John was staring off into the distance. I was just getting ready to say something when he said, "Yes, that's odd. Tell you what Matt, I'll look into it and get back to you."

"No John. That's not good enough." John frowned. "I want access to the files. Now! I'll investigate it. You're a busy man. Obviously, I have a vested interest in getting to the bottom of whatever this is. I want, no, change that to I need to know what's going on. Are Walter and I in danger?"

"Have you told Walter about this?"

"I left a message on his voicemail this morning. I asked him to make sure to take precautions and then call me when he could."

"You haven't heard back yet?"

"No. But I'm not worried about him. Unless you know where you're going when you hike to his cabin, you can end up in serious trouble. Nobody is going to find him."

"Okay. Let me think about this. I'll get back to you."

He started to rise. "John, sit down!" I demanded. "You're not listening. I'm not going to let you blow me off. You're going to arrange for me to investigate what's going on. Either you, or whoever it takes is going to give me clearance to access to those files. If this means calling in all my markers, so be it. You owe me big time, my friend. Do I really have to remind you of all the things I've done for you under the table? Are you really going to make me beg?"

"Damn it Matt, you don't understand. You're asking a lot. You want to go places and look at things you're not authorized to see. Leave this alone. I'll investigate it. I promise."

"I do understand what I'm asking. And I've done a lot for you. It isn't like I haven't earned the right to ask. Grow a set of stones will ya? I need access to those files, and you're going to arrange it for me! I have a bad feeling about this and I need your help."

Orchard sat for a long time; arms folded across his chest staring off into the distance. I've seen him like this before and the only thing to do is to wait him out. There are times he can make a snap decision and times when he needs to mull things over. This was one of the times he needed to mull.

Eventually, he looked at me. His blue eyes were like ice. "Okay. I don't want to do this, but I will. Give Lois your fake credentials and I'll have her issue you legitimate creds for my department. I'll even put you on the payroll as a GS-15. That way if anybody does run a check on you, there won't be any red flags."

John heads a clandestine department with lots of letters in the name. Very few even know of the agency's existence.

"I'll have her make a list of the five ghosts who passed away recently. It will give you a starting point."

"Thanks. This is important."

John and I stood, tossed our empty cups in the trash, and headed back to his office. I knew I was lucky to have Lois in my corner. John tends to put things aside and they stall, but she had my back.

This was going to happen.

SEVEN GHOSTS

CHAPTER THREE

John made dinner reservations for Lois and me at his private club and Lois and I discussed the reason for my visit, and my chat with John over dinner. "What did John tell you about our talk?"

"He told me I was to set it up so if anybody checked on you, you'd appear to be a member of our organization. He also mentioned you needed to access some files that are deemed NTKO. Need to Know Only. In addition, he asked me to make a list of the five ghosts who've died recently. I waited till the waiter had taken our drink order, then asked her, "Were you able to get the five names?"

She reached into her purse. "Yes and no. This is a list of their real names, but I don't have any way to find out their ghost nicknames."

"Did you get my new creds?"

"Yeah, and you even get a paycheck."

"I didn't want that."

"I know, but it's important to be exactly what you claim. You're a GS-15 and you're on our roster. You should have no problem."

There were only a couple of pay grades higher than GS-15. In the world of government employees, I would have some clout. "Do I thank John for this, or do I thank you?"

"John told me to do it, but he didn't make it sound very important. I'm the one who made it happen. You know John."

"What can I do to show my appreciation?"

"Gee, I don't know honey. Let me think about it. I'll see if I can come up with something."

When we got back to her place, she came up with a way for me to thank her. Considering how things were going between us, I was surprised by her suggestion and how well it turned out.

~ ~ ~ ~ ~

My first stop was Leavenworth, Kansas, where the military records I wanted to see were kept. That meant flying to Kansas City and driving to Leavenworth. I discovered our air service didn't make a lot of flights to Kansas City. My request was only our third trip to Kansas.

At Lois' insistence, John notified the records office I was coming, and that I was authorized to see anything I wished to examine. John tried to drag his feet, which I expected, but Lois kept poking him until he did it.

My new identification said I was *director of field operations* within John's organization. A GS-15 rating is the equivalent military rank of a full bird Colonel, but the division fell under the broad umbrella of enforcement. Enforcement of what is purposely left vague. On paper I had the juice to do whatever I wanted.

My ace in the hole was newly elected President Albert Bradson's personal private phone number. I'd called the President and warned him I might need a little help with something. Albert and I go all the way back to Seattle when he opened his first office, just after law school. I had resolved a couple of issues that cropped up during the run up to the election and help resolve them for him. Let's just say he owed me one.

On the way to KC, Henry and I discussed a name for our little company. So far, we were an air service used by the government and a few people in business who knew about us. Those who used us called us "Henry's Air".

We wanted to advertise our company, but secret groups like Johns didn't want us to advertise. Many of our government customers wanted us to stay low key. We were flying to places we were not supposed to go, in planes nobody knew we had, and we were doing things we were not supposed to do. Since these secret groups kept us very busy, and even more important kept out coffers full, Henry and I didn't feel a rush to come up with a company name.

Upon my arrival in KC, I got my rental car and headed for Leavenworth. That's when I discovered there are no direct routes from the airport to Leavenworth. You drive a couple of blue roads to get there. (For those of you who don't know what a blue road is, they're the secondary roads and on the printed maps you used to get at a service station, they're printed in blue ink.)

Pulling up to the main gate at the fort, I presented my credentials to the guard who examined them carefully, came to attention, saluted, and passed me through. I found the correct building and parked. At the front door, a guard relieved me of my briefcase and put it through a scanner and I walked through another. An attractive young woman in uniform met me on the other side. Her blond hair was cut short, and her blue eyes looked at me through gold rimmed glasses. She had a nice smile, and I liked the way she filled out her uniform. (Of course, I'm going to notice that!) The uniform was army, three stripes up, one down. Her name tag indicated she was Sergeant Small.

As I recall, there weren't any sergeant's that looked like Sgt. Small when I was in the Army.

Before we left the entrance, she asked, "May I see your identification?" I handed everything to her. When she read my authorization, her eyes widened. "Follow me sir."

We took an elevator deep into the basement and when it finally stopped, we walked down a long hall to door guarded by a MP. He came to attention and the put out his left hand. "Sir, may I see your identification?" he carefully inspected it and waved me forward. I was cleared.

Sergeant Small opened about four different locks and finally led me into a huge room with rows and rows of filing cabinets. "What exactly are you looking for sir?"

"I'm looking for a roster of the Phoenix Project during the Viet Nam war."

She seemed surprised. "Just a minute, let me see what I can find." She sat down at her computer, typed, and studied the screen. "I understand you've been granted special access but the file you're requesting requires security clearance well above GS - 15."

I was surprised. John said he'd cleared me for everything. Trying to get ahold of him to straighten this out would take a lot of time. I wanted access *now*. Time to cash in a marker. I handed Sergeant Small a piece of paper with a phone number on it, President Bradson's phone number. "You need to make a phone call. I'm authorized to see those files and anything else I want to see. Call this number."

"Whose number is it?"

"The President."

"The president of what, sir?" She queried with a smart-assed attitude I didn't care for.

"The President of the United Sates, President Albert Bradson."

She leaned back in her chair. "Bull-shit!" She blushed and said, "Excuse me. That just popped out. But I have a hard time believing this is the President's phone number." She waved the paper at me.

"Just call." There was indecision on her face. "Call." I barked.

She dialed the number and asked for President Bradson. She was put on hold and when Bradson answered, I could hear him. "This is President Bradson."

She sat up and stuttered, "I... I have a Matt Preston here. He wants to see some files, but he doesn't have clearance. When I told him that, he asked me to call this number."

The President asked, "Who is this?"

"My name is Staff Sergeant Lenora Small, sir."

"Sergeant Small, if you still want to be a sergeant to-morrow, help Mr. Preston in any way you can. If he tells me you're obstructing his investigation, I assure you that you will be on your way out of the Army. Am I making myself clear?"

"Yes sir. I'm sorry to have bothered you. Goodbye sir."

When she hung up, her hand was shaking. I considered being snarky and saying, *I told you so*, but I took the high road.

She asked, "Who the hell are you?" But her phone rang, and I didn't have to explain. It was the president's secretary. Sergeant Small assured her I would be well taken care of.

She shook her head and remarked, "I'd love to know exactly who you are sir. You look a little old to be a spy or something."

"Let's just say back in the day I was an underwater as-sassin in Viet Nam, and let it go at that?"

"Huh? That doesn't make sense."

"I was a bandsman too." The look on her face was price-less. "And anything else I told you wouldn't make sense ei-ther, so let's just get on with it."

She shrugged and asked to see my credentials again, this time pulling one of the cards from the pack. "What are you going to do with that?" I asked.

"I must use it to check out the file you want. I'll be right back."

Sergeant Small returned carrying a metal box. She motioned for me to follow her. As we wandered through filing cabinets, I thought her uniform fitted her bottom very well which was replaced by the thought that I should be ashamed. She is young enough to be my daughter.

She stopped at an old microfiche machine. "I'll be right back," she said. When she came back, she had a key that unlocked the box. She opened it, flipping through the contents and came up with a roll of microfilm. "Do you know how to use the machine?" she asked.

"I was running one of these before you were a gleam in your daddy's eye."

She turned red. "Excuse me, I'm used to people not having a clue how to run one. If you need anything else, I'm up front."

It took a long time before I found the listing of personal from the Phoenix project. The first thing I did was look up my own name and read my bio. On my bio page, I noticed a mark in the upper right-hand corner. It looked like a star, but it was a fat, fluffy star with a face on one of the points. Eventually, it occurred to me it was a cartoon of a ghost, hence the face. After I figured that out, it was a lot easier to find what I wanted. I went to Walter's file next. His had the same symbol. The file gave me his ghost name: Dog. Walter had a long face and with his big brown eyes, he looked like a sad puppy.

I looked up Trey, and there was the same mark in the corner. I was on to something. He was still listed as alive and I wasn't surprised, but I wondered how often the files were updated.

I started at the beginning, checking each name for the symbol and against Lois's list. The first name I found in both places was Akioka, Bruce, AKA Kapuna. Bruce was a Pacific Islander from the big island in Hawaii and because he was a surfer, the crew at first called him Kahuna. Bruce wasn't a large man, but what he could do with his hands and feet was frightening. Later when we found out he had been a world champion surfer we started calling him Big Kahuna. He finally explained the word Kahuna means Witch Doctor, it had nothing to do with surfing. If they meant the leader in a village, the word they were looking for was Kapuna, the senior person, or Kapuna of a village. Apologies were offered and accepted. From that moment on he was Kapuna. He was a couple of years older than the rest of us anyway and the name just fit. He was quiet, but there something about him that made you want to treat him with respect. He was listed as still alive, but John told me he was dead. I took out my cell phone and took pictures of his file.

The next name I found was Johnson, Adam, AKA Moose. We called him Moose because he was a big guy, just a fraction under the height limit for service. He'd been playing college ball, but his grades were too low, and his coaches were fudging things to keep him eligible. It caught up with him and he was kicked out of school. The army found out and drafted him. How he made it through ghost school was beyond me. For Moose to go out in the field and stay hidden was a miracle. No way could he hide in a bush --- he'd have to pretend to be a tree. He was also listed as alive.

I kept searching and found Taylor, Timothy, AKA Bullwinkle. Taylor hung out with a guy we called – naturally – Rocky because he was lightening quick and really squirrelly. Rocky never made it through the school, but Taylor's name of Bullwinkle stuck.

Taylor didn't look anything like the cartoon moose, he looked more like a mouse. Where Moose Johnson had pushed the upper limits of size, Bullwinkle was on the low end the of the size spectrum. He was a skinny little guy, but he could run all day with a heavy pack, and ate enough food for three people, but never gained an ounce. Looking at him, it was obvious his nickname had nothing to do with his size.

One thing about Bullwinkle was how tough he was. I saw him get in a fight with three marines one night and he cleaned their clocks. They were so embarrassed by the beating they took; no charges were ever filed. There was no date listed for his death, which wasn't strange.

The last name I found was Williams, Jamir, AKA Snowflake. In our politically correct world today his nickname wouldn't be allowed since it was totally racist. Jamir was the darkest man I'd ever seen. He picked his own name. I guess he was afraid if he let anybody else pick it, it would be far worse than Snowflake. He was a big guy, soft-spoken. When he did talk, he showed a high degree of intelligence and you always wanted to listen to him. There was no date of death listed for him either.

I leaned back in my chair, folded my arms across my chest, and closed my eyes, remembering the various individuals I served with. In an instant I was back in-country. I could feel the heat, the humidity and smell of the jungle and rotting foliage. It was all so vivid. My mind was no longer in Kansas but in some isolated jungle in Viet Nam. I shook my head.

I wondered if there were up to date files on these men. Four men, all dead. Five if you counted Trey. Five members of an elite super-secret group that died within a couple of weeks of each other. Five men who had worked together in-country. I ask you, what are the odds?

I had taken cell phone pictures of all the service records, and I had enough information to start asking questions. I stood, stretched, and then reached alongside of the machine to turn it off. Accidentally I bumped the advance button and another file appeared.

Spielman, Joseph David. AKA Talon. Ol Joe looked like a hawk, but we already had a Hawk, so he ended up being Talon. He was the only ghost listed as MIA. He hadn't returned from his last mission and his body was never recovered. He disappeared without a trace, and I asked our CO about him one time and his reply was, "That's none of your fucking business, Tudor." It was the one and only time he'd ever spoken to me like that.

I removed the roll of film from the machine and put it back in the box. I noticed a piece of paper on the bottom. It was supposed to be a list of everyone who'd checked out the file, but the bottom half of the paper was missing. I wondered what other names had been on that piece of paper and who had seen the file.

I found Staff Sergeant Small at her desk.

"Are you finished sir?"

"I have a couple of questions. May I?"

"Yes."

"The bottom of the sign out sheet is missing. Any idea who else checked the file out?"

"That's strange. I didn't notice it was torn. I'm sorry sir but I have no idea who else checked it out. The woman who used to work here was killed in a car crash. I've been here less than a month. I can ask my supervisor."

"How was she killed?"

"I was told she lost control of her car and ran into a tree at high speed."

I handed her the box. "Some of the people on that list are dead. Can you find out the dates of their deaths?"

"Let me check, sir." Sgt. Small typed in a few commands. "I'll need the names of the people you want to know about."

I gave her the names and thanked her for her help. She handed back the list. "They are still listed as alive. But then I have no idea who has access to these files, and I don't know who would update them." She paused, "If I asked you a question, would you answer me?" It was obvious she was consumed with curiosity.

"Tell you what Sergeant, let's not find out. That's easier on both of us."

It was obvious she still had questions, but I had to give her credit, she kept silent.

When I got to my car, I decided to check on Walter again, but my call went straight to voicemail. His cell service is spotty at times, and I promised myself I'd try again later.

I wanted to start looking into the deaths of my ex-service mates. The closest one was Snowflake. The address listed for him was in Kansas City. Since I had to go back to Kansas City to catch my plane, it made sense to start my investigation with him.

CHAPTER FOUR

On my way to Snowflake's house, I tried calling Walter's cell phone again and was pleasantly surprised when he answered.

"Matt, nice to hear from you."

"Did you get my message?"

"Yeah. But dude, why are you worried? You know the trail to the cabin is boobytrapped."

"I wanted you to know I've discovered some strange recent happenings about our old unit."

"Really? Like what?"

"In less than two months, five of us have mysteriously died. You and I are the only ones left. Do you remember Trey?"

"Yeah, you helped him out on one of your missions. What about him?"

"There was an article in the local newspaper about him. Trey died crossing a street in Cape Coral."

"So what? I've heard you bitch how crummy drivers are down there. What's so unusual about Trey getting killed crossing a street? Was it a busy street?"

"Yes, an extremely busy street."

"So, what's the issue?"

"Trey was killed at 3:30 in the morning by a stolen car."

"Was it a hit and run?"

"It was a hit and run and I called a friend on the Fort Myers police force. Unofficially, they think it was murder."

"You said five deaths. Who were the other four?"

"Moose, Bullwinkle, Kapuna and Snowflake. Snowflake lived in KC and that's where I am now. I'm going to see what I can find out."

"You said Kapuna?"

"Yeah, why?"

"Damn! We did a mission together one time. Long story short, it got really ugly, and he bailed me out. I should be dead. I've always felt beholden. Damn, damn! I hate to hear he's dead. Always wanted to find him and see how his life turned out and thank him again."

"I'll let you know what I find out about the others."

"What do you mean? What are you doing?"

"I want to know how they died. Trey's death is weird. A hit and run at 3:30 in the morning? A stolen car the kind of car thieves don't usually steal! Wiped totally clean! That's strange. I don't think it was an accident and neither do the police."

"I agree."

"I've been able to get addresses for the other four and I'm going to see what I can find out."

"Do me a favor and watch yourself."

"The same back at ya. Say hi to Thien and the kids."

"Is Lois with you?"

"No!" I thought about saying more but stopped. "I'm alone."

"Problems?"

"I really don't want to get into it right now. Okay?"

"It's cool. Please be careful." I was about to end the call when Walter shouted, "Stop. Are you there?"

"Yeah. What?"

"Look, I know you're busy and you know how grateful I am about the money you send us every month and all..."

"Yeah, and...?"

"We've been putting the bread aside for the kid's education, so this next question is more for them than for me."

"And?"

"There haven't been any deposits for a couple of months."

"No shit? I didn't know that. Let me check with my bank and find out why."

"Do you ever communicate with Jennifer?"

"Haven't spoken to her in a couple of years. I need to see if everything is okay with her. I don't understand why the deposits stopped."

"I'm sorry to bother you. I know you're busy. Go, find out what's up with our fellow ghosts dying."

"No, it's cool. I'm glad you said something. Something might be wrong. I'll get back to you."

Jennifer is a woman I helped a long time ago. Her father was murdered, and I helped the police solve the murder. Her father had been a wealthy man and there was some question regarding the estate. I helped her receive her inheritance and since she was already a wealthy woman, and because I'd helped her, she started sending me a check every month for a vulgar amount of money. I didn't need the money, so I'd been depositing it in an account earmarked for Walter's kids for college.

Something else to solve along the way, like I didn't have enough on my plate.

~ ~ ~ ~ ~

SEVEN GHOSTS

Thanks to the Garmin that came with the rental I found Snowflake's house without problem. The house wasn't in the best neighborhood, but it was clean and tidy. The yard needed a little attention and there were some weeds in a few small flower gardens. There was a for sale in the front yard with a realtor's name and phone number. I parked on the street and walked up to the front door.

Just as I was about to knock, I heard a woman's voice behind me. "Ain't nobody there mister."

I turned and saw a slim, older African American woman with streaks of grey in her hair in the yard next door. She was wearing a dark blue patterned dress and a white sweater. Her black shoes were well worn, and she was leaning on a cane, but her eyes were bright and intelligent behind her glasses.

"Good afternoon ma'am. Does anybody still live here?" I asked.

"You need to come closer. My hearing ain't too good."

I crossed the yard and joined her. "Does anyone still live here?"

"Mr. Williams owns that house. Jamir Williams. A fine man he was, too. He's dead now. What do you want with Mr. Williams?"

"Sno— I mean Jamir and I were in the service together. I just found out where he lived, and I stopped by to say hello."

"You were with him in the Navy?"

"No ma'am, we were in the Army."

She nodded. "What did you play?"

"Ma'am?"

"You said you were in the same outfit as Mr. Williams. He played in the band. What did you play?"

"Oh! I played piano and drums. When we marched, I played drums and for stage band I played the piano." I'd told the lie so many times I didn't have to think about it.

"I never heard Mr. Williams play the clarinet. He any good?"

"He was great. He played extremely well."

"What did you say your name was?"

"I didn't. My name is Matt Preston."

"Well Mr. Matt Piano Man, you're full of shit! Mr. Williams didn't play clarinet, he played trombone. The band story was a cover story anyway. Now what's your business with Mr. Williams?"

If Jamir had told this woman what he'd done in the army, I supposed I could do the same.

"Yeah. Jamir and I were in the same outfit in 'Nam and the band was our cover story."

"If you were with him in Vietnam, you should know his other name."

"We called him Snowflake. He picked the name because he didn't want to get stuck with something more offensive."

"Like that name wasn't offensive?"

I smiled and shook my head. "Like I said, he picked it. And I know it was offensive. That's how things were back then."

"Let's say I believe you. What are you doing here?"

"I just found out about his death. I'm trying to find out how he died."

"He was shot."

"I knew that. What I want to know is, what were the circumstances?"

"It was a drive by shooting. And he was…" She stopped, turned and started to walk away.

"Stop! You started to say something, but you stopped. What were you going to tell me?"

"The best thing you can do is get your car and drive away. This isn't a neighborhood you want to spend time in— you're not welcome here."

"Ah, Mrs…"

"Davis. My name is Abigail Davis."

"Is there a Mr. Davis?"

"He died from a heart attack six years ago. Mr. Williams has been looking out for me. His wife died of cancer a few years back. We talk. He confided in me what he did in the army when he was over there in that awful place."

"Mrs. Davis, you started to tell me something about the shooting, what was it?"

"It was supposed to look like Mr. Williams was killed in a drive by. I was at my kitchen sink when it happened. It was a white man. I didn't even tell the police. They're not going to do anything about a white man shooting a Black man."

I tried to look as trustworthy as I could. (Or at least as trustworthy as a white man can be to an older woman of color.) "Please tell me about it. What did you see?"

Her voice was soft, and I had to strain to hear her. "A white man was sitting in his car in the alley. You don't see a lot of white men in the neighborhood, anyway, especially not watching a house." It seemed like Mrs. Davis suddenly became aware she was telling a white man what she saw. She stopped speaking.

"Go on, Mrs. Davis. What happened?"

"Are you going to tell the police what I'm telling you?"

"Not if you don't want me to. Please go on."

"Well, Mr. Williams, he rides the bus. The stop is at the end of the alley, just around the corner."

The look on her face told me how difficult it was for her to tell her tale.

"Mr. Williams always comes up the alley from the bus. When he passed the car, the man inside said, "Williams! Hey, Snowflake!

"Mr. Williams turned, and the man in the car shoots him in the chest. He gets out of the car and asks Mr. Williams if he remembers something. I couldn't hear what. I didn't hear Jamil's answer either. But when he answered, the white man shoots him in the head. Then he spit on Jamil got in his car and drove away."

"What do you think Jamil said?"

"My hearing isn't so good. It sounded like Mr. Willimas said, 'Tell him', and then, 'Don't do this, please tell him.'"

"Tell him?'"

"That's what it sounded like. But I can't be sure."

"What did he look like?"

"Tall and kinda skinny. His clothes were old. He had marks on his face, and he didn't walk right."

"Marks? Like tattoos?"

"No, like deep scars."

"And you didn't tell the police any of this?"

"I don't need the problems."

I understood what she was saying. "Mrs. Davis, you've been a big help. I promise I won't tell the police about our conversation." I pointed to the house behind her. "Is that your house?" It was, and I took note of her address. I pulled out my wallet and withdrew a card along with a hundred-dollar bill I keep hidden. "If you can think of anything else, please call me."

She looked down at the bill in her hand. With surprise on her face, she asked, "What's the money for?"

"In case you remember something, that's to pay for the phone call."

"They don't charge for long distance anymore."

"Consider it a thank you trusting me enough to tell me what you saw."

"What are you gonna do now, Mister Piano Man?"

"More guys have died lately under strange circumstances, like Mr. Williams. I'm looking into it. But you're right, it wasn't some drive by shooting. He was murdered."

"I knew that Mr. Piano Man." Mrs. Davis turned and headed for her front porch. "Have a good day."

"And you as well."

Before I drove away, I put Mrs. Davis' address in my wallet. I was going see to it that she got a good hearing aid.

35

SEVEN GHOSTS

CHAPTER FIVE

I felt I was on to something. I got out of the neighborhood, pulled into a parking lot and dug out my cell phone. The next closest ghost was Bullwinkle in Denver. I decided to drive.

Once on the road, I called Walter and told him what I'd just learned.

"Who do you think shot him?" Walter asked.

"I don't know. The fellow who shot Snowflake had a lot of scars on his face and a limp. That description doesn't ring any bells for me. You?"

"Nope. Where ya going now?"

"Denver. That's where Bullwinkle lived."

"Not to be a pest, but did you check and see if Jennifer was okay? I'm not reminding you because I want the money."

"I know Walter. I'll call the bank when I get a second. I'm worried, too. But what with this crap about ghosts dying, I need you to keep reminding me. Thanks."

"I don't want to make you angry."

"No sweat. I'll call you and let you know what I find out in Denver."

"Thanks. And thanks for the phone call."

~ ~ ~ ~ ~

Unless you enjoy flat and tan, there's not a lot to see in Kansas from a freeway. The joke in Kansas is my dog ran away and I could still see it two days later.

Driving along, I let my mind wander to an afternoon back in Seattle when I watched a tall, dark-haired beautiful woman stroll through a restaurant and every male in the place watched her. Jennifer knew how to make an entrance. I'd enjoyed our lunch and I was happy I was able to help her. I hoped there was nothing amiss with her as she was one of my favorite daydreams. I always wondered what would have happened if we'd done the big nasty. But she had two lovers back in Europe, one of each sex. And I can't compete with that.

Halfway across Kansas I remembered another trip I'd done driving across the state and how boring it was.

Guess what?

Driving across Kansas is still boring.

~ ~ ~ ~ ~

Many cities complain about their infrastructure. Denver is right up there. The roads are atrocious. The freeways feel more like a heavily potholed country road. Considering their weather I understand, but it doesn't make the ride any more comfortable.

The place I was looking for was in Lakewood, which is Southwest Denver. It was an attractive condo complex. I found the street I wanted, parked and started walking down the side street that serviced his condo. I lucked out and found a man washing his car in the street.

"Howdy," I greeted him.

"Hello." He turned off the water. "I don't think I've ever seen you before."

"No, Tim Taylor is an old army buddy of mine. I know he lives on this street, but I can't seem to find his place."

"You're correct, it was Taylor's Street. He doesn't live here anymore."

"Did he move?" Of course, I knew better, but I wanted to see what he might tell me.

"You could say that."

"Where did he move to?"

"I understand they buried him with his kinfolk out in Washington State somewhere."

I tried to act surprised. "Buried? What? When did that happen?"

"Almost two months now, since he died."

"What happened?"

"They say it was a heart attack, but I'm not so sure."

"Can you think of anyone who might know what happened?"

"Well, Mr. Keys knew him better than anybody else around here. They were really good friends."

"Where would I find Mr. Keys?"

"You might still find him in the morgue."

"The morgue?"

"Yeah, he was killed the other day in a hit and run. Happened late one night, or I guess I should say, early one morning."

"This is important—do you know who the investigating agency was? What city was he in when he got killed?"

"Well," he said, "My guess would be the Lakewood police department. I'm not sure where he was when he got hit."

"Thank you."

At the police department I parked in the visitor's lot and entered the building. A pleasant looking woman in uniform was behind the desk.

"How may I help you sir?"

"I just got into town, and I wanted to see an old army buddy. I found out he was killed in a hit and run. Nobody seems to know much about it, and I was wondering if I could speak to the investigating officer."

"What was your friend's name?"

"Keys."

She wrote it down on a pad in front of her. She looked up at me. "First name?"

I didn't know his first name. The fellow on the street just called him Mr. Keys. "I don't know."

She looked at me over the top of her glasses. "Excuse me? This was an old friend, and you don't know his first name?" I shook my head. "Have a seat. I'll see what I can do."

She sounded like an elementary school secretary, and I was going in to see the vice-principal for some rule infraction.

I waited for about an hour before a large African American came out. "I'm Captain Harris. The desk sergeant said you were asking about Mr. Keys. What's your interest?"

"Is there a place where we can speak in private?" I asked.

He looked at me strangely and then motioned for me to follow. "Come on."

He led me to a small room with a well-used table and four chairs, two on each side. He motioned for me to sit, and he took a seat on the other side. "Now what is it you want?"

I pulled my cred pack and laid it on the desk. Officer Harris looked it over very carefully and put it back on the desk. "So you have some juice. What do you want?"

I handed him a piece of paper. "If I asked you to call a captain in the Fort Myers PD, would you do it?"

"Why?"

"I'm going to tell you a couple of things I'm not supposed to."

Captain Harris leaned back in his chair, motioning for me to continue.

"When I was in the service I served in Viet Nam. I was part of a super-secret group that even today the government says never existed. A few days ago, another guy who was in the unit was killed in a hit and run in Florida. The accident happened around three in the morning and the car had been stolen and when the police found it, the car had been wiped clean.

"I came to Denver to investigate the death of another soldier from my unit. He was supposed to have died of a heart attack. Mr. Keys knew him the best and I wanted to interview Keys. Now I'm told Keys was killed in a hit and run. There seems to be a lot of hit and runs lately. I was hoping somebody might give me some information about it."

Harris held up the piece of paper with Polk's number on it. "Why do you want me to call this fellow in Florida?"

"He can confirm what I told you about the Florida death."

"Okay, let's say I believe you. What do you want from me?"

"Were you the investigating officer in Keys' hit and run?"

"Yes."

"Did you find the car?"

"We did."

"It was an older Chrysler Sebring 2000?" I volunteered.

He just stared at me. I assumed that was an affirmative answer.

I continued, "And the car was wiped totally clean, it appears to have been started with some sort of a key machine. It hadn't been hotwired."

"How do you know all of this?"

"The hit and run car in Florida was the same make and model and in the same condition when it was found."

"What's the name of the man you're here to investigate?"

"Taylor, Tim Taylor." I gave Harris the telephone number.

"I'll be right back."

41

Right back turned out to be just under an hour. "Sorry about the wait. Can I get you a soft drink or water or…?"

"I'm good. What did you find out?"

"I found the initial interview sheet between Keys and one of the officers who investigated Taylor's death."

I opened the folder and started to read.

> OFFICER: *"Why did you contact us?"*
>
> KEYS: *I was told Taylor died of a heart attack.*
>
> OFFICER: *The way you say it, I get the feeling you don't agree."*
>
> Keys: *"I'm no doctor, but he was pretty damn healthy for his age. Shit, he ran almost every day.*
>
> OFFICER: *"There was a fellow a few years back that ran all the time and he dropped dead of a heart attack.*
>
> KEYS: *Look officer, I knew Tim pretty well. We drank a lot of beer together. Right before his supposed heart attack he had his annual physical. The doctor told him how healthy he was. Said he had the body of a man half his age. There was no sign of any heart problems.*
>
> OFFICER: *Who said he had a heart attack?*
>
> KEYS: *The EMT'S that came out to pick up the body. They checked him out and said he died from a heart attack.*
>
> OFFICER: *Who called them? Who found the body?*
>
> KEYS: *I don't know. I didn't know anything was wrong until I saw the ambulance parked in front of his house and the EMT's bringing the body out."*

OFFICER: You don't know who found the body? Did he have a wife?"

KEYS: He had a lady friend, but they broke up a few months back. He wanted to marry her, but she said she'd never get married again. They had a big fight over it, and she moved out.

OFFICER: So, you have no idea who found him?"

KEYS: No. And I think it's kinda weird.'

OFFICER: Why?"

KEYS: Well, I was as close to him as anybody and I asked around, but nobody seems to know who found the body or called the medics."

OFFICER: Were the police called?"

KEYS: "I don't know. A police officer did show up, but the EMT told the cop it was a heart attack."

OFFICER: Do you recall where the EMT's were from?"

KEYS: Nope. But it wasn't a normal EMT vehicle like from the fire department. It was a private ambulance."

OFFICER: And you don't remember the name?"

KEYS: Sorry. It looked like an old station wagon with a red cross on it. Oh yeah, and there were no red lights on it either."

I put the folder back on the desk. "It looks like you have no idea who took the body."

"That's why I was gone so long. I was trying to see what I could find out."

"And?"

"Nothing. Sorry."

"What did the autopsy show?"

"There was no autopsy."

"What? Why not?"

"I don't really know. The body just showed up at the morgue. There's an intake sheet listing the cause of death as a heart attack, and there was a signature from the attending physician. There was no reason for an autopsy."

"Thanks Captain, I appreciate your help."

"I did call your friend Captain Polk. He told me some interesting things about you."

The smile left his face, "Look mister there's something strange about the way Taylor died. Our unofficial feeling is your buddy was murdered.

"I'm not at liberty to tell you much, but I can tell you, I agree something is very wrong and that's why I'm investigating his death.

I thanked Harris for his time and left. I was satisfied that Taylor was killed. I didn't know how, but I was positive it had something to do with being a ghost.

I decided my next stop was going to be Hawaii. I headed to the Denver airport and called Henry. "When's the soonest somebody can pick me up in Denver?"

"Where you wanna to go?"

"Hawaii."

"We have at least two or three flights to Hawaii a week."

I was stunned.

"It's a popular destination. If you can get over to the Rocky Mountain Metropolitan Airport in the next hour, you can catch a ride right now."

On the way to the airport, I made arrangements with Martha to stay at the house and watch the dogs for a while longer. I dropped the rental car and ran for the plane. I'd just fastened my seat belt and we were moving.

Damn, I love having access to a private plane.

CHAPTER SIX

It doesn't matter if you're sitting in the back of the plane or sitting in the right-hand seat, the flight to Hawaii is boring. You can only look at so much blue ocean and white caps before you get bored. Really bored.

I was glad when we arrived. I rented a car and debated whether to see Kapuna's sister or talk to the police first. I decided my best course of action was to learn as much from his sister as I could. The sister's house was small, as were all the houses on the street. All were well maintained.

I parked in the street. Approaching the house, I stepped up to the screen and knocked. A heavyset Pacific Island woman with long flowing white hair came to the door.

"Yes, may I help you?"

"Hi. My name is Matt Preston. I'm looking for Bruce Akioka's sister. Are you his sister?"

"No, I'm his ex-wife. My name is Vivian, Vivian Akioka. Why are you looking for Bruce's sister?"

"Bruce died recently, and I have questions about his death. I hoped his sister might be able to help."

"His sister lives on the other side of the island. You know he committed suicide?"

47

"I know there was a report that said he committed suicide. Can you tell me anything about it?"

"Yeah! He didn't commit suicide. We were divorced, but we were still friends. Bruce would never commit suicide. He was happy, well-adjusted and had no reason to kill himself. Would you like to come in?" I entered and Vivian pointed to a large couch.

"May I get you something to drink?" she asked.

"No, I'm fine."

"You never told me why you're looking into his death."

It was decision time. How much did I want to share with Vivian? "Did you know what Bruce did over in Viet Nam?"

"Yeah. He was in some special thing that he wasn't supposed to talk about. But you can't be married as long as we were and not learn something about each other. Why do you ask?"

"I was in Viet Nam with Bruce."

"What was your name?"

"Matt, Matt Preston."

"No! I mean your name over there. I know what they called Bruce. What were you called?"

"I was called Tudor, because of my car."

She laughed. "That was you?" I looked at her strangely. "Bruce told me about a fella who had a picture of a car in his locker. He had a picture of me naked wearing a little grass skirt in his locker. Most of the other guys had pictures of women, but you had a picture of a car. He couldn't remember your name, but he talked about you a lot. He always called you The Car Guy. Bruce also spoke about someone called Dog."

"That's Walter."

"Bruce said he wasn't supposed to know real names. But he knew Dog's name because that wonderful man saved his life."

"Walter said it was the other way around. Bruce saved Dog's life. I have a question. You said Bruce didn't commit suicide and you seem very sure. Why?"

"Mr. Tudor, I'm a retired nurse. I have seen lots of things in my life, and I can tell when a person is considering taking his life, or if he is even close to killing himself. Kapuna, as you call him, was very content with his life. He'd put things he did over in that awful place away and made peace with it.

"He lived out by the beach. One day he saved a young woman who was surfing. They ended up living together and she'd do anything for him. Do you know what it's like to have a beautiful young woman doting on you?" I indicated I could guess. "She waited on him hand and foot. He was so happy. He wanted for nothing. He had no reason to kill himself."

"Do you think she would talk to me?"

"I'll go with you. We're friends."

We got into my rental and with her directions, we drove to the young woman's place. Vivian told me, "Bruce called her Lani, which means heavenly woman. I never knew her real name."

"You know what we called Bruce?"

"You called him Kapuna and that meant a lot to him. Around here he was the Big Kahuna. His neighbors looked up to him, he was both a leader and big medicine. When you talk to people who knew him, you'll see he had no reason to commit suicide."

I pulled up in front of another house on posts; this one was completely open under the house. It had a thatched roof with a veranda that circled the house, and chickens running around under it.

A well-tanned blonde woman came out of the house. She was stunning. Barefoot, bare breasted with a long bright-colored piece of cotton about her waist. She was one of the most beautiful women I'd ever met.

"Hello Vivian. What brings you out here?"

"Lani, this is someone from Bruce's past. He knew Bruce in the service. Tudor."

Lani's eyes opened wide, and then she smiled. "The car guy? Kapuna spoke of you many times. You had a friend named Dog and the two of you were very kind to him in the war."

"Kapuna? You called him Kapuna?"

"He liked Kapuna better than Bruce. Everybody here in the village called him Kapuna or Big Kahuna. Sometimes he would smoke a little bud and share some of the things he did with me. He was a special man. I was lucky to spend the time with him that I did."

"I assume you don't think he committed suicide."

"No fucking way!" she snapped. "Excuse my language. But there was no way he killed himself. He really was our village Kapuna. People came to him for advice. He held this village together. He would never consider suicide. If he *had* committed suicide, he wouldn't have done it with a bunch of pills. He would have used one of his pistols. But it doesn't matter - the police won't help us. Why are you asking about it?"

I decided I was going to be honest. "Did you know what we were called over in Nam?"

Lani answered, "You were called ghosts."

"A few days ago, a ghost was killed in a hit and run. Another ghost was supposedly killed in a drive by. A third was supposed to have been a heart attack. The problem is the body just showed up at the morgue with an intake sheet all filled out. There was no autopsy, and he was cremated so it can't be proven he was killed. I believe they were all murdered."

Lani had tears running down her face. "I knew it. I knew he didn't commit suicide."

"Do you have any more questions?" Vivian asked.

I shook my head.

"Why don't you go. I'm going to stay here. I'll find a way home."

I'd been dismissed.

Call me a pig, but Lani was breathtaking. If I was waking up every morning and seeing her in bed with me… well, I damn sure wouldn't be considering suicide. There was no way Kapuna had committed suicide with somebody like Lani waiting at home.

~ ~ ~ ~ ~

I thought my next stop ought to be the police.

I try not to be judgmental, but sometimes stereotypes are spot on. The desk sergeant was a caricature of a fat donut eating cop. There was even a box of Krispy Kreme donuts on his desk.

But I kept my opinion to myself.

I said, "I'd like to talk with whoever is handling the Bruce Akioka investigation."

"That would be Sergeant Kahale. He's off until tomorrow. What's your interest in the Akioka case? It's a suicide."

I handed him my cred pack. "I'm investigating the death. Mr. Akioka was in the service and served in Viet Nam. We've been looking into suicides of vets from that era." I hoped the desk officer bought it.

"Do you have a card?"

"Yes. Here's my cell phone number. Would you ask Sergeant Kahale to call me when he gets in?"

"Yeah." The way he said it didn't give me a lot of confidence.

Our air service has an arrangement with a hotel in town. We get a good deal on rooms and in turn, we recommend the hotel to our passengers. It's very nice with an excellent restaurant and I arranged for a room. After a great dinner, I crashed. I was operating on a different time zone, and it was after my bedtime.

I was having breakfast when my cell phone rang.

"Good morning. My name is Sergeant Haverly Kahale. I'm told you have questions about Bruce Akioka?"

"Yes sir." I went into my spiel about looking into suicides.

"I'm sorry you came all the way over here. You've just wasting your time. We don't discuss ongoing cases. Have a nice day." The phone when dead.

Excuse me?

Since when do they have an ongoing case with an open and shut suicide? That didn't sound right to me.

I finished my breakfast and since it was just a few blocks back to the station I walked over. Today there was a different desk sergeant on duty, but he seemed to be cut from the same mold as yesterday's overweight officer. At least this time there wasn't a doughnut box in sight. "May I help you?"

"I'd like to see Sergeant Kahale." I showed the desk sergeant my creds.

"Why do you want to see him?"*Regarding*

"I'm sorry, I'm not at liberty to discuss that with you. May I please see Sargent Kahale?"

"Just a sec." The desk sergeant held his hand over his mouth when he made the call. He hung up the phone and said, "Go wait on the bench and someone will be out to talk to you."

My radar went off. Something wasn't right. I pulled out my cell phone and dialed Admiral Orchard. The call went straight to voicemail. "John, this is Matt. I'm at the Honolulu police station and I think I'm going to need the cavalry. The officer who investigated Akioka won't speak to me. I'm waiting to talk to someone at the station and I have a feeling something bad is going to happen. Use your magic and give me a hand here, would you?"

Two very large Pacific Islanders in uniform appeared in front of me. "Please come with us."

"Why?"

"We can do this the easy way, or we can do it that hard way. Your choice."

"I haven't done anything wrong. Why should I go with you?"

"If you haven't done anything wrong, then there's nothing to worry about."

"Am I under arrest?"

"We have some questions for you."

"I'm here to see Sergeant Kahale. If he has questions, I'll be happy to answer them. If he's not here, I'm leaving."

One of them put his hand on me.

"Stop," I warned him. "I don't know who sent you out here, but you're about to make a big mistake."

The phone on the sergeant's desk rang. He answered, then asked me, "Are you Matt Preston?"

"Yes."

He waved me over to the desk and handed me the phone. "Hello."

"Matt, this is John. What's going on?"

"I'm being held against my will and two very large cops are about to manhandle me."

"Put the desk sergeant back on the line."

I handed the phone back to the sergeant. I couldn't make out what John was saying, but the buzzing sounded angry.

The sergeant listened to the Admiral for a moment and then said, "Listen asshole, I don't give a shit who you think you are. You don't call here and tell us what to do." He hung up.

I shook my head at the Sergeant. "Sarge, you're making career decisions right now. I don't think you understand what you just did."

"Shut up!" he barked. "Get him out of here."

One of the cops said, "Are you going to come without any problems, or do we have to use force?"

"I'm coming, but only because you threatened me with physical violence. Lead on."

I was taken to a small room with a badly scarred wooden table and three chairs where I waited for a long time. Like Goldilocks, I tried all three chairs but none of them were comfortable. After what seemed like an eternity, a new officer of Pacific Island extraction came into the room.

"My name is Sergeant Kahale. We spoke earlier today. Why are you asking questions about the Akioka case? What's your interest?"

I wasn't impressed with his attitude. "I explained my interest on the phone this morning."

He leaned back in his chair, folded his arms across his chest and smiled at me. "Do you really expect me to buy that cock and bull story?"

"Why do you say that?"

"Because I ran your name past a buddy of mine in Washington. You don't work for any research group. When my buddy started checking up on you, he got a nasty phone call from way up the food chain telling him to cease and desist. Or else. He was to stop asking questions about you. So, let's try this again? What's your interest in the Akioka case?"

"Let's play show and tell. Since you know a little about me, how about you tell me what you know about Akioka's death? If it's open and shut, why is there still an open investigation? The case is either open or closed. Correct? And why threaten me?"

Sergeant Kahale considered my words, "Okay, there's a rumor Akioka was part of a black ops group in Nam." He proceeded to tell me he'd learned about my former outfit. He finished and smiled. "Now it's your turn."

"Sergeant Kahale, you seem to have some well-connected sources. You've gathered a lot of information you are not supposed to have. However, from here on in, you need to understand the conversation we're about to have never took place. If you say anything about it, I will deny it and there could be repercussions."

"I understand that too, go ahead."

It took me a full ten minutes to bring him up to speed. When I finished Kahale stared at me for a long time and I wondered if he was going to tell me anymore. Eventually, he shrugged his shoulders, "Do you understand the term, 'staged' when it comes to a crime scene?"

"Yeah, a body is arranged so it appears the death was caused by a different means than what actually happened."

"Exactly. I've been on the force for a long time, and I've investigated a lot of deaths. I'm usually right when I suspect something is staged. It had the appearance of a suicide—he overdosed on pills. But it didn't feel right to me. I asked around and found out he was well-respected and had a lot of friends. His girlfriend was adamant he didn't commit suicide and if I was living with a woman who looked like her, I sure as hell wouldn't be thinking about killing myself. His friends all told me he wasn't depressed. Everyone was shocked about the suicide.

"I told my captain and he told me to leave it alone, it was a suicide. When I pressed, he got very angry. I was ordered to leave it alone. The case was closed. That bothered me. I've never been ordered off of an investigation before.

"I have a friend over at the coroner's office and as a favor he ran a couple extra tests. I was right, they found other shit as well that didn't make it into the final report.

55

"Mr. Preston, it wasn't a suicide; the body was staged. I have no doubt he was murdered, but I've been ordered not to go further, I have to walk away and leave it alone."

I leaned back in my chair and folded my arms over my chest. "And that makes three for three. Actually, it makes four for four because what got me started on all of this was a ghost who was killed crossing a busy street."

"So, what's so strange about that? People get killed all the time crossing a busy street."

"True, except it was a hit and run at 3:30 in the morning. The car had been stolen and wiped clean."

"You're right, that does sound strange. Why the song and dance about investigating suicides?"

"It was a ploy."

"Well, when you started asking questions, the captain heard about it, hence the holding cell. I have no idea who you called, but your phone call got the governor and the mayor involved and now the captain's ass in big trouble. Since shit rolls downhill, the desk sergeant ended up getting his butt chewed. As of a few minutes ago he's on suspension for a few days. The captain ordered me to come see you, find out what I could about you and then cut you lose and make sure you leave the islands. But I was curious, so I ran the check on you. Sorry about the holding cell and all, it wasn't my idea. You're free to leave."

"Thanks. What's going to happen to the desk sergeant?"

"I have no idea, why?"

"He really pissed off my boss, who has a lot of juice. I wish him luck because I'm not going to try to help him."

"You need to see this from our perspective—"

"No." I interrupted. "You need to see it from our point of view. People are turning up dead that shouldn't be dead. We're trying to find out why. Having some fat desk cop get in my way and then hang up on my boss does not help anybody see it from any perspective!"

"Sorry. What are you going to do next?"

"I don't know. I don't think I can do any more here."

"So, what's next?"

"Another strange death left. In Napoleon, Ohio."

"There's gonna be a big difference between here and there."

I laughed. "No shit! Thanks for your help, Sergeant." I extended my hand, and he took it.

"Can I ask a favor?" Kahale asked.

"Sure, what?"

"If and when you get this figured out, please let me know what happened. I had a favorite uncle who died from shit he contracted in Viet Nam, and I've always had a soft spot for those vets. By the way, thanks for your service."

"Thank you. I'll get ahold of you and tell you whatever I'm allowed to tell you."

"Well, tell me what you can, when you can. Okay?"

"It's deal. Thanks for finally coming clean with me.

"Have a nice trip to Ohio."

SEVEN GHOSTS

CHAPTER SEVEN

Being able to land at the Toledo Express Airport, which is home to the 180th Fighter Wing is one of many reasons I love having access to a private plane. I'd arranged a rental and was immediately on my way to Napoleon. My first stop? The police station.

Walking into the station it dawned on me I was spending a lot of time lately in police stations. However, since the police seemed to have the information I needed, it was the correct place to start. I told the desk sergeant I wanted to speak with the investigating officer on the Adam Johnson case. I was asked to take a seat and they'd have Lieutenant Irving McCready come up and talk to me.

After ten minutes, a pleasant-looking man with a fringe of grey hair surrounding a bald head came out. His tan slacks were rumpled, and his blue blazer looked like it had seen better days. His white shirt was wrinkled, and his striped tie was partly undone. McCready extended his hand, and I took it.

"How can I help you sir?"

"Is there a place we can chat? I have some questions about Adam Johnson."

McCready led me to a small room in the back of the station.

"What's this all about?" he asked.

I handed him my creds. He looked them over and handed them back to me. "Same question, what's this all about?"

I decided I wasn't going to try anything cute. I was going to come right to the point. "Adam Johnson served in Viet Nam."

"We knew that."

"He served in a clandestine unit."

"That I didn't know."

"Over the past few weeks, four members of that unit have been killed under suspicious circumstances. I'm trying to find out why those men died. What can you tell me about Johnson's death?"

"Basically, it was a mugging that got out of hand. I don't know what you know about Johnson, but he was a large man. He was part of a local biker gang, and we think whoever robbed him got scared and hit him too hard. They cracked his skull and he bled to death."

"Lieutenant, you just said Johnson was a large man." McCready nodded. "How well did you know him?"

"I knew him. I arrested him a couple of times."

"What for?"

"Dealing drugs."

"Drugs? What kind?"

"Marijuana." I couldn't help it, but I reacted. McCready held up a hand. "I know it's legal in some states, but when I busted him, it wasn't legal here. He got off with a warning the first time and he did sixty days for the second offense."

"Then you know how big Johnson really was?" McCready smiled. "Okay, if you were going to rob somebody, would you have picked him?"

McCready thought for a moment. "I see where you're going with this. If it wasn't a mugging turned bad, what do you think?"

60

"Johnson knew several ways of ending a life, especially if they were stupid enough to try and rob him. Over the past couple of months five members of our group have died in strange circumstances."

"Five people ain't that unusual."

"Considering there were only twenty-three of us to start, and over half of us didn't come back from rice-paddy land, yeah, it's unusual! I've been looking into this. All of them were murdered. Now you tell me that Johnson dies of a mugging that went wrong. Sorry, I'm not buying it."

McCready mulled over what I'd said. "You've said US a couple of times. Were you a member of that group?"

"Yeah, but I'm asking you to keep that information to yourself. Right now, there are only two ghost members alive."

"Ghosts? What are ghosts?"

"Sorry, that's what we were called. We slipped into a place, did our mission and left. We were like ghosts."

"I get what you're saying, but I don't understand why you're involved in this investigation."

"I want to know who killed all of them, and I want know how much danger I'm in."

"I can understand that."

"Did you talk to any of the other bikers?"

"That gang is a true died-in-the-wool biker gang. They don't talk, especially to the police. Ever! Johnson was killed in an alley by an unknown assailant during a mugging the went bad. That's the official police position."

"What's the gang's name?"

"They call themselves Phoenix."

That was interesting. "What was Johnson's position in the gang?"

"He was their leader. Do you have any more questions?"

"Does the gang hang out anywhere in particular or have a clubhouse?"

"Yeah, down on the river there's a place called Outlaw Smokehouse. Killer BBQ, no pun intended. The place is owned by two brothers who are both in the gang. A question if I may?" McCready asked.

I motioned for him to continue.

"Is your being in town going to cause me any problems?"

"I hope not. I'm not planning on it. I guess it depends on how well my meeting with the members of Phoenix goes."

"Good. Well, if you learn anything of interest, let me know."

~ ~ ~ ~ ~

Bikers. I could see Moose being a biker. Besides being huge, he had a hard time with military rules. Actually, any rules. The problem for me was bikers tend to be a very closed group. Outlaw biker gangs don't take to strangers, especially when they start asking questions. I needed an in with this group. I needed a bike! I saw there was a Harley dealership in town, but I needed a bike that would be unknown to them. I assumed most the members frequented the dealership and knew every bike there. I needed a bike that was unknown to them, and it had to be bad ass enough to give me some street credibility. I checked online and found a Harley dealer in Toledo. That was probably far enough away.

On the drive to Toledo to pick out a bike, I called Walter. He answered, "Matt, what's up?"

"Just wanted to let you know about Kapuna."

"Hearing about him really hit me hard. I've still got a case of the blues. What did you find out?"

"Supposed to be a suicide, but the investigating officer didn't like the way it looked. For sure it wasn't a suicide."

"Damn! Where are you now?"

"Toledo. I need a bike to try and fit into a biker group. I'll keep you up to date."

"I have a million questions, but I know you're busy. Fill me in later. Thanks."

"Walter, I haven't forgotten about the bank thing."

"Not to worry, You're busy."

"Ciao."

It was getting late, and I decided I'd find a motel and go motorcycle shopping in the morning. I called Lois and we talked for a long time. I told her I missed her, and I was sorry we were having problems. I wanted to tell her I loved her, but it just wouldn't come out. She said she felt the same way and then talked a little dirty to me and I reciprocated. By the time we rang off I was feeling horny. I needed to get information on Moose fast and then see about getting back home.

~ ~ ~ ~ ~

It was a nice clean dealership with several new bikes set up in the middle of the showroom and a few used ones parked along one wall. There were lots of racks with T-shirts and riding gear and a couple of attractive salesladies were waiting on customers. My problem with the used bikes on display was they were all either too upscale, or too vanilla for what I wanted. I explained to the salesman I really wanted something used. Something radical. Something really bad-assed.

He smiled. "Ah, sounds like you want to see the Widow Maker!"

"The what?" I asked with trepidation.

"The Widow Maker. It's scary fast, hard to handle, looks really mean and takes balls of steel to ride."

"Let's look at the bike. It just might fit the bill." I tried to sound confident, but it wasn't exactly how I felt.

We went back into their repair shop and then across an alley into an old warehouse. There were bikes scattered throughout the building. Some of them were still in crates, new ones waiting to be detailed and put on the showroom, and some of them were obviously old, waiting to be either wholesaled or scrapped.

In one corner a bike was covered up. Underneath the covering was an old school chopper with a Sugar Bear front forks protruding --- exactly what I had in mind. Menacing black fenders with red flames curling down the tank. The front forks stuck out with a typical chopper rake, and ape-hanger handlebars on top. The motor was deceiving. There was very little chrome, but I recognized much of it to be high end speed parts. The bike looked mean and nasty and if you understood what you were looking at, you knew it was fast and not everyone could ride it.

The salesman explained, "This is a 1992 Mad Dog Custom Santee Softail Chopper. It has a S & S 143 CID engine with Super E carbs married to a Revtek six speed transmission. The bike has low mileage, and it's in excellent condition. This is a one-off custom build. The previous own-er only rode it a few times and decided it was way too much bike for him. The bike does not come with any warranties of any kind. What's you sees is whats ya' get! You buy it, we don't want it back."

"Understood. May I ride it?"

"Think you think you can handle it, pops?" The sales-man chuckled.

I gave him a cold stare until he looked down, then growled, "I'll let that slide, sonny. This time. Let me put it this way, I've was riding before you were a gleam in your daddy's eye."

The salesman held up his hands. "Okay, sorry. You'll have to sign a waiver releasing the dealership from any li-ability. And I need to see your driver's license with an en-dorsement and some sort of a deposit."

I was sure glad I'd kept the endorsement when I'd renewed my license. I showed them to the salesman, signed the liability waver and handed him my Titanium Mastercard.

"What's this?"

"My deposit. That's a Titanium Mastercard. That will cover the cost of the bike if I mess it up."

"Just a sec, I need to ask my boss about this." In just a couple of minutes the salesman came trotting back. "Would you please come with me?"

I followed him to the sales manager's office. The manager wore a shirt with a collar unbuttoned and a tie with the knot loose. His face was well tanned, and he had a scar running across his forehead. His salt and pepper hair was combed straight back and his eyebrows and mustache were still black. He stood and extended his hand.

"My name is Carl Magno, I'm the sales manager." Magno held up my credit card. "I don't understand what you're doing. With this card you can buy any bike on the premises. Why are you looking at that piece of shit out back?"

"What's it to you?" I asked.

"Just asking. I want to make sure you really want that bike. We don't want it back and I wanted to know why you were interested."

"It's a long story. But to speed things along, here are my federal credentials." I laid my cred pack on his desk and his eyes popped open when he saw who the issuing agency was. "I need the bike for cover. I wanted to ride it and see how it handles."

"Have you ever ridden a bike before?"

I put on the same cold face I'd used on the salesman. "Sonny, I've backed up more miles to the curb than you've ridden in a straight line. I'll let the insult slide... this time."

The manager paled and held up his hands. "I'm sorry." He looked over at the salesman. "Let him take it for a spin."

I left the credit card on the edge of his desk. Magno looked at it like it was a dangerous snake.

It had been a few months since I'd ridden, but some things you never forget. I walked around the bike and then got on. The bike was more comfortable than it looked. I checked the shift pattern and opened the gas tank and wiggled the bike back and forth to see how much gas was in the tank. The gauge said it was about a third full and the slosh sounded like that was accurate. I fired it up and the noise in the enclosed shed made my ears ring. I'd noticed it had straight pipes, but it hadn't dawned on me how loud it was going to be when it started.

I eased the bike out of the shed and while it warmed up, I put on a borrowed helmet. I got on and rode to the end of the alley and looked down the street and when a window in the traffic appeared, I pulled out. I was stunned at the pickup. I'd expected it to be quick, but this was plain stupid. No wonder it was called The Widow Maker. I was going to have to be careful riding this puppy.

Very careful.

I rode for about ten minutes and was pleased with the way the bike handled. The bike was just what I needed. When I went back into the dealership I went straight to the sales manager's office. He looked up and started to stand when I entered.

"Just a sec and I'll get your salesman."

"Don't waste my time, please. You're the one who decides what you'll let the bike go for, so you're the man I want to deal with."

He sat down and motioned for me to do the same.

I continued "I can tell from the dust on the seat the bike's been here for a while. It's going to take a very special person to purchase the bike. Quite a few birthdays could come and go while it sits out back waiting for a buyer. Now, with that said, what do you want for the bike?"

He named a price.

I pushed myself up from the chair. "I was mistaken. And here I thought you really wanted to sell the thing." I was standing and as I turned to leave, I picked up my credit card. "Have a nice day."

"Hang on. What are you offering?"

I gave him a number. He asked me to do a little better and I came up a small amount.

He bent over the adding machine on his desk. It's an old ploy used by managers to act like they're working the best deal they can. When he looked up, before he could speak, I said, "The only thing I want to hear from you is that you accept my offer or goodbye."

"How about—"

"If you say another word, I'll leave. That was my final offer and considering what you have out there, it's a good offer and you know it."

He was a good enough manager to know I was serious. He stood and extended his hand, "You have a bike."

"You have an hour to put this dealt together. While you do the paperwork, I want the oil changed and the tires properly inflated. In one hour and one minute I'll be leaving. If you're not done, you'll still own the bike. I'm going next door for a cup of coffee and a bite to eat."

Forty-five minutes later the salesman came into the café. The paperwork was completed, and the bike was serviced and ready. I signed the necessary paperwork and arranged to leave my car in the employee parking lot. It was time to go back to Napoleon and deal with Phoenix.

It wasn't the most comfortable ride I've owned, but it was far from being the worst. As with most custom bikes, it had its quirks, and it would take time to get used to them. Halfway to Napoleon, I pulled over at a rest stop. Using a knife I keep hidden in the heel of my boot, I cut the sleeves off of my shirt. My left shoulder has a tattoo from my days in the army. I don't like ink on me, or anybody, as a rule, but one night in Nam several of us got drunk and had our unit insignia tattooed on our left shoulders. Moose had one. I was positive some or all the biker club would have seen his, and hopefully someone would recognize mine. It would give me an in.

Several miles outside of town several bikers rolled up on me. The leader glared over at me and then swerved into me. I was expecting the maneuver. His intent was to try and force me off the road. When I saw him start his swerve, I slowed down and he passed in front of me. He dropped back and rode next to me for about a mile. when he tried the maneuver again, harder this time. I nailed the throttle and my bike leaped forward. In the mirror, I saw him fighting to keep his bike upright.

He opened his throttle and raced to catch me and for a very short time he stayed with me. But I was tired of his antics and since my bike totally outclassed his, I opened the throttle wide until he was a dot in my rearview mirror. I was pleased at the way the bike handled at high speed. It was steadier than I expected, and I was comfortable going as fast as it would go. When I got to the edge of town, I throttled back to sub light speed before I got picked up by the police. The bike was running exactly as it should. It was turning out to be a nice bike.

I cruised through town and since I'd located the Outlaw Smokehouse before I went back to Toledo, I knew where I was going. A dozen bikes were parked in front of the restaurant and I pulled up at the far end and rolled my bike back into position.

Two bikers were standing out front having a smoke and after I put the kickstand down, they came over and checked out my bike. They asked a couple of questions about the motor, and I answered them. I put my helmet on the seat and left it there. Basically, I was saying I was one bad dude and if you dared screw with my helmet, there'd be hell to pay. As I opened the restaurant door, the bikers I'd seen on the way into town rolled up.

Inside the floor was covered with cigarette butts and old peanut shells. A huge bar stretched across the far wall with liquor shelves up to the ceiling. It looked like they had every kind of liquor known to man.

The restaurant smelled of good BBQ, stale beer and old smoke. The room was smoky. I wondered how much longer Ohio residents were going to be allowed to smoke cigarettes in restaurants. Several states already had laws prohibiting smoking and it was just a matter of time before you wouldn't be able to smoke inside anywhere.

I took a stool near the end of the bar. The bartender wore a white shirt and a Bolo tie with a Harley clasp. Over black pants he wore an apron I assumed at one time was white. He wiped the place in front of me and asked what I wanted.

"What do you have on draft?"

He ran through a lengthy list, and I stopped him when he named one that interested me. The riders I'd seen on the highway came in and joined a table with a couple of bikers seated at it. I was about halfway done with my beer when I felt a person sit down on each side of me. Looking in the mirror behind the bar, I saw the guy on my right was the biker who had tried to swerve into me. He asked, "Are you riding that piece of shit parked out front?"

"Who's asking?"

"Me."

"And who is me?"

"I'm the owner of the bike next to yours and cooties are jumping from your bike and infesting mine. I want you to go and move that piece of shit, now." He guffawed at his feeble joke and the biker on my other side snickered. I ignored him and took another sip of my beer.

"What are you, deaf or sumpin?" he asked.

I met his eyes in the mirror and said, "What's your name?"

His stringy, black hair was greasy, and his face was dirty and unshaven. He had brown eyes set too close together which made him look like he wasn't very bright. His teeth were yellowed from smoking and one of his front teeth was missing.

"Why, you written' a book or sumpin?"

"No, I wanted to know what to put on your tombstone."

"Your funny, old man. Not that it's any of your business, my name is Dick, but they call me Junior."

"Dick, huh? I can see why you want to be called Junior. But Dick fits you better. Moose told me to stop by sometime. He told me about the club, and he made it sound like most of you were at least of average intelligence. But he was wrong about you. You're sitting here making an ass of yourself and you have no idea who I am."

He paled a little under the dirt on his face. "You knew Moose?"

"Yes, I knew Moose. We were in the service together." I turned my shoulder so he could see the ink. For the first time in my life, I was glad I had the stupid tattoo.

He slid off his stool and took a few steps back. "You were a ghost?"

"Moose told you about the ghosts? He wasn't supposed to tell anyone, ever. It's too bad you know anything about it. You need to hope certain government agencies never find out. If Moose told you about the ghosts, for sure he was murdered."

"Murdered! What the hell do you mean? Moose was killed by a mugger."

"Really?"

"Yeah, really."

"Did ya ever see Moose fight?" Junior indicated he had. "Think about it. Think real hard, Junior. You still think Moose was mugged?"

Junior considered my words.

"If you were going to rob somebody, would you really pick Moose?"

Junior shook his head.

"Moose was silenced because he told some of you about the ghosts. I wonder how long before you guys end up like Moose?"

"Who are you?"

"Well, Dick, isn't it a bit late to be asking that question? Maybe you should have asked yourself that before you tried to kill me on the highway. I'll tell you right now I'm probably your worst nightmare."

Junior started to take a step forward. I held up my hand. "You need to stop right there."

He reached behind his back and before he had a chance to pull whatever he had hidden; I kicked my booted foot as fast and hard as I could at his kneecap. A pistol dropped to the floor along with Junior followed by the loud pop from his knee and then his scream as he lie there holding his leg.

While Junior distracted everyone, I swung around and chopped his buddy across the throat with the side of my hand. Not too hard, just enough to get his attention.

I slid off my stool and scooped the pistol off the floor and stomped on Junior's chest. I returned my attention to his buddy. "It's your play Skippy. What ya gonna to do?"

He shook his head.

With that taken care of, I addressed the room. "I was a friend of Moose's. We served together." I showed them my tattoo. "He's dead and I want to know why.

"Moose wasn't killed by a random mugger. Like I said, we were friends. We were more than that. We were brothers in arms. I have no beef with any of you. I think Dick here has figured out he fucked up."

I handed Junior's pistol to the guy closest to me. "Here, hold on to this. What's your name?"

"Jughead."

"Well Jughead, you have the gun now. I need you to answer some questions. Are we cool?"

There was a murmur agreement.

"The obvious first question is, did anybody hate him enough to want Moose dead?"

Jughead said, "We're bikers. But we're not organized like the Hells Angels or anything like that. We don't wear colors and we're not outlaws. But we ride bikes, and it freaks people out. They may dislike us for what we represent, but I can't think of anybody who would want us dead. Or should I say, anybody who would act on their feelings."

"Did any of you notice any change in Moose's attitude? Did he seem edgier lately?"

It was unanimous: Moose was the same ol Moose as always.

"Did anybody see any strangers lately doing anything unusual, or paying too much attention to you?"

Jughead replied, "Funny you mention that. A guy showed up a couple of months back and hung around here for a week or so. He had a nose that looked like he'd had too much Scotch and way too much of the good life. He dyed his hair jet black – you could tell since it didn't match his gray stubble or his wrinkles.

"How did he dress?"

"He wore a wrinkled brown suit."

"Looked like he slept in it?"

"Yeah, we joked about it among ourselves. He'd come in and sit at the bar and watch us in the mirror. Do you know who he is?"

"Maybe. What happened to him?"

"One day he didn't show up. Never saw him again"

"Was that before or after Moose was killed?"

"I think the last time he came in just before Moose was killed. I'm not positive. He didn't bother anybody and after a while we didn't pay him any attention. You think he had something to do with Moose's death?"

"I don't know, but he's the only strange thing that happened around here?"

"Yeah."

"Thanks guys, I'll be leaving now."

"Hey, stop and have a beer with us."

"I'd love to, but I have to get going." I added, "By the way, somebody should get some medical attention for these two clowns." A couple of the bikers said they had a car and would get the two of them to Urgent Care. I asked, "You've all seen my bike, anybody interested in buying it?"

Somebody asked, "Is that really a Mad Dog Chopper?"

"What's your name?"

"Dan, but they call me Pops."

"Why?"

"I don't drink liquor; I just drink soda pop."

I laughed. "Yep, it's a Mad Dog custom, and if you were out on the highway, you saw how well it runs."

"How much do you want for it?" Pops asked.

"Name a price," I told him. Pops gave me a stupid figure and I told him he had just bought a bike.

"No shit?"

"No shit!"

Someone else said he would give me five hundred more than Pops offered.

"Sorry, he was first." I turned to Pops, "You ride back to Toledo with me and then you can have the bike. I'll give you an address where to send the money."

"Are you serious, you trust me that much?"

"Do you want me to come back and find you?" I pointed at Dick, lying on the floor. "And have to do that to you?"

Pops put his hands out as if to ward me off. "No! I'll send you the money. I promise."

"I know you will. Let's ride."

The trip to Toledo was fast and without incident. I handed Pops the keys to the bike and got in my car. I called Henry and asked when I could catch a ride back to DC. He told me it would be the next day before somebody could pick me up so I needed to find a place to crash for the night.

CHAPTER EIGHT

The next morning, I caught a ride back to D.C. in one of our new planes with a pilot I'd never met before — Oliver, a friend of Dominick's from Germany. We were growing so fast I didn't know how many planes we had and there were a bunch of pilots I'd never met.

On the way I called Walter to give him an update. I ended with, "Please be careful. I don't know what's going on, but both of us need to be very careful."

"I agree."

"Yeah."

"Have you had a chance to check with your bank? Is Jennifer all right?"

"Oh shit! Sorry. Plate's too full."

We hung up and I made a mental note to check with my bank. More importantly, I needed to find out what was going on with Jennifer.

~ ~ ~ ~ ~

When I got to Orchard's office Lois gave me a hug along with a kiss on the cheek, but it didn't feel the same. She didn't seem a bit uncomfortable with me. I wondered what was going on with her.

When John came out of his office to see why the commotion. I asked him if he had a moment; I needed to talk to him. He started to take me into his office, and I asked him to go and have coffee.

John and I walked down the street toward our usual park.

Once we were seated on our favorite bench, he asked. "What have you found out?"

I cut to the chase. "All five ghosts were murdered. This isn't speculation, this is fact. I spoke with the local police departments and in some cases the official view was different from the cops who worked the cases. Every officer I talked to said they thought the victim was killed.

"When I was checking on Moose Johnson, I was told about a stranger who started appearing at the gang's hangout just before he was killed. The guy they described sounds like John Mescher. He disappeared around the time Moose was murdered."

John frowned and he growled, "I don't think you should be making accusations with no evidence. Besides, what makes you think it was Mescher?"

"I didn't make any accusations. I'm saying the bikers described somebody just like Mescher. From his big red nose to his rumpled brown suit."

I phrased my next sentence carefully. "John, I've done a lot for you over the years. I think I've earned a little honesty here. What can you tell me about Mescher?"

"Matthew, you have no proof it was Mescher—"

"I never said it was him," I interrupted. "I told you what the bikers told me, and now I'm asking for information about Mescher."

Orchard shook his finger at me. "Damn it, you're putting me in a difficult situation. If it *was* Mescher, and I'm not saying it was, I'm not supposed to discuss who or what Mescher is or does, with anyone. That includes you. I have my orders. I'll tell you this much, several people are aware of your investigation and your questions are upsetting them."

"Like who?"

"Never mind. I have my orders."

"What does that mean?"

"It means I'm ordering you to stop your investigation. Leave it alone."

"No! Does McNaulty know about any of this?"

"Shit, Matt. You know we have McNaulty on ice? He doesn't know a thing."

"McNaulty's been a thorn in my side for years."

My history with McNaulty goes all the way back to Nam. There were others in Phoenix Project, but he ran the ghosts. "Are you insinuating McNaulty and Mescher are in this together? I don't understand, what does McNaulty have to do with Mescher?"

"I can't tell you where McNaulty is, but he is not part of anything going on today. Let's just say some of Mescher's people are doing a lot of the things McNaulty's people used to do. Now, stop making waves. Forget about Mescher and listen carefully. I'm ordering you to stop. Do you understand?"

I stood and started to walk away.

"Where are you going?"

"Back to your office before I say something we both regret."

We got back to the office and Lois said, "I just had a call asking if the two of you were here. They hung up when I asked who they were."

"What did you tell them?" Asked John.

"I told them I expected you to return shortly?"

Orchard motioned me into his office. When the door was shut, he said "Last time I'm telling you this. You have to stop asking questions about Mescher and McNaulty, or I can't help you. Is that clear?"

"So Mescher is doing McNaulty's dirty work now?"

He didn't answer me.

"Come on, since when are you afraid of guys like Mescher? What does he have on you? Why are you afraid to discuss him with me?"

Orchard snapped, "Damn it, leave it alone. I think you need to leave, now."

"After all I've done for you, this is how it is? This is your attitude? You're throwing me out of your office?"

"Take it however you like. Right now, I don't really give a shit. Just leave, please."

"Can you at least tell me if Mescher's people had anything to do with the five dead ghosts?"

"I honestly don't know, but I doubt it. Why would his people be involved?"

Over the years, I've learned usually when people use the word honestly, chances are they're not being honest.

"That's why I'm asking you, John! Tell me what's going on. Was that Mescher hanging around the biker bar in Ohio? Did he off Moose, or have something to do with it?"

With no warning, the door to John's office flew open and three good-sized men wearing dark suits entered.

"What's the meaning of this?" John barked.

One of the men pointed at me said, "You're to come with us, now."

"Who are you?" I asked.

"By what authority do you come barging in here and demand anything?" John roared.

One of the men pulled out his cred pack and handed it John. "That's my authorization."

John's face turned white and when he handed the cred pack to the man, his hand was shaking.

The man turned to me. "Come with us now."

"And if I don't?"

Orchard said, "Go with them. I'll get to the bottom of this."

They marched me through the outer office past a wide-eyed Lois. A black Chrysler van with blacked out windows and blue lights flashing waited at the curb. The side door slid open, and I was told to get in. We rode for a while and then the van pulled into a parking garage under a tall building. We took the elevator and when the door opened, one of the muscles tried to escort me off by the elbow.

I pulled my arm loose. "If you value your hand, you won't put it on me again."

"Come on, pops. You're wasting time." He grabbed my elbow again and started to push me forward. Bad move! I may be getting old, but the training I received so long ago still works. I broke his wrist with a quick twisting maneuver. One of the other two reached for his gun and found himself on the ground with one of his kneecaps in the wrong place and his privates cupped in his hands in pain. His gun was in my hand.

I handed the pistol to the third guy and growled, "I'll go with you, but you're not going to touch me. Understood?"

"Understood." He motioned me forward.

We ended up in a luxuriously appointed office with windows on one wall. The windows were fake—there were no windows on this floor. This was both to keep people from listening in and charmingly enough, shooting through the windows. The man behind the desk was larger than average, but he carried the weight well. Anywhere between forty and seventy, he was well dressed with an intelligent face. The nameplate on his desk said: John Cole, Director. He was the director of some super-secret agency and reported directly to President Bradson. He didn't introduce himself. He didn't need to.

His voice was calm, and his diction perfect. "Mr. Preston let's get to why you're here. You're digging around in information that's still classified. Why?"

There was a chair in front of his desk, and I moved to sit down.

"I didn't give you permission to sit down."

He hadn't raised his voice, or change his tone, nevertheless, I recognized the warning.

"Why are you asking questions about things you have no business inquiring about?"

His attitude was starting to piss me off. "What *business* is it of yours?" I snapped back.

Cole's eyes narrowed but his voice remained cool. "I'll ask the questions."

"Well John, if you want answers, you have to answer some of mine," I said insolently.

"That's Mr. Cole to you."

"Whatever." I snapped back. I wasn't going to be intimidated by this man. "I want to know why men from my old unit are dropping like flies."

"You're investigating things you had no right to, and you've been told to stop. You need to leave this alone. There are issues you don't understand and that don't concern you." He still hadn't unfolded his hands.

I replied, "I disagree. Somebody's been killing off members of the ghost squad. And I got a description of a potential suspect that sounds a lot like John Mescher. Is he responsible?"

"Don't be ridiculous. Besides, it's none of your business."

"I don't see it that way. Since I was a ghost, and they're dying at an alarming rate, it damn well is my business. I have the right to protect myself."

"I'm trying to give you some good advice, Mr. Preston. I know who you are and what you did in the past, but now you need to step back now. This is way above your pay grade. Do you understand?"

I decided the best thing was to keep silent.

"I asked you a question mister!" Finally, he raised his voice. "Do you understand? Do not ask questions about John Mescher."

He hadn't asked me if I was going to stop, he asked if I understood I was supposed to stop. There's a difference.

I nodded.

"Good. You're dismissed."

I stood there for a moment staring at the man. He looked up at me and snapped, "What?"

"I wanted to take a long look at you, I don't want to forget your face. If anything happens to Walter McLaughlin I'm coming for you. Orders or not!"

"Get out. Get out of my office. Now!" He pointed at the door, his face red and his hand shook. I'd managed to break his cool. The problem was I had no idea if I'd done something unwise.

Time would tell.

The two men I'd put down were nowhere to be seen. The remaining man walked me to the elevators, staying well away, and escorted me to the waiting van.

They left me outside the admiral's office. When I walked in Lois asked, "What happened?"

I shook my head and headed into John's office.

"What happened?" John asked once his office door was shut.

I told him.

"You saw Director Cole? You actually said that to Director Cole?"

"Yeah. He tries to act like he's one mellow dude, but he's wound pretty tight. I think I lit a nice fire under his ass."

Orchard said, "Show some respect. I didn't know this went that high. What are you going to do next?"

"Since nobody will tell me what the hell is going on, I think I need to have a chat with ol Mescher. I'm gonna find him and then we're gonna have a nice long talk."

"Listen to me, this is a warning and an order, leave Mescher alone. Back off."

"You can't order me around."

"Do not push this. Didn't you hear what Director Cole told you? You're messing with things way above your, or my, pay grade. Do us all a favor and leave it alone. Stay away from John Mescher."

"Not until I get some answers."

I leaned forward and put my fists on his desk, my face close to his. "This is your last chance to come clean with me. What's going on?"

"I won't help you. Actually, I can't help you."

"You know, you've turned into a bitter disappointment. I thought you had balls. See you around and thanks for nothing."

He called my name as I walked out of his office, but I slammed the door behind me. I stopped in front of Lois' desk and before I could say anything, the phone on her desk rang.

"Yes," she said and listened again. "I understand."

I told her, "I'm going back to Florida. The guy in Orchard's office has turned into somebody I don't know. I could use your help and I'm asking you to come with me. John will just have to get by without you."

"You want me to leave now?"

"Yes. I'm asking you to come with me… right now."

"Matt, I can't. That was John warning me to keep my distance from you. I have no idea what's going on, but you need to think about what you're doing. Go to my place and wait for me. We can talk this over tonight."

"Lois, something's not right. It's decision time, babe. Are you coming with me or staying here?"

"Matt, you don't understand…"

"Last time I'm asking. I hate to do this to you, but it's either John or me."

"Matt, I won't leave. I can't leave. You have to trust me."

"I thought I could, now I see I can't. Right now, the only person I trust is me. Goodbye."

"Go and wait at my place," she implored.

"No." I left the office.

That answered the questions about where our relationship was going.

I called Henry. "What time can I catch a ride back to Florida?"

"Tomorrow morning. Be at the airport by 9:30." Since I had no place to stay, I found a hotel near the airport. Something told me I should keep my cell phone turned off and just in case, I pulled the SIM card. I also paid cash for the room, leaving as little trail as possible.

Something was wrong, very wrong, and I needed time to think it over before I did anything.

CHAPTER NINE

The next morning Henry met me at our office and took me out the back door. We got in a car I didn't recognize and drove to a smaller airport we'd never used before. On the way Henry told me. "We need to use a different airport. A friend called me this morning and warned me. They don't want you leaving D.C. I have a plane nobody knows about stashed and the plane isn't on our company records. Since nobody knows about Ruth either, I'm going to have her fly you down to Florida."

The flight went quickly. Since Ruth was a new pilot, I made a mental note to get to know our new pilots. Our government contracts are double our regular business; and best of all, the government ones are the most lucrative. Of course, they're lot more dangerous, but the pilots who do them know what they signed up for and are well paid for the danger.

I tried to keep my mind off Lois since I didn't understand why she chose John over me. I feel she should have walked out on Orchard and left with me if she cared for me as much as she professed. Was I being unreasonable?

I don't think so.

Max and the puppies were delighted to see me, and I could tell Martha was happy to get away. She loved the dogs and all, but they can be a handful and I'd been gone longer than anticipated. I took them for a long walk and by the time I got back I was all hot and sweaty and ready for a swim. My pool is secluded, and I stripped beside the pool and dove in. When I surfaced, I found the puppies had joined me and Max running around the edge of the pool barking. Max does not like the water. We splashed around and I made sure both puppies knew how to get out of the pool in case one of them accidently fell in. The water felt great.

I had a great steak in the freezer, and I pulled it out to thaw. Later I remembered I'd turned off my phone and I'd pulled the card. I reinserted the card and turned it back on. My phone had several calls from Orchard and one from Lois. I ignored them. There was one call from a number I didn't recognize. Out of curiosity I hit redial. "Hello." A voice answered.

"Hello, this is Matt Preston. I see you called, I apologize, I missed your call. Who is this please?"

"Hello Mr. Preston, this is John Mescher. Thank you for returning my call. Did you get my voice mail?"

"Please call me Matt. I'm sorry, I just noticed you'd called and I'm returning your call. I didn't listen to my messages. Anyway, how can I help you?"

"Mr. Preston, I'm told you're asking questions about me and looking into my business."

"That's true." I could see no reason to lie.

"And I also know you've been told to stop asking questions about me. True?"

"Yes, however I have unanswered questions and until I'm satisfied, I'm going to keep prying."

"Why? What do you want to know about me?"

"Let's start with your interest in Phoenix Project. Do you know why so many of the ghosts from the old Project died lately?"

"Why are you asking me? I don't understand."

"Well, I know you were in Ohio checking on Moose, Adam Johnson. The members of his biker club described you right down to your rumpled brown suit. What's your interest in him?"

"That's none of your business Preston."

I decided to let that slide. "Okay, but answer this, why'd you leave so quickly after Moose was dead?"

"He was dead. There was no reason for me to stick around."

"Are you implying you had something to do with his death?"

"Of course not!" He snapped back.

"Then why were you there to begin with?"

"I've already told you, it's none of your business."

"Why did you call me yesterday anyway?"

"Because I'm ordering you to stay out of my business. Stay away from me. You have no idea what's going on so stay away from me. You're to stop asking questions about me. That's an order? Do you understand? "

"No! I don't understand. You have no authority over me, and you can't order me to do a damn thing."

"Mr. Preston, I know Director Cole has already ordered you to leave this entire business alone. By ignoring me, you're ignoring both of us, and if that's the case, you're making a bad decision."

"I don't know who you think you are, or what you think you are, but now you really have my interest. I'm coming for you."

"We shall see." And the line went dead.

For a long time, I sat staring at the phone wondering exactly who, and what Mescher was. I had to admit, I never knew exactly what group McNaulty belonged to either. I knew he was part of Phoenix Project but after that I had no idea what else he was involved in.

I grilled my steak and was enjoying my evening with a small but nourishing when my phone rang. I'd forgotten to turn it off. "Hello."

"Matt, this is President Bradson."

I was stunned. "Good evening, sir. This is a pleasure."

"Perhaps you won't think so after I explain the purpose of my call."

"President Bradson, I have to admit you've piqued my curiosity."

"This is regarding John Mescher."

Right then I knew he was correct; I wasn't going to like where the conversation was headed. "Let me guess, you're asking me to stop poking around and asking questions about him?"

"No Matt, I'm not asking you, I'm ordering you to stop asking questions about Mescher. I'm ordering you to leave Mescher alone. You're not to talk to him, ask questions about him or do any form of investigation regarding him. Do I make myself clear?"

I was totally pissed. "Albert, you know you and I go a long way back. All the way back to the beginning of your career. We've been friends for years and now I see this president thing has gone to your head. If you think you can call me and order me not to do something, you don't know me as well as you think. You must know you don't have the authority to…"

"Matt, you're wrong!" He interrupted, "I do have the authority to order you to stop investigating Mescher and I have the power to back it up. Leave him alone. Don't make this difficult. Stop looking into anything Mescher is doing. Please don't make me do something that I'll regret later."

"Are you gonna have the FBI come after me if I don't?"

"Yes Matt, and the CIA and Homeland Security and Army Military Police and organizations you have never heard of if necessary. Matt don't fuck with me on this. You're going to lose."

"Ya know Albert, I never thought I'd say this to the President of the United States, but why don't go fuck a rolling donut. I'll do what I want." And I hung up.

This whole thing was quickly getting out of hand. I had no idea how far Bradson would push this, and I didn't want to find out. I needed to find a place to hide and the safest place I could think of was Walter's cabin.

I needed to get to Walter's and fast.

I still wanted to try one last time and talk to Lois, but before I could call her, my cell rang. It was my old childhood friend Jeff L. Davenport who was the Commissioner of police for Seattle. "Jeff ol buddy. How the hell are you?" I greeted him.

"Hello, Matt. Ummm... you may not feel that way when we're finished with this call."

"So help me, if you're calling me to say something about my investigation about why so many of my fellow ghosts are dying, I'm going to hang up on you and I'll be very disappointed with you."

"That's exactly why I'm calling. Do you know who just called me?"

"Let me guess. Albert Bradson?"

"Yes, and he's pissed as hell at you. Did you really tell him to fuck off?"

"No, I told him to go fuck a rolling donut."

Jeff's voice rose several octaves. "You can't talk like that to the man. That man is president of the United States of America."

"I knew 'that man' as you call him when he was just starting. He had a one room office off Pioneer Square, and I was one of his first clients. I don't give a crap who he is now!

He's still the person I knew from back in Seattle. Have you forgotten how he used to kiss your ass for favors when you were chief of detectives, and now you're his lacky?"

"I didn't call to have you belittle me. I called to help you, my friend. You're in a lot of trouble. As an old friend, you need to listen to me. Whatever you're doing, you need to stop. Now! Do you hear me?"

"You know some of what happened to me in Nam. Jeff, in the past few weeks several of the members of my old outfit have died under weird circumstances. To put it bluntly, they were killed! I need to know if Walter and I are in danger. You can't ask me not to investigate that."

"Oh shit! I know even if I tell you to stop, you won't quit. You do what you want. I tried to tell you to stay out of... well stay out of whatever you're doing. I can't help it if you won't listen, and I sure as hell can't help you when you get your ass in a bind."

"Goodbye Jeff. Thanks for the call. Who love's ya baby?"

"Obviously not you. Goodbye."

Somebody was pulling out all the stops. First Orchard, then Bradson and now Jeff Davenport. Who's next? My junior high school heart throb Cheryl Quinn? Not that I wouldn't mind hearing from her. What was going on?

I decided to call Lois and see if she would tell me anything. When she answered, I heard fear in her voice. "Matt, what are you doing? President Bradson just called John. He ordered John to send people to find you and arrest you. John asked me if I knew where you were. John said President Bradson told him he didn't care how it got done, they were to bring you in."

"I need to run for it. I need to go, and I need to go now."

"Why are you doing this?"

"I told you what was happening to past ghosts. I have good reasons to find out why."

"What's the point in telling me all this? You're not asking me to come with you, are you?"

"Yes. I was."

There was a hesitation before she answered. "Matt, I need to talk to you. I want to be with you. Where are you? Are you at your house?"

"Are you saying yes, you want to come with me?"

"Let's meet and talk about it. Where are you?"

"Why the change of heart?"

"I'm worried about you. Are you at the Florida house?"

"Why? Are you coming?"

"Umm, I want to know where you are and that you're safe."

And at that moment I knew Lois was no longer on my side. She wanted to know where I was so either Orchard's people or Mescher's could come and pick me up. "Sorry. I can see this is something I need to do on my own. Goodbye." As I hung up, I could hear her calling my name. I turned off my phone, opened it up and pulled the SIM card and dropped the pieces into the waste can.

I needed to get out of town!

Fast!

I went into the extra bedroom I'd made into an office and from a bottom desk drawer I pulled out a couple of the burner phones I keep. The phones are not registered to me and for the call to be traced it would take a long time.

I was concerned about what to do with the puppies and Max. I grabbed them and put them in the car. On the way I called my veterinarian friend, Dr. Lesley Oldman on one of the burners. After our greeting I got to the point. "I need to be gone for a while and I don't know how long. I need a safe place to put the dogs. Do you have room for them?"

"You know better than to ask that question. For you, of course."

"I'm on my way. Thanks Lesley.

CHAPTER TEN

After dropping off the dogs, I called Henry. "What the hell are you doing Ma…"

"Shut up!" I cut him off. "Do not say my name. I need to get to the other coast, and I need to do it as fast as possible, and nobody can know about it. Can you help me"

"That explains the call I just received."

"What was the call?"

"Somebody called from one of the agencies we do business with and warned me if you called, I was to report it to a number they gave me. I was warned if I didn't do what they said I'd find myself in deep shit. Then some dude named Cole called and asked me if I understood what I'd been told. He also ordered me to call him the second you contacted me. Was that *THE* John Cole who called me?"

"Yeah, it was. Feel honored. So, what ya gonna do? Turn me in?"

"Get serious. No way! You've done so much for me, there's no way I'd rat you out. Can you hide some place for 24 and then come to the hanger after midnight?"

"Yeah, why?"

"Just come to our hanger after midnight tomorrow and come in the back way. See if you can find a car nobody knows. The plane will be in the larger hanger and after you're aboard, I'll have it towed out. I'll file a flight plan for D.C. I'll explain the rest when we're airborne."

I still have access to several old cars Snooker left for me to auction off for his granddaughter after his passing, and there was one car I never understood why he'd purchased. The car was a triple black 1986 Cadillac Seville. Not really a collector car, even if when the car was new and was the top of the line. The windows of the car have been blacked out. It was such a strange car for Snooker to have since most of his collection were muscle cars. I wish I'd asked him when he was still alive why he bought it. But when he was alive, I had no idea he had such a massive car collection. However, the car was exactly what I needed.

Thank you, Snooker!

I hid out at Snook's old car warehouse and at the proper time, drove the old Cad to behind the airport. Sticking to back roads I still watched to see if I was tailed. Twice I timed a stop light as it turned red and squeezed through. I didn't see anyone trying to follow. However, the way people run red lights in Florida that didn't mean much.

I'd fixed the interior lights in the Cad so they wouldn't come on when the door opened. Just past midnight I rolled into the parking lot across from our hanger and drove to the end of the lot. I parked the car at the back of the long-term area and sat in the car for a couple of minutes, waiting to see if any strange cars were in the lot, or if I'd been followed. After waiting without seeing anything unexpected, I felt it safe to head over to the hanger.

When I stepped into the hanger Dominick was waiting for me. "Get in." he told me.

I climbed on board and found Henry behind the stick going through the pre-flight check list. Dominick opened the hanger doors and then pulled up in front of the plane with a tractor. He hooked it up and pulled the plane out. Once the plane was outside and the tractor was clear, Henry started the motors. Dominick ran towards the plane and leaped through the hatch, slamming it behind him.

Once Henry heard the hatch shut, he started to taxi. Over on the port side of the plane I saw a government Chevrolet Impala pull up between the buildings and when the person got out of the car, the streetlight illuminated him, and I could see he was on a cell phone.

I heard Henry call out, "We have a problem, the tower is denying us permission to take off. I'm going to ignore it."

Henry pulled the plane onto a runway, shoved the throttle forward and we immediately picked up speed. I noticed two cars with flashing blue lights coming towards us. Henry continued down the runway and at the last second one car veered off and the plane lifted over the top of the other. Henry hollered out, "Who the hell did you piss off?"

Dominick came into the cockpit, and I offered to move. Dominick motioned for me to stay, and Henry handed me a headset which I slipped on. He showed me the switch to talk. "Is this going to create problems for you?" I asked.

"I don't know. But I really don't care. There are several important people, both here and abroad we've done big favors for, and I've never collected on a lot of them. I'll be fine. Now, hold on, we need to get you to Washington State."

We were out over the Gulf of Mexico and with no warning, Henry put the plane in a steep dive. He dropped the plane so low I thought we were going to clip a wave. Back in Viet Nam I'd flown on a couple of missions to my jumping off point by chopper. One of the techniques pilots used to avoid getting shot at was flying at maximum speed while we were between 20 to 30 feet above the ground. It's called "NAP of the earth". It's simultaneously amazing, and terrifying. It had been a long time since Nam, and I'd participated in NAP flying. I found I didn't like it any more now than I did back then.

We flew NAP for half an hour when Henry finally pulled the nose up. I was most grateful. We leveled off at a higher altitude and then he slipped directly behind a large commercial jet. "Now we're hidden in their radar blip. I've turned off our transponder when I put back us down on the deck, nobody will have any idea where we are."

Twice we changed altitudes and followed a different commercial jet. When we were over the Pacific Ocean, Henry dropped down again and did more NAP flying. Eventually we turned eastwards to follow the Straits of Juan de Fuca. When we were close to the airport at Port Orchard, Henry turned the transponder back on. "Won't they pick up your signal now and find us?" I asked.

"It's against FAA regulations, but we have three transponders. Right now, we're shown as a FedEx plane coming in for a landing."

"Ya know, if I'd known what a crook you are, I don't know if I'd have wanted to be your partner?" I told him. We both laughed.

CHAPTER ELEVEN

Henry landed and taxied to a deserted part of the field. He'd planned for a rental car to be waiting and I found the car and drove to the drop off spot where I could hike into Walter's cabin. I'd hiked into his place enough times and I knew where his traps were set, and about the different false trails.

Rounding the rocks behind his place, I was again dazzled by the beauty of the surroundings. The mountains in front and the valley below were stunning. What a place to live. I stepped up onto the deck and called out his name. Without a sound, Walter suddenly appeared in front of the deck before me with a rifle in hand. It was like he came out of thin air. "Hello Matt."

"Walter, how the hell did you do that? You came up beyond the deck. It was like you were walking on air or you flew in."

Walter laughed and motioned for me to come forward. There was a platform in front of the deck he was standing on. "This is cantilevered so I can stand on the platform, and it will drop down below the deck. If I want, it can lift me up to the deck again."

"It gave me a scare. It was like you were floating on air when you appeared before me. Very cool."

Walter stepped onto the deck, and I wrapped my arms around him. I was glad to see he was still alive. He'd shaved off the beard he'd worn since he got out of the service and without the wild and wooly beard, he was handsome. "You look great without the beard. And appearing out of thin air was amazing."

"Okay, you're stunned and amazed. And Thien likes me without the beard. Now, don't take this the wrong way, but what the hell are you doing here?"

"Can we sit and chat for a bit?" Walter called for Thien and told her it was safe. We all embraced. "Where is Lois?" Thien asked.

"She's having problems with me right now, or perhaps I'm the one who's having the problems. Let's sit and I'll tell you what's going on."

We sat on chairs Walter had created out of old wood he'd found. I told them about the past few days and what I'd learned about our fellow ghosts. When I finished, Walter stood and walked to the edge of the deck. He stared out over the valley and when he finally turned back, he had a grim look. "You're sure, everyone was killed?" I indicated yes. "And we're the only two left?"

"You're batting 1000%."

"Any ideas who is doing this?" I told him my ideas about John Mescher and why so many agencies were after me when I told them I wanted to ask Mescher questions. When I finished Walter asked, "Who is this Mescher cat and any idea why he'd do this?"

"I hoped you might have an idea. I don't remember any missions where all of us were involved, so it isn't like we all saw something, or did something somebody still wants kept secret. The thing is, Mescher isn't from our time. He's not

98

old enough to have been involved with anything we did over there. And I'm told McNaulty is locked up somewhere."

"And Orchard told you to stop looking into Mescher and investigating why ghosts have been killed?"

"No, he *ordered* me to stop, and President Bradson also called and ordered me to stop my investigation."

"I can guess what your response was."

"Walter, someone even tried to keep me from leaving Fort Myers. Had it not been for Henry's amazing flying skills, I wonder where I'd be right now, or if I'd even be alive."

"Who all knows my location?" Walter asked.

"I believe Orchard kind of knows where you live, but not precisely. Somebody could come in here with a chopper and fly up and down the valleys and search for your cabin. It would take a long time. If they did happen to find it, do you have a place to hide?"

"First, they have to spot the cabin. You see how well it blends with the surrounding foliage. You know I'm into survival? Sometime I'll show you a place I've set up just in case."

"Ideas on what we're gonna to do now?"

Walter sat for a moment staring off into space. "We need to go on the offensive. But how can we get information where Mescher lives? It sounds like he's the one we need to talk to first."

We sat on Water's deck until dusk discussing ways to get an address for Mescher. During our discussion Walter asked again if I'd had a chance to check with my bank. I hung my head and told him I hadn't; and to please forgive.

"Do you have access to a vehicle?" I asked.

He smiled. "Tomorrow morning I've got something to show you. Let's get some sleep."

~ ~ ~ ~ ~

The next morning was cool, but the sun was shining. We had a cup of coffee, after which Walter gave his little family a big hug and then turned to me. "Follow me."

We hiked back to the main road and headed for the little general store. Next to the store was an older farmhouse with a dilapidated barn in the back. Once inside the barn, I noticed the barn wasn't in as bad a shape as it appeared on the outside. Inside was what appeared to be a ratty 1956 Chevy three quarter ton truck. "Where did this come from?" I asked.

"I bought it a few years ago. I own the house thanks to some of the checks your bank sends me every month."

"I'm sorry, I've been so busy I just haven't had the time to see why the check's stopped."

"That's not why I said that about how I bought the farm."

"I'm sorry anyway. But I'm also wondering what happened. I promise when I get a chance, I'll call the bank and see what's going on." I was angry with myself. Jennifer was someone I cared about. We'd been together long enough I'd grown very fond of her. I wanted to know she was safe.

"I rent the house to the owners of the general store and part of their rent is giving me the space in the barn. The truck may look old, but it has a completely new chassis with four-wheel disk brakes, rack and pinion steering and all new suspension. It also has a new fuel injected 383 crate motor mated to a 7-speed automatic transmission. The truck is registered to Jacob McNaulty." I laughed. "His mailing address is the little post office at the general store. The tabs are current, and I have a driver's license that says I'm McNaulty."

"Brilliant."

"Where do you want to go first? Any ideas on who might be able to give us a handle on Mescher?"

"Yeah, I need for you to get me to Port Orchard. I know somebody there."

~ ~ ~ ~ ~

Normally on my missions I worked alone, but on a rare occasion I was pared with a fellow ghost and sometimes we had to use other groups, like when we needed a ride up one of the rivers on a Swift Boat. A Swift Boat's normal crew was six, but on one trip when we went deep into the jungle and there were only four. A gunner was missing as was the engineer. On the way up the river, the skipper was picked off by a sniper and the other gunner. That left just the radarman, the boatswain's mate and me.

Somehow, we had to find our way back to the base and lucky for us the boatswain's mate was able to navigate, while the radarman and I filled in as gunners. We ended up in a fire fight and the mate was shot. I remembered a place down-river to run the boat ashore and the radarman and I packed the mate out of the jungle. The mate kept demanding we leave him behind and both of us kept telling him to shut up. I was lucky because I knew the area we landed well. When we got back to safety both the mate and radarman were grateful.

We kept track of each other until the radarman died of cancer five years ago. The mate became the manager of a marine supply company, and he has two brothers, both of whom are high ranking officers stationed at the Pentagon. I wondered what help he might provide getting an address for Mescher.

Walter drove to Port Orchard and dropped me off at the supply company. I entered my friend's store and when he spotted me, I gave him the signal I wanted to speak to him. He showed me the sign he'd understood. I went outside and when I saw him coming, I turned and walked towards a near-by park. I picked a bench in the middle of the park where I could see anybody coming. My friend walked up and sat down. "Matt, what's going on?"

"I'm dealing with some problems left over from Nam."

"You're shittin' me? That was like forever ago."

"Yeah, I know. But part of my past has come back and is biting me in the butt."

"What do you need?"

"I hesitate to ask you. I need you to make sure none of this shitstorm comes back on you. I'll tell you now, I'm wanted and there's a price on my head."

"You're kidding, right?"

"No. There are some agencies who've put a bounty on me. If you want me to go away, tell me now."

"Get serious. What do you need?"

"I need for you to see if either of your brothers can dig up information for me. But it must be done carefully. I don't want them getting burnt by any fall out."

"Matt, you don't screw with two and three-star generals."

"This time I don't think it matters how many stars they have on their shoulders. If certain agencies find out one of your brothers is asking questions about what I need to know, there'll be serious trouble. Again, if you don't want to get involved, tell me now and there'll be no hard feelings."

"I'd be dead if it wasn't for you. I owe you my life."

"This is a lot more serious than you know. This is about as nasty as things get. Don't tell me I didn't warn you."

"Matt, what do ya need."

I proceeded to tell him about Mescher. "Okay, and what do you need me to find out?" He asked.

"I need an address. I need to find him and ask him some questions."

"Come back tomorrow and I'll see what I can find out."

"Good. I'm going to stay here for a while and make sure we're alone. You go on ahead."

~ ~ ~ ~ ~

The next morning, we went through the same ritual. This time I headed straight to the same park bench. He came and sat down. His face was ashen, his hands shook, and he looked frightened. He kept gazing around until finally he said. "Shit Matt, do you have any idea what a shitstorm your request created?"

"I can guess. I warned you yesterday you didn't have to get involved if you didn't want to."

"Yesterday I had no idea exactly what kind of shit you're in. Did you know there are orders in place you're to be shot on sight?"

"I told you that!"

"Not exactly, anyway I called one of my brothers and told him I wanted information on John Mescher. An address and so forth. He told me he'd call me right back. My other brother called me about an hour later telling me that David, the original brother I'd called, had just been arrested." My friend's voice raised. "A two-star general was arrested! The brother who called me was on the phone and as we were talking, I heard someone banging on his door. He left his phone on speaker and I heard him arrested. Now this morning I saw two strange vehicles in front of my house. I snuck out my back door to get to my shop and wait for you. Now I wonder if I even want to go back to my shop."

"I'm sorry I got you in trouble. I should have stayed away."

I looked up and from the other side of the park I saw two men in suits headed our way. I had no idea if they were government, but men in suits in the middle of a park is a strange sight. I told my friend goodbye and we each headed off in different directions. I glanced back and the men had separated and one of them was following me.

At the end of the park was a wall with a tunnel through the middle. As soon as I exited the tunnel, I turned right and climbed up on the wall. The man pursuing me was running as he exited the tunnel and when I dropped behind him, he heard me. He turned and I made my fingers stiff as I drove them into his Adams apple. He was gasping as his hands flew to his neck, and I lashed out at his left knee with my right foot. There was a popping sound and he dropped to the ground. I knelt, putting a knee on his chest. Reaching inside of his jacket, I removed his pistol and found he had hand cuffs on him. I waited a moment to see if he was going to be able to breath. I only wanted him out of action, I didn't want to kill him. When I saw he was breathing I cuffed his left wrist to the ankle his right leg. I threw the key as far as I could and I left him.

I got to the parking lot where Walter was waiting and there was a government vehicle parked a few rows over. I got in the truck and told Walter to leave, now! We had to drive by the fed's car, and I was relieved to see it vacant.

I wondered what to do next.

CHAPTER TWELVE

I had no way of knowing how many people knew I was wanted, but I still needed information on Mescher. I remembered a lady friend I hadn't spoken to for ages. The last time we talked I recalled she had some super-secret job at the Pentagon. I wanted to call her, but I didn't want any cell site to accidently disclose our location. To keep distance between Walter's cabin and a cell tower, we looked for a tower outside of a village. When we found what we wanted, Walter parked next to the tower.

I called my old friend. A familiar voice answered, "Hello. This is Colonel Liisa Curtis. Who is this?" I loved her accent. Her father was an American who married a Finnish woman and Liisa was born in Finland. Because her father was American, she was automatically an American citizen.

"Hi Liisa, this is a voice from your past. If you know who it is, please don't say my name."

Silence.

"Liisa, are you there?"

"Oh my God, do you have any idea how much trouble you're in?" Her voice tinged with fear.

"Oh yeah, that's why I asked you not to say my name."

I got a call the other day. You know I'm under orders to turn you in? They know we're old friends, and I got a call from Director Cole himself telling me if you called, I was to contact him immediately. He also threatened me with dire consequences if I didn't." I knew the kind of place where Liisa worked wasn't the kind of place where one asks questions. I'd been told if you ask the wrong question to the wrong person there was a chance you'd just disappear. It was no surprise she was aware of my problems. "What did you do now?" She asked.

"I really don't have time to tell you the story. My question is what will you do?"

"Oh darling, you know I'd never rat you out. You and I have history. You know it could have been so much more. We never had a chance with our relationship, but it doesn't mean I don't have special feelings about you."

"I know Liisa, and I have feelings for you as well. But I refuse to bed another man's wife, regardless of how many problems you were having. I may have my faults, but I won't do that. Besides, that's in the past, I just couldn't do it, regardless of what you wanted."

"And that's why I still love you?"

"Yes Liisa. But this isn't the time to go down that path."

"What do you need, I remember what you did for me."

"Thanks."

"Why did you call me?"

"Can you get me an address for John Mescher?"

"Holy shit, you don't want much." A pause ensued. "I'll try and get the information and I'll make sure nobody knows we've been in contact. I'll text you if I find the information and if I don't, call me back in half an hour."

"Be careful. Asking questions can be dangerous."

I called back at the appointed time. "We're in luck. I found two addresses for Mescher, and I think the first address looks the best. I'll text you the information. Good luck and I don't want to know why you were even asking."

My phone notified me I had a text message. I checked and found two addresses for Mescher. One of them was in Ohio and the other was in D.C.

We started back to Walter's cabin and on the other side of the village four black Chrysler Town and Country vans with flashing blue lights in the windows went speeding past. I ducked and Walter drove on. We'd already been located. Making sure we were some distance from the cabin to make the call had been a good idea. I just hoped my friend didn't get caught.

It bothered me that I'd been found so quickly, and I wanted to check back to see if Liisa was safe. I had Walter turn around and we headed for the ferry to go over to the mainland. After I copied the two addresses, I removed the sim card from the phone I'd used and pitched it out the window. Later I broke the phone in half and tossed the pieces off a bridge. The fact they'd found me so fast meant Liisa's phone had been monitored. The bad news was now some of the agencies that wanted me knew I was in Washington State.

"Walter, I think we need to stay away from your cabin." Walter dove us to the ferry landing. We boarded and I went up on deck and took out the other burner phone. I called Henry. "Wow dude, I'm continually amazed at the number of people you've pissed off! Everybody wants your ass, now! They wanted me arrested but I convinced them I had nothing to do with your escape. I blamed another pilot. We have a couple of fictitious names on the books because of the clandestine missions we do. Whoever called checking up on me is now looking for somebody who doesn't exist.

"Anyway, Orchard is fit to be tied and he has a lot of people riding him to bring you in. I'm under orders to call him immediately if you contact me. I've had at least four calls from various agencies I'm to bring you in. Director

John Cole even called me again and threatened me with a long stay at Git Mo."

"Have you changed your mind about things? Are you gonna call Orchard or Cole?"

"Screw 'em. Come on Matt, what ya need?"

"Back to Ohio. I think I have an address to find... ah... somebody I need to find."

"K! Know where I dropped you off?"

"Yeah."

"Be there, 1:00 AM."

"Can I put it off for 24 hours. I need to make a stop."

"Yeah, same place 24 later work for you?"

"Great. I'll let you know if things change."

"Take care my friend, a lot of really dangerous people are gunning for you, and when I say gunning, I mean just that."

"Understood."

Hearing what Henry told me, I was worried about Liisa. I called her back and a strange voice answered.

"May I speak to Colonel Liisa Curtis?" I asked.

"Colonel Curtis isn't here."

"When will she return?"

"She's gone, she's been transferred."

"I just talked to her."

"And she has been transferred since then. Who is this?"

"Transferred where?"

"That's on a need-to-know basis. Who is this?"

I pushed the off button, opened the back of the phone, pulled the SIM card and threw it overboard. I broke the phone in two and threw the pieces into the sound. I returned to Walter's truck.

"What's up?" He asked.

"I just tried to call Liisa Curtis, and they told me she's been transferred. In less than a couple of hours she's gone, and they won't tell me where."

"Damn! That was fast. What ya gonna do?"

"I need you to get me back to the Port Townsend airport tomorrow night. Henry is picking me up at 1:00 AM."

"NO!" Walter said forcefully. "Henry isn't picking YOU up, he's picking US up tomorrow night. I'm coming with you. Remember, this affects me too." I had to agreed. He should be coming with me. We both needed to have a long talk with ol' Mescher.

"What are we gonna to do till tomorrow night?" Walter asked.

"Get me to Seattle, I need to see Mouse." Mouse is an old friend who has mysterious contacts all around the world, and an armory in the lowest level of his parking garage that would put several small countries to shame.

"Did you get any information on Mescher?"

"Yeah, I got two addresses. Will Thien be safe if you go with me?"

"I pity anybody who tries anything with her. I've never told you some of the things she did back in-country when we first met. I have all sorts of weapons stashed about the cabin and there are several early warning devices I have scattered along the trail. Not to worry. She can be a very dangerous person."

We drove off the ferry and headed for Seattle. Pulling away from the ferry landing, two black Suburbans with flashing blue lights went speeding towards the dock. I'd been traced to the ferry.

On our way down to Seattle we stopped at a truck stop where I purchased more burner phones and gave Walter a couple.

CHAPTER THIRTEEN

Walter dropped me off by Mouse's condo and I took my time walking around the block and those surrounding it. I didn't see any vehicles I felt were out of place and because I had no idea how many of his phone numbers had been compromised, I didn't call ahead.

When I felt it was safe, I turned down the alley behind the condo building and hid behind a dumpster. I waited a couple of hours, watching the door to the loading dock. I watched several delivery vehicles come and drop off deliveries. Each time the doors were open I could see into the building, and I didn't see anything peculiar. I slipped from my hiding place and moved up to the loading dock door. The doors have a combination lock and I know the combo.

Opening the door, I entered the building and crossed the hall. The stairwell door was unlocked, and I descended to the second parking level. Each level has a house phone next to the elevator and I called Mouse's condo. He never answers a call if he doesn't recognize the number and when his answering service kicked in, I told him, "Do not say names. This is Jade's guardian angel. Go to your armory. Now! I'm there." I hung up.

I'd saved Jade's life one time and I knew Mouse would know who'd called. In the lowest level of the garage, Mouse had a large room full of various weapons. When he heard the message, which would be soon I hoped, he'd come down to the armory.

It took over an hour before I heard the elevator doors opened. I was hiding behind one of the columns and I waited to see if he was alone. He called out, "Matt, are you here?"

"Are you alone?"

"Yes."

I stepped out from hiding. When the two of us were close, Mouse stepped up and strapped his arms around my waist. He gave me a hug and then stepped back and looked up. "What the fuck have you done my friend? I've getting calls from all sorts of agencies, as well as Bradson himself. The President of the United States called me to tell me you are a crook. Everybody wants your ass, and they want it now. What gives?"

"You know the group I was with over in Nam?" Mouse nodded. "We were called ghosts. A couple of months ago there were seven of us still alive. Now there are two, Walter and me. The other five were all been murdered.

"One of the ghosts was a biker. He had a strange person spending a lot of time around the bar where he hung out and after he was killed, the stranger disappeared. From his description, it sounded like John Mescher."

For the first time in my life, I saw a person's eyes bug out. "Mescher?" I nodded my head, "I know who he is, but I find it difficult to believe."

"Not only has Bradson told me to cease and desist, but I was taken to see Director John Cole who threatened me if I don't stay away from Mescher."

"Cole is Mescher's boss, and what you say is a stretch to believe, but if you say so, I believe! No wonder the world is after your scrawny ass. Do you know what Mescher's actual position is?"

"No and nobody will tell me."

"Ever since 911, all of the secret government agencies have been pulled under the NSB, the National Security Bureau umbrella. Name any agency and if you look deep enough, one way or another they all report back to the NSB. Somewhere near the top of the NSB is none other than John Mescher. I think he's number three man. Director Cole is above him and I guess that makes Bradson the top dog."

"Holy shit! Okay, now I understand how he has the juice to make my life hell. But I don't understand why he has this vendetta against former ghosts. We were way before his time. We never did a thing to cause him grief now. None of this makes sense."

"You were the one who brought up Mescher, I don't know what else to tell you. You're aware that Mescher's people do a lot of the dirty work McNaulty used to do. Someone put out the word you're wanted, dead or alive; preferably dead! I can see Mescher doing that. What do you need?"

"Are you going to turn me in? I know you deal in gathering and selling information and I'm sure knowledge of where I am is worth a lot."

"Go to hell Matt! Every time I look at Jade, I thank heaven for you and for what you did for us. You know I'd do anything for you. Your comment offends me. You know now how Jade and I feel about you. Name it and it's yours."

"Can I shop in your armory?"

"Let's go."

We went to the bottom floor and in the middle was a large, locked cement vault. At the entrance Mouse went through security procedures to gain access. I picked up a duffle bag from a pile on a shelf by the entrance and proceeded to load it up. I picked up two pairs of night vision glasses, a communication system so Walter and I could be in touch along with several handguns and a few sniper rifles with scopes. I selected several boxes of various types of ammunition. One box I selected was HELAP, which stands for high explosive incendiary/armor piercing ordnance. It was a fifty-caliber round which had a thirty-caliber tungsten penetrator built into in. The round was capable of blasting through tank armor, brick walls and concrete blocks. I thought the rounds might be a little overkill for what Walter and I might have to do, but it was better safe than sorry.

"Here is something you might want to have with you." Mouse extended his hand.

"What's it?" I asked.

It looked like a gumball. Mouse handed me a pistol which used a gas-cartridge to fire it. "The friction of the round passing through the air makes the covering very soft and sticky. The idea is to aim it at a window. Inside of the covering is a soft plastic sticky ball, when it hits the window, because it's soft it won't break the window. Inside of the sticky ball is a miniature microphone connected to a radio transmitter. The battery is good for a week. Its voice activated and you can listen to a conversation inside of the room where the window is located. Inside of this box are a dozen balls."

"You're kidding? I've never heard of such a thing."

"I know, one of my companies developed it. Take four pistols and a box of the balls. The pistols also fire tranquilizer darts. Take a couple of boxes of the tranquilizer darts. Be careful, the balls are still highly classified. If you get caught, you're not to disclose how you ended up with them or what you know about them."

"Know about what?"

Mouse smiled. He handed me two cell phones. I shook my head, "I have several burner phones. I don't need these."

"Yes, you do. For starters these can be linked to the little transmitters I just gave you. Also, the way these phones connect can't be immediately traced. Plus, I have the num-bers plugged into my phones and I will answer whenever you call. These are as safe as you can get with a cell phone. I would suggest however you don't stay on a conversation for more than ten minutes tops. After that, chances increase you'll be traced."

I thanked Mouse and we back to the lobby level. I called Walter. "Come down the alley and call me as you turn in. I'll be ready."

I had the duffle bag in the back of the truck and myself in place before the truck came to a stop. Walter pulled up to the one-way street at the end of the alley. There were no cars coming our way and he turned against traffic. At the next corner he turned again, and we were off. I looked back over my shoulder and saw two individuals running for a parked black Suburban, but we had turned the corner and were gone before they even got to their vehicle.

~ ~ ~ ~

The airport parking lot was dark except for one light pole at the far end. I used the pellet gun Walter kept in the truck cab to shoot that light out. Now the parking lot was completely dark. We left Walter's truck in the long-term parking area and walked over to the private plane area. I looked around for one of our planes, but I could see nothing like ours. I was starting to worry when a voice from behind me spoke my name. I turned and Dominick stepped from the shadows. "Where is the plane?" I asked.

"Who is this?" Dominick pointed at Walter.

I made the introductions, "Walter and I did the same kind of things back in Nam. We are together."

Dominick nodded, "Follow me." We went to the far end of a series of hangers and behind the last hanger was an older single engine Piper. "This is our ride."

"You're kidding." I groused. "This ain't gonna take us any place. Where's one of our regular planes."

"Right now, every plane we have is being watched or is under armed guard."

"What? Every plane?"

"Every plane they know about. Get in, we have a short hop to where I have a better plane waiting."

Once we were airborne, Dominick explained. "After your calls yesterday, federal agents showed up at every location of our planes and placed armed guards around them. Henry warned me what was going to happen, and I was able to get away with a plane.

"We had a few charters we had to finish, but those planes were tracked until they landed and then impounded. However, we still have a couple planes they don't know about. Due to some of the missions we fly, we have planes nobody knows about, and can't be traced. In a way the federals screwed themselves since it was at their behest we keep them secret."

"Are you going to get in trouble?"

"Are you kidding? Ask me if I care. Anyway, we've worked for so many agencies doing shit they don't want made public, I'm not worried. S'ides, I owe you, my friend. Whatever you ask, I'll do. By the way, where are we headed?"

"I need to get to Toledo. There's a town a little west called Ottawa Hills. I was just in Napoleon, and I've been told the person I'm looking for might be in Ottawa Hills. It's between Napoleon and Toledo. Where are we going now?"

"We're going to Marysville, where we have a better plane hidden. Then we'll work on getting you two to Toledo."

We landed in Marysville and taxied to a row of hangers. Dominick shut down the motor and Walter and I pushed it into an empty hanger and closed the door. I picked up the duffle bag and the three of us entered the next hanger. Waiting for us was a Bombardier Challenger 350 which has a range over 3,700 nautical miles. The plane was hooked up to a tactor ready to pull it out of the hanger.

I fired up the tractor and pulled the plane to one of the runways. Once the plane was in position, Dominick fired it up and we took off. Three hours later we were landing in Toledo. "How long do you think we will be here?" Dominick asked.

"Walter and I want to get a look at where we think Mescher might be hiding. Maybe he's so well protected, we may have to wait for him to move to another location."

"I'm going to move the plane to a private airfield half an hour from here. Call me when you need me, I'll be waiting."

Dominick had arranged to have a car waiting for us. We found it and I drove while Walter plugged the address we had into the Garman system. I knew we ran a risk of being detected using the Garmin, but I hoped nobody would discover us.

We found the address and I drove past Mescher's street which was blocked off with two black federal Suburbans with blue flashing lights flashing. In front of the vehicles were four army personnel in combat gear. Two of them were carrying M16A2 rifles and the other two were carrying M14 enhanced battle rifles. Nobody was driving down that street without permission.

I drove around looking for access to the house. The Garman showed a small stream flowing through the woods about half of mile behind the house which started in a bird sanctuary. We agreed the best way to approach the house would be after dark and enter the stream in the sanctuary and then wade down until one of us was directly behind the house.

We returned after midnight and the sanctuary was locked. Walter picked the lock and once inside, arranged the lock to appear locked. We flipped a coin to decide who was going to wade down the creek. I lost. I'd be the one navigating the stream while Walter found a place to wait until I called him.

I donned a pair of the night vision glasses and put on something to wear while wading downstream. It was a little cold but not so bad I needed to quit. Staying in the middle, I kept watch for roving patrols. Tree branches arched over my head and sometimes touched the stream and I'd dip under the water. I knew exactly when I reached Mescher's property due to the barbwire fence stretching across the water. The wire extended over the stream but nothing under the water. I submerged to slip under the fence.

Getting closer to the house I smelled cigarette smoke, wondering who supplied security. Back in the day, smoking on duty was forbidden, plus it was a good way to get yourself killed. It would have been easy for me to take out the smoker, but that wasn't the objective tonight.

I came to a break in the bushes where I could crawl up on the bank. Hidden under the brush, from my position where I had an unobstructed view of the back of the house. A light shone in one of the downstairs windows and inside I could see a large bookshelf. I assumed it might be an office and I took aim at the lower corner of a window with my pellet gun. There was a soft popping sound when I pulled the trigger followed by a soft thud when the projectile struck the window. I aimed for the next window to the right and one to the left beside the one I'd just hit. The small balls stuck to the lower corner of each window exactly where I aimed.

I sent Walter a text asking him if the listening devices were working. He replied one of them was working because he could hear a TV playing. I moved back to the center of the stream and waded back to my starting point.

When I got to the car, Walter had the receiver on, and we could hear voices from one of the rooms. Two people were talking, and I recognized Mescher's voice, but I didn't recognize the other person. "Listen to me," Mescher shouted, "I want Preston and McLaughlin found, and I want them on ice one way or another. I don't care how or what you do."

"We're doing everything we can sir." The other voce whined. "We've arrested all the pilots from their air service except for the faggot Walbourn. We can't find him. We've also impounded their planes. However, we think there may-be a couple of planes we don't know about."

"What do you mean by planes we don't know about."

"Because of the secret things they're hired to do, they've been instructed not to disclose all their planes. However, after interviewing their pilots we feel we have accounted for most of their planes. We have them under our control."

"They better be. And, what about the pilot shot up a few months ago? Where is he?"

"He disappeared. Nobody has seen him since he was released from the hospital. We believe he's gone back to recover in Europe where he has family."

"Do you have any idea where Preston and McLaughlin are right now?"

"We know Preston was in Washington state, and he visited his friend Steve Fox in Seattle, whom we have arrested and locked up." I was saddened to hear Mouse was being detained. "Preston managed to escape. He had a plane hidden somewhere. We know he flew somewhere but we don't know where the plane is now."

"Who flew him if you have all of their pilots under arrest."

"It's our belief that Preston can fly a plane. Walbourn taught him, but he doesn't have a license. When that pilot was shot, Preston landed the plane. The plane exploded after it was on the ground, but it was from the fuel tank being shot-up."

"Well, what about his old boss, Admiral Orchard?"

"He claims he has no idea where Preston is, and Orchard's orders are to report any contact he has with Preston, immediately. However, I don't trust him, so we have him under surveillance, very close surveillance.

"We've also spoken to Preston's girlfriend, and she swears she has no idea where he is, plus she knows what will happen if she helps him. I believe she'll turn him in if she can. She seems very upset with him for some reason."

"Not nearly as upset as I am," I muttered under my breath.

"What about McLaughlin?"

"He has a cabin in the Olympic Mountain range, and he's there with his family."

"You're sure?"

"Yes sir."

"Have you relayed all this to Spielman?"

When Mescher said the name, Walter and I looked at each other. He mouthed the word, "Spielman?" I shook my head and held my finger to my lips

The voice continued, "We've been relaying everything we're doing, sir."

"What does he say?"

"It's dragging on too long. He demands we take care of Preston and McLaughlin. He's given you a few more days and then he's going public with his information."

"You know that can't happen. I swear, if I go down, I'm not going alone. I'm taking several people with me. Now get the hell out of here and go do your job." Mescher shouted, "Find Preston and take care of things."

"Yes boss."

The receiver went silent. Walter and I looked at each other in stunned silence. The only Spielman I knew was the former ghost, Talon. It had always been assumed he'd been killed on a mission.

Or was he?

From Mescher's conversation, it sounded like Talon was still alive. But how? And what was he holding over Mescher to make him liquidate old ghosts?

"What do we know about Talon?" Walter asked.

"Not much. I only know his real name, which is Joseph David Spielman because I saw the info in the flies I was looking through. I didn't read his file carefully since I thought he was dead."

"Any idea what his mission was when he disappeared?"

"No. After he disappeared there was lots of rumors. One of them was he'd gone to China to assassinate some person who was helping the North Viet Nam troops, and there was the rumor about something in North Korea, but they were rumors. You know how rumors get started! But if either one was even partially true or it got out, I don't even want to consider the fallout."

"Who could we contact to see if we can get any more information?" Walter wondered.

"We can't ask Liisa anymore. I sure hope she's okay. I feel bad that I might have gotten her in trouble. The Boatswain Mate and his brothers are also out of the question. It sounds like Mouse is also in trouble. But I know he can take care of himself."

"I can't understand what Talon has to do with Mescher. It sounded like Mescher had to report to Talon for some reason."

"I agree, but it doesn't make sense. Like you said, all of us, including Talon, were way before Mesher."

"Any idea how can we find out about Spielman or where he might be? Who do we know that could get the information?"

I was stumped. Everybody I knew had been warned to stay away from us. And what was worse, anybody who we communicated with was under orders to immediately report their contact with us, in addition they'd been threatened with dire consequences if they disobeyed.

I needed somebody from my past. A distant past! A person who Mescher and crew would have no possible way of knowing about. The problem is what I did in the past was a small world and it had gotten smaller over time. But there had to be somebody I could ask. Who in my small world could help us?

Then I remembered an old friend who had recently passed away, everybody called him Snooker, his real name was Tom Frost and he'd been a command sergeant major. Snook had a couple buddies who might have access to the information I needed. An old friend of his I'd met, and Tom said he saved this fellow's life. I needed help one time and Snook set me up with his buddy, Elmer. Elmer had been a huge help and if anybody could help, this fellow could. Time to look up Elmer.

~ ~ ~ ~ ~

I contacted Dominick and asked him if he could get me to Portland, Oregon. We met at the airport, and since the plane we were using was unknown to Cole's staff, we were safe. Once in Portland, Walter rented a car and we drove south to Salem. Walter checked into a hotel, and I called Dominick back. "I just found out Salem has a small airport. Is it safe to have the plane here?"

"I can see no reason not to. Is it okay if I fly down in the morning? I have a…"

"Friend, you want to see." I interjected.

"Yeah, right." He laughed and hung up.

A few miles west of Salem is the farming community, Dallas. It has nothing to do with the big D in Texas. Snooks' friend worked in a mall between Salem and Dallas.

I parked at the mall and went inside. I found Elmer's store and I entered. I was looking at things while Elmer was waiting on a customer and when he glanced at me, I knew he recognized me. He gave a nod and I pointed at the front of my pants, indicating I'd meet him in the men's room. He gave another barely perceptible nod. I left the store and took a seat in the walkway between the stores.

Ten minutes later I watched Elmer walk out of his store and head for the men's room. When I entered, he was standing at the urinal. I checked both stalls which were empty. Elmer finished and zipping up his slacks, he looked at me. "Matt, it's been a long time?"

"Yeah. Is it okay to contact you?"

Elmer smiled. "You're a very popular man. All the way out here in the boonies I've heard about the hunt for you. Seems a lot of people want you either locked up or dead, and from what I understand, it really doesn't matter which."

"And where do you stand? Are you going to rat me out?"

"I owed Snooker a large favor I never properly paid. I know the two of you were friends, so I'll help you and, in that way, I feel I'm paying off my debt. No, I'm not going to rat you out."

"I need information. Do you still have access to your old sources?"

"Most of them. What do you need?"

I proceeded to tell Elmer everything I knew about Talon. "I know it isn't much. I just found out that he's still alive. What can you do?"

"Be at the store tomorrow, same time."

"Thanks."

~ ~ ~ ~ ~

The next day when I returned, I parked my rental towards the back of the lot and as I walked to the mall, I kept my head on a swivel. I doubted Elmer would rat me out, but I've been known to be wrong.

I went into Elmer's store, and he was with a customer. I stayed away from them until I saw him turn and come towards me. He called over to his customer, "I have a different model here." As he passed by me, he softly said. "Parking lot. Go stand by your car."

After waiting by the car for a few minutes Elmer, came out to the parking lot. Opening the passenger door Elmer got in the car and we moved to a different spot on the lot. "You didn't give me much time to look up the information you wanted. I've asked a couple of people I know to investigate this. Both wanted to know why I was researching old ghosts."

"In the past you didn't need much time. Am I wrong? Losing your touch huh?"

"Before I couldn't get in trouble. Even the two guys I have looking into this were scared shitless."

"Did you find out anything?"

"I tired, but this is all I could find out." Elmer started to reach into an inside pocket of his jacket when I glanced beyond him into the parking lot. A car was coming towards us at high speed. I reached inside my coat and drew out my pistol. The speeding car turned at the last moment and pulled up on the passenger side of my car, screeched to a stop. Both front and rear passenger windows of the new vehicle were down. A shotgun appeared in the back window, and I opened my door.

I was rolling onto the ground when I heard gunfire. The person in the front seat opened fire with what sounded like an automatic pistol against my windshield. Lying on the ground I felt glass from the shot-out windshield raining down on my back. Looking under my car I saw the other car driving away. Jumping up, I used my car roof to steady my arm and emptied my pistol towards the departing vehicle.

One bullet broke out the back window and the next round struck the driver in the back of the head. Another bullet hit one of the rear tires causing the vehicle to veer into a lamp post and slam to a stop. Another bullet must have hit the gas tank because I could see liquid dripping from the bottom of the car. The gas hitting the hot exhaust pipe caused the fumes to explode and withing seconds the vehicle was engulfed in flames. The resulting explosion knocked me to the ground.

I peeked inside the rental at what was left of Elmer. The shotgun blast had removed most of his face. I picked myself up and limped off. I didn't need to stick around and answer questions. I felt badly. I'd needed Elmer to help me, and it had gotten him killed.

Luck was with me when I exited the other side of the mall. A taxi was just dropping off two ladies and I got in the back and told the driver the name of the motel we were staying at. He made some comment about how far it was, and I pulled out my walled and handed him a hundred-dollar bill. "Will that get me there?" I asked.

"Yes sir. On the way."

When the cabbie pulled up in front of the motel, I pulled out another bill and tore it in half. I handed him half, "If you wait, you get the other half when I get back to your car."

"It's a deal."

I stepped away from the cab and called Dominick. "Where are you?"

"Salem airport. Why?"

"We need to leave town… now!"

I called Walter and told him he needed grab the duffel bag and immediately come to the parking lot. We got in the cab, and I handed the cabbie the torn bill along with another hundred-dollar bill. "Take us to the private sector of the airport."

"You're the boss."

When he dropped us off, I handed him two more bills. "If anybody asks, you know nothing. Okay?"

The cabby held up the two new bills and smiled. "Right, I know nothing about anything. Anytime you need a ride, you ask for me." He drove away and we headed off in search of Dominick.

~ ~ ~ ~ ~

We were airborne before Walter and I had a chance to talk. "What happened back there?"

"Evidently one of the people Elmer talked to was the wrong person. We were in the rental, and he told me he hadn't found out much. He was ready to show me the little he'd learned when I saw a car speeding towards us. There was no time for Elmer to react. The person in the back had a shotgun and the person in front used an automatic pistol. One of my return bullets put a hole in the gas tank and the car exploded. I had no idea I'd been exposed so quickly. Now we're back to where we started. We need someone who doesn't give a shit about any government agency, but still has access to government information. Somebody who is unafraid of any government agencies. Some sort of an outlaw group."

"Can Zampuchini help us?" Walter asked.

"I'm so stupid! Why didn't I think of him first, you're right? I can't think of any group who is more anti-government than Sal's. I'll call him when we land."

Salvatore Zampuchini was the head of an American crime organization which is decades old, and I won't name. I'd done him favors and he gave me a phone number one time, and a code to use if I ever got in trouble. I never thought I'd use it.

It was time.

Because I had no way of knowing if Sal was being monitored of not. I needed to find an old-fashioned pay phone. I remembered Orchard mentioned most of the agencies tended to focus on cell phones and texts and emails now days. He said there were so few pay phones left very few agencies bothered to monitor them. That would be the safest form of communication with anybody.

Walter and I started looking for a pay phone. We quickly learned pay phones really are a dying breed. It was over half an hour before we found one, that worked! I called the number Sal had given me and a voice answered me by repeating the number I'd called.

"Give me a number where you can be reached for the next half hour?"

I read off the number from the pay phone. The line went dead. Less than twenty minutes later it rang. "Matt?" I recognized the voice.

"It's good to hear your voice Mr. Zampuchini."

"Please don't call me mister. What's the problem?"

"Sir I'm in trouble and I don't know where to turn. You're my last hope. I need your help."

Sal laughed. "No shit you're in trouble. I've heard all about it. I received a call from a couple of agencies both of which are known by three letters. They have given me grief for decades and the interesting thing is they've offered me amnesty for any crimes that are on the books, plus forgiveness for any future problems I might encounter. Very tempting, don't you think? All I need do is call them and tell them if you contact me. And they would also like for me to set you up to be picked up. Complete amnesty if I do Matt."

I wondered where I stood with Sal. "What's ya gonna do?"

"You and I have had our ups and downs, but you're more valuable to me alive and on the loose than locked up or dead. Besides, you know how I feel about the government."

I snickered. "You're right, we've had ups and downs. But I've always been honest and fair with you, and I believe you've been the same with me."

"Why'd you call?"

"I need to find somebody. All I have is a name. I need an address if possible and any other information you can come up with. Also, up to a short time ago, this guy was missing in action presumed dead."

"Where are you, Matt?"

"I trust you, but I'd prefer my location remain a secret. The air has ears."

"I understand. I'll make you a deal. Come here, I'll protect you."

"Where are you?"

"I have a house on the Idaho panhandle. I'm near a town called Sand Point."

"I have a friend there."

"I know, you call him Digger."

"You know where he lives."

"Not too far from me. Do you have a way to get to me?"

"If I do, I'll call you when I get to Sand Point."

I knew if anybody was going to find info about Spielman, it would be Sal. I'd given him all the information I had. "Don't be surprised if I show up at your doorstep."

"You're always welcome. By the way, we have an airport less than six miles from the house. Just wanted you to know."

"Thanks Sal."

"Do you want me to call this number if I learn something about this Talon fellow?"

"No. This is a pay phone. I'll contact you later."

"How the hell did you ever find a pay phone?" He laughed. "And one that works! I'll hold on to any information I get till I see you."

Because we were desperate for any information on Talon, Walter and I returned where we could eavesdrop on Mescher. We waited a few hours without hearing anything. I took out one of my burner phones. Walter knew how to set up the listening device to forward any messages from Mescher and it would be recorded.

It was time to see if we could get to Sal. I called Dominick on the device I'd received from Mouse. He picked it up on the second ring. "Is this who I think it is?" Was his greeting.

"Yes. Are you still where you said you'd be after you dropped us off?"

"I will be shortly."

"Come, get us."

"In a few."

We drove back to the airport and grounded the car. I decided not to turn it in case we needed it later. We went to the spot where Dominick had dropped us off. No Dominick. There was an empty hanger with a door opened across from where we'd last seen him. We went inside and hid.

Half an hour later Dominick came sauntering between the two buildings with an unlit cigarette in his mouth. He stopped in front of the open door, took a stick match out of his pocket and scratched the tip with his thumb. When the match was burning, he lit the cigarette and once lit, shook the match and I heard him, "If you're out here, make a noise." I picked up a pebble and tossed it against the building behind him. "Okay. In a few I want you to follow. Go down four buildings and then turn left. The last building in the row will have the main door partially open. Do not move the door, just step into the building." Dominick walked off.

We waited a few moments and Walter started after Dominick. I waited a few minutes and as I was about to step out, I heard footsteps on the gravel coming my way. Two men walked past, obviously trying to stay hidden. Inside of Mouse's bag was a pump shotgun. Stepping behind the two men, I racked a shell into the chamber. Both men stopped walking when they heard the sound. "Put your hands on top of your head." I told them. One of them complied, one of them didn't. "Last warning, hands on your head or I shoot. If you know who I am, you know I have nothing to lose. Do it NOW!' The other fellow put his hands on his head. "Turn around, both of you."

Just at the right moment Walter came around the building and walked up behind them. He grabbed one of the arms of the man on the right and pulled it behind him and then the other. Using a Zip-tie he secured the man's hands behind him. When the man on the left started to move Walter clocked him.

We first took the man who was still mobile into the empty hanger. We made him lie down and we Zip-tied his feet together. Next, we carried the unconscious man into the hanger and laid him down. While I Zip-tied his hands and feet, Walter looked around to see if he could find anything to cover their mouths. He found a couple of filthy, oily rags and we stuffed them into their mouths and using some old ropes we found, tied the rags into place. Before we left them, I used the tranquilizer gun on both.

Quickly we ran down the row until we reached the place where Dominick said to turn. We found the hanger with the door partially opened. We stepped into the darkened area. "Dominick?" I whispered.

"Over here. There were a couple of men following me."

"I know. Walter and I have them tied up right now."

"Come on. I have a plane back here for us to use." The plane looked like an old, well used crop duster. I looked at Dominick. "Are shitting me? You're going to fit three people in that thing?"

"One of you will have to sit in the other person's lap. We're not going far. I have another plane stashed. There are a lot of people looking for the three of us and we need to leave now."

Thank God the fight didn't take too long. Sitting in Walter's lap I could see we were barely flying over treetops. I prayed we didn't clip one. I saw a small field ahead lit by marker lights and Dominick aligned the plane between the lights, and we landed. He taxied to the end of the field where Walter and I jumped out. There was an open hanger, and we pushed the plane inside and shut the doors.

"We're staying here for twenty-four hours. There is a commercial jet that leaves for Spokane Washington, and we can hide behind it. When we get over Montana I'll drop down and come into Sand Point undetected." Dominick informed us.

"Not in that puddle jumper!" I exclaimed pointing at the plane we'd just flown.

"Don't worry, I have a plane hidden a couple of hangers over. This one belongs to my cousins and nobody who's looking for us knows about it."

"What do we do for the next twenty-four hours."

"Follow me." Dominick motioned for us to follow him up a set of stairs. There was an apartment located in half of the hanger and he showed us where we could shower and then get some sleep. I was ready, I was tired.

SEVEN GHOSTS

CHAPTER FOURTEEN

Next morning, we checked to see if there were more recordings from Mescher. There was one with a lot of background noise, but we were able to hear Mescher's voice. "Look Spielman, we're working on trying to locate Preston. Somebody is helping him. We also have people working on exactly where McLaughlin is hiding." We could hear a buzz of somebody talking on the phone, but we could not make out the words.

Mescher continued, "I swear we're doing our best. Do you really think we want anything made public?" More buzzing. "I know you have those records." Buzzing again. "Don't threaten me. I'm doing everything I can. Besides, why'd you wait so long to start this vendetta?" Buzzing. "You're correct, it's none of my business, but if you want things done so fast, it will help if you let me know why it's so important." Loud buzzing. "Okay. I don't need this. All of us are working our asses off to get the two of them. I'm sorry if this isn't going as fast as you'd like. We're trying."

I heard the phone slam into the cradle and then Mescher mutter, "Fuck him. You just can't show up after 40 years and expect things to happened overnight, regardless of what your threat may be."

Walter and I looked at each other stunned. "What does Talon have that has everybody running scared?" Walter asked.

"I think we need to get out to Idaho and see if Zampuchini can help."

~ ~ ~ ~ ~

The flight to Idaho went without problems. We landed and Dominick taxied to the end of the runway and then behind a couple of hangers. We aligned the plane next to a couple of tie-downs and then covered it up like it was in storage. Unless someone wanted to start counting planes and comparing it to an inventory sheet, the plane was safe. Dominick said he had a friend who lived close and was going to crash at his place. He promised me he'd keep his cell close by.

Luck was with us, and we found a working pay phone behind the main office. I called Sal and waited for him to call us back. This time it went a lot faster. Sal told us a car would be around to pick us up. Shortly an older Cadillac limo pulled up and we got in the back. Sitting across from us in the jump seat was an acquaintance who I guess could be called a friend. Guido grinned at us and stuck out his left hand. A long time ago I'd damaged his right one. He was laughing as he asked. "How does it feel to be a wanted man?"

"It sucks. Now I understand why you've always been so paranoid. I don't know who to trust."

"I promise, you can trust me."

"No offense Guido, but I don't trust anyone right now, even you."

Sal's house was incredible. The house was stone and cedar and fit in well with the surrounding forest. We were taken to the top floor where we looked out over a large lake. Sal was dressed more casually than I'd ever seen. He was wearing a western style tan wool shirt made in Oregon and Levies with western style boots. He still looked like Gentleman's Quarterly material.

Coffee was offered and after we were served, Sal handed me a folder. On top of the folder were two pictures side by side. The one on the left was a picture of a face from my past. It was Talon, Joe Spielman, and the right was a picture of an older man. The face was haggard with several deep scars across one cheek and forehead. He was a resemblance to Joe, but I wasn't sure it was really him. I handed the picture to Walter, and he shook his head. "Could be, maybe?"

"Yeah, hard to tell. The person in this picture looks like he's lived a hard life."

"Agreed."

I pointed to the picture of the old person and looked at Sal. He leaned back in his chair and explained. "That's the passport photo he's using. He's traveling under the name Joseph Spielman. I was able to get if from a friend who works in immigration. Spielman came to the states about seven months ago from Toronto by way of Poland. I'm told we have no way to find out how he got to Poland."

I opened the folder. There were just two sheets. one was a copy of the entrance form Spielman filled out and the other sheet was information about his brother with an address of the brother who lived in Travis City, Michigan. At least it was more information than we knew earlier. We might have found a starting place. "What are you going to do?" Sal asked.

"Don't take this wrong, but I'm having a hard time trusting anybody, even you. I'm leery of telling you too much because I don't know what sort of position you might find yourself in. This way if you must tell something, the less you know, the less you can tell. Whatever Walter and I are going to do needs to stay with us. "

"I understand. You're correct. Why don't you spend the night and then get on your way?"

"Will do."

~ ~ ~ ~ ~

At first, I didn't know what woke me, but I was awake. I lay there for a moment trying to figure out why. When I looked up, Walter was standing over my bed with a finger against my lips signaling me to be still. The house was quiet. Walter motioned for me to come to the window. At the window I looked out at the dark night. Walter pointed at the forest shadows and a movement caught my eye. I was able to follow the shadow by subtracting the darkened silhouette from the darkness around the person. I concentrated on one spot and waited for more movement to cross the spot I picked. I stared at it and eventually something darker than the spot moved.

"There is somebody outside?"

"Did Zampuchini turn us in?" Walter asked.

"I doubt it. I have no idea, but I doubt if he would."

"There is no reason for anybody to be lurking around outside. I think we need to assume they mean to harm us. Agreed?"

I nodded. "Can you get the bag I got from Mouse?" I asked.

Walter had the bag hidden in his room. Walter told me to stay where I was, and he retrieved the bag from its hiding place. Opening it I found the small flashlight in one corner. Locating the night vision goggles I slipped them on. When I powered them up the outside became visible. I could see four people standing just beyond the tree line. I turned to Walter, "We need to go. Now!" I whispered.

We rummaged in the bag and removed two Glocks, two of the air pistols along with some darts tipped with a fast-act-

136

ing knock-out drug and our two com units. We slipped on the pistol holsters, headed downstairs and out the back door.

Before parting, we powered up the com units. Walter went into the woods while I slipped around the front of the house. With the night goggles on, I could see the four men hadn't moved. I had no idea who these men were, but I assumed they were armed and must be here to either take us in or eliminate us. Either way, it wasn't going to happen.

I pulled my Glock from the holster and screwed on the silencer. Putting the Glock inside my waist band for a fast draw, and with an air pistol in each hand, I aimed at one of the men. I heard Walter say "Left" in my ear and I knew he was going to take out the two men on our left. I heard Walter say "Now", and I pulled the trigger.

Walter's darts struck their target. He had new darts loaded and fired before the anyone realized there was a problem. Only one of my darts was successful. When the first man went down, the second man was alerted and moved. The remaining man aimed in my direction and Walter pulled his Glock and shot him in the leg. His scream broke the quiet night. Walter's man was down, and I moved to the men on the ground, making sure their weapons were removed. I put zip ties on all four and we moved into the woods.

The scream brought reinforcements and we heard them coming. Walter and I took aim and shot at the advancing men. I shot one man in the knee and the other was hit in the ankle. Walter had aimed higher and now one of his targets was missing fingers and the other was holding his right shoulder. All the reinforcements were on the ground.

Walter stepped over to Missing Fingers and put his knee on the man's chest. Pointing his pistol at the man's forehead, he asked. "Who sent you?" The man shook his head. "How did you find out where we were?" Again, he shook his head. I heard Walter cock his pistol. "At this point, I really don't care if you live or die. You were here to take us out, so I don't care one way or another. This is your last chance, how'd you find us."

Fingers moaned, "Shoot me. It doesn't matter. If I tell you anything I'm dead and if I don't tell you, I'm dead. Shoot me."

I told Walter to step back, and I aimed the air pistol at the man. When he saw me start to pull the trigger he screamed, "Stop". Woops, too late.

Walter turned and looked at the man lying on the ground who I'd shot in the shoulder and pointed at me. "My partner is just itching to pull the trigger again. You see what he did?" Walter pointed to the man I'd shot. Shoulder had no idea I'd only shot his partner with a dart.

"Don't shoot. We were sent here by…" I heard a bullet go past my ear before I heard the rifle shot and I watched the man's head explode. Whatever he was going to tell us was gone.

Walter and I reached down, and each grabbed an arm of Missing Fingers and moved him behind a tree. We split up and I heard over my com, "Left of my position, 200 yards out, on top the rock." We both drew a bead and shot the man at the same time. I watched him tumble off the rock.

The commotion caused the lights in the compound to flood the area with bright light and Sal's soldiers came running out of the house. All were armed and quickly fanned out into the surrounding woods. Two of Sal's people took Missing Fingers into the house. Sal's resident nurse came and performed triage. We decided to wait and see if we could get information on who'd sent out the attack on us. As Sal's people returned, they brought the three bodies with them. However, they told us that at least two men had gotten away.

It was late that afternoon before Fingers was in any condition to answer questions. The nurse gave him a lot of pain killers but he seemed ready to talk. "How did you know we were here?" I asked.

His speech was slurred, but still understandable. "We were sent here to wait and see if you might show up."

"Who sent you?"

"We were told the orders came from Director Cole himself." The NSB was behind this? The National Security Bureau. That totally sucked!

"How did you receive your orders? Verbally or by message?" Walter asked.

"Our leader got a text. We're out of Portland and drove here."

"Where is your leader?" I asked.

"He's one of the people you shot. I think he's dead."

"What were your orders?"

The man paused a second before he responded. "To kill the two of you."

Walter stood and motioned for us to leave the room. Before we left, the man asked. "What are you going to do to me now?"

Walter snarled. "Your orders were to kill us. You fucked up and didn't get it done. Now that's what's going to happen to you." He turned and I followed him. As we left, I heard Fingers pleading "Please don't kill me, I have a family. Please don't kill me."

Sal was waiting in the hallway and told us to follow. We went to his study where we were served drinks. After we were comfortable, Sal asked. "I guess I was wrong, my phones seem to be under surveillance. I can't come up with any other way they could have known you might be here. What do you want us to do with him?"

Walter replied, "Are your people still in the woods looking for any others?" Sal indicated they were. "How about taking the men who attacked us and stage a bank robbery. Make sure it goes wrong. Leave the bodies behind, and any still alive who were trying to take us out. Make sure they get caught and make it difficult for them to get out of the mess."

Sal laughed. "I think that can be arranged. But what are you going to do now?"

I replied. "Missing fingers mentioned the NSB. That's Mescher's group which mean this all leads back to John Cole who is at the top."

"Can we somehow get to him?"

"I'd doubt it. I'll bet right now he's very well protected, probably even more than President Bradson."

"Okay, let's see if we can find Talon. We have a starting place in Michigan." Walter said.

"First, let me see if I can find Dominick."

~ ~ ~ ~ ~

I called Dominick's number. I heard the phone stop buzzing and I knew it had been answered but there was only silence. "Dominick, are you there?" I finally asked.

"Who is this?" A frightened voice aasked.

"What do you mean who's this? Who else would call you? It's Matt. Can you come and get us? We need to go."

Another long pause ensued before Dominick asked, "Where are you?"

"Where you left us."

"Idaho?"

"Yeah. Why?"

"Idaho? Right? Answer me."

"Yes, Idaho. I just said that. What the hell's going on?" I didn't understand, and I was really getting tired of his crap.

Another long pause. "You haven't heard?

"Heard what? Damn it, Dominick, what the hell's going on?"

"Mescher!"

"What about Mescher?" I almost shouted.

The fear in Dominick's voice was something I'd never heard. "Please tell me you had nothing to do with Mescher's death."

"What? Mescher's dead?" I shouted. Walter's mouth dropped open.

"Somebody broke into his house and killed him, along with several of his aides and then got away. Cole is blaming you and Walter! Every agency has orders to shoot to kill. If either of you are spotted, you're to be put down on the spot and anybody with you. You're not to be interrogated. There are to be no questions asked. You two are to be liquidated."

I was stunned. "Fuck me!"

"You might say that." Dominick said.

"What you gonna to do?"

"Excuse me, I thought for a minute you two had something to do with his death, but I couldn't figure out how you got there. I'm here to help. What do you need?"

"We're trying to get to Michigan. Can you get us there? Or do you want to stay away from us?"

"Dude, I've lived on the edge for a long time. This is nothing new. By the way, they have Henry locked up, but I'm still on the loose. They think I'm in Europe" I was saddened to hear Henry had been arrested. Dominick continued. "Come to where I dropped you off before. Understand?"

"Yes."

"Come tonight at 1 AM. I'll be there, but I have no idea how safe it will be. A lot of people are after both of you. Cole's pushing since everyone thinks you and Walter killed Mescher. There's a bounty on you. I don't know exactly how much, but I've heard it's over seven figures, each, for your bodies. You know I'd never be tempted."

Arrangements were made with Sal to be taken to the airport later. Walter and I were having coffee with Zampuchini, and I asked Sal if he had any more information on Mescher's death. "I thought you guys had a listening device set up at Mescher's house."

Walter and I looked at each other and stupidly hung our heads. I called the number to access the recording to check. We had a message and I put it on speaker phone. The recording started with a noise that sounded like a pistol with a silencer shoot several times and bodies falling to the ground. Mescher's frightened voice asked, "Spielman, what are you doing here?"

"I'm tired of waiting; tell me, where's Preston and McLaughlin?"

"You need to believe me; we're working on it. We've tracked them to Idaho, and I sent a team to take them out. I'm waiting to hear from them."

A phone rang and Mescher's voice answered. "Hello."

The buzzing sound of someone talking over a phone was heard. Then Mescher's panicked voice. "What? All of them? Killed or captured?" Silence. "Okay. Take care of any fall out from this." And then the sound of a phone being hung up.

Talon's voice, "What happened?"

"For some reason it didn't work. Some of my men were captured and others have been killed."

Talon snarled, "Your people are incompetent. I'll take care of it myself."

Mescher's fearful voice whined. "I don't understand. Why now? Why go after those two at this late date?"

"I wanted them dead before I killed you. Now it doesn't matter, I'll take care of it myself. I spent so many years in that fucking North Korean prison and none of you tried to get me out. Not McNally or you or Preston or anybody. You all left me there to rot."

"You can't put that on me. It was before my time. Until you contacted me, I didn't even know you existed. Besides, you knew from the start what the deal was. If you were caught nobody was coming to get you."

"Yeah, but none of you had the authority to order me to do that mission. I did what I was ordered to do. When it fell apart, not one of you tried to help me, you just left me there to rot." The cough of a silenced pistol was heard.

We heard a scream. "You fucker, you shot me." Another shot and Mescher screamed several times, "My finger's gone."

Maniacal laughter was heard and then a shout, "Yeah. Watch! I'll do it again it felt so good." We heard the pistol cough again.

More screams were heard and Mescher begged, "Don't shoot me again. Please."

"Why not?" More shots.

I heard a crash. "My foot. You've shot my toes; I can't stand up." More shots and more screams.

"How do you like it? My toes were frozen off while I was forgotten, rotting away in that hell hole."

"It wasn't my fault. I had nothing to do with that mission." Mescher moaned.

Talon screamed. "I don't give a shit. You people lied to me. You owed me. Somebody should have come and got me." We heard another shot and then more screams. "I want you to feel pain. Pain like I had to deal with every day."

Mescher begged. "Wait, if you kill me, who's going to get Preston and McLaughlin for you? You can't kill me."

"I'll find them on my own. I'll find the two of them, kill them and then I'm going to release all of the information I have on what I was ordered to do."

"You can't do that. That will start a war between our countries; they have the atom bomb now."

"Perhaps you people should have thought about that." Talon shouted.

"Talon, your orders didn't come from any authorized source. You were sent in, and it never should have happened."

Talon shrieked. "But it did. I did what I was ordered to do. That was a fuck-up on your people's end. Because of that fuck-up, you owed me. You should have gotten me out of there. But nobody ever came." We heard another shot, Mescher's pained squeal followed. In the background there was the sound of somebody pounding on a door. The sound of an unsilenced gun firing several shots was heard. The pounding on the door stopped. Talon must have shot through the door because whoever was pounding the door stopped.

"It's time for me to leave. Say hello to the rest of your buddies in hell."

Mescher cried, "No..." A shot was heard and then moaning. "Talon, please. End this. I hurt so bad."

Talon's demented laughter. "It will end, in a while. As you bleed out, you will pass out and then die. But you get to think about why you deserve to die. I wanted to die every day, but I didn't. But you will... eventually."

A door opened, footsteps and maniacal laughter faded away. All that was left was Mescher moaning. The moaning and crying continued for a few minutes and then silence. The tape shut off shortly afterwards.

We sat there stunned, looking at one another for a long time as we tried to process what we'd heard. I had my issues with Mescher, but I didn't want him to die that way.

Walter and I got up and walked outside. I was having a difficult time with what just happened. It was apparent Mescher had been involved in the death of at least one ghost, and perhaps all of them. Because of that I was glad he was dead, but I still had a hard time with the way he died. To listen to the death of a person and be helpless to stop it was terrible and extremely unsettling.

Later Sal, Walter and I gathered again in Sal's office. I asked Sal if he had any more information on where Talon might be hiding.

"Nothing so far." Sal said. "If that's really Talon on your recording, he took out the guards behind Mescher's place before he entered the house. When he went in through the back door, the guards inside were killed. You heard Mescher being tortured before he was killed, and two bodies were found outside of the office where Mescher finally died. Until I heard that recording, I didn't exactly understand why Spielman finally killed him. Anyway, since nobody else knows about Spielman, nobody has any idea who killed him. It's assumed you two are the ones who did it in retaliation for your ghost comrades."

I pointed at the phone. "Of course, that wasn't the case and now with the recording Walter and I should be off the hook."

Sal laughed. "Yeah, I know, but how are you going to release the recording? And who is this Spielman guy?" Sal asked.

"The information you got for us is basically all we have. His name is Joseph Spielman nicknamed Talon. We thought he'd wait for people to find us, but it sounds like he got tired of waiting." I told Sal the little I knew about Talon and the rumors regarding his last mission.

"But we still have no idea what Talon has or what his orders were. If there was just some way to find out for sure what the assignment was for the mission." Walter wondered.

"I wonder if Orchard would tell us." I asked.

Walter looked at me like I was crazy. "Are you serious? He's under strict orders to turn us in. How can we possibly talk to him?" Walter said.

"I think I know a way to contact him. Gypsy Queen showed me one time how to hack into anybody's email server. I could send him a message and see what he has to say."

"Is there any way he could come back on us?"

"I don't know. That's something I need to ask Gypsy. I wonder if her phones are being watched?" I asked.

"Why not use one of my cell phones to call her?" Sal volunteered.

I called her number. Since it was cell to cell, I knew the number I was calling from would show on her screen. I wasn't surprised when she didn't pick up and the call went to her mailbox. "Gypsy. This is 347 million calling. Call me back at this number when you get a chance. Thanks."

An hour later the phone rang. Her voice sounded fearful. "Hello. Is this who I think it is?"

"Yeah, this is Ralph's poker buddy." She started to say my name and I cut her off. "No names. The air has ears. I don't want to get you in trouble, so if you want, hang up now."

"I think we're safe. What's going on?"

"I need to hack into somebody's email. I want to leave a message, but I don't want anybody to be able to follow any sort of a trail and find me. Can I do that?"

"Yes. How about you give me the message and I'll send it for you, and you can trust me when I tell you nobody'll be able to trace it. We're both out of the loop."

"I want this person to call me." I told her John's email address and gave her a number from one of the cell phones Mouse provided. "This is important for him to call. Tell him it's his Alaska fishing buddy. He'll understand."

"Okay, I'll do this. But it'll cost you."

"What's the price?" I slowly asked.

She giggled when she told me. "When this is over, you'll take me, and only me to dinner at Hanney's Hideaway and then tell me what this was all about. Deal?"

"Deal." I hoped I'd be able to make good on the deal. For all I know I could end in prison, or dead.

Walter and I were at the airport getting ready to board the plane when my cell phone when off. I recognized the number and I figured I was safe for a couple of minutes. Since we'd be taking off any second, I didn't think there was time for anybody to trace the call. I answered. "John?"

"You have no idea how much trouble you're in since the two of you went rogue. I won't say your name, however…" He didn't have to finish. I knew exactly what he meant. "What the hell are you doing? And more important, why'd you kill Mescher?"

"John I can prove I was over a thousand miles away when he was killed. I believe Talon, Joseph Spielman, killed him."

"What?" He shouted. "You're crazy. Spielman's dead."

"No, he's not dead. I can't tell you how, but we overheard Mescher talking to Talon before Talon killed him. I'm sending the link to your number for you to listen to the recording of Mescher and Talon. Talon was threatening Mescher with something about his last mission. Whatever Talon has is the reason Mescher was having old ghost members killed."

"What the hell are you talking about? Where are you coming up with all of this?"

I gave him the information on how to access the recording of Talon shooting Mescher. "John, listen to the recording. Then find out what Talon's mission was when he went missing. I think it's the reason all this is happening."

John repeated. "Talon has been missing for years, he's presumed dead."

My voice was rising. "He's not dead!" I took a deep breath and lowered my voice. "I have a recording of him and Mescher talking before Talon killed him. I'm sending it to you. Talon's body was never found. I understand he entered the states through Canada using his real name. You can check that with immigration."

"Listen, come in now and we'll get to the bottom of this. Trust me. I'll protect you."

"Sorry, but right now I don't trust anybody. Particularly you old friend. And especially not Director Cole. I have no idea what he has on you to make you to turn on me. Anyway,

I can't, and won't come in. Now, please do what I asked, find out Talon's last mission. I'll call you later. Bye"

"Do not hang up. I ..." It was too late. Dominick had moved the plane into position. I got in the plane, and we immediately started to taxi. We were gone before anybody could possibly show up. I didn't know if Orchard was lucky or what he would have to deal with from my phone call, but it wasn't my problem. We were on our way to Michigan and find Talon's brother and hopefully Talon.

CHAPTER FIFTEEN

Our plane landed at Cherry Capital Airport where Walter and I loaded the gear from Mouse into a car Dominick coordinated for us. "I'm going to leave," he told us, "I have a better place to wait for you. I don't think anybody knows about this plane, but I'm not taking chances. I'm making it as difficult as I can."

The car Dominick arranged for us wasn't much. The car didn't have a Garman and I pointed it out to Walter. I had no idea where Talon's brother's place was located. "How are we going to find the house?" I asked Walter.

"Oh shit. What do we do now?"

"Look in the glove box. Perhaps there's a map." I started pawing through the glove box and along with old candy wrappers, several insurance papers and registration papers, much to my surprise I found a well-used local map. When I picked it up it fell apart in three sections. The map was old, but it was even longer since I'd used a map. Now days I use a Garman.

Oh well, old-school works just as well.

I looked for the street name in the index, found it and after locating which piece of the map we wanted, we headed out. I didn't know much about the area, but from the little I knew I'd always thought Travis City was an affluent area. I guess all areas have pockets of downtrodden people and this town was no different.

I had two addresses and we had a choice of going west or north. We decided to try the north address first since it appeared more secluded. We were at the end of the map before we came to the correct area. A dirt road led off from the main highway and we parked in a wide spot. Rifles in hand we started walking down the dirt road.

Trees lined the sides of the road, branches reaching across to form a tunnel and we moved carefully down the lane until we came to a gated fence blocking the road. Several signs posted on the gate told us we were on private property; we were not wanted and to keep out. Undaunted we opened the gate easily and went through. We walked on opposite sides of the road and rounding a turn, ahead we saw a rusty shipping container blocking the road. Walter took a couple of steps towards the container when he hollered, "Get down."

I dropped to the ground and from that position I could see a trip wire directly in front of me. Glancing over at Walter, he pointed at a different trip wire on his side of the road. Taking the end of the barrel of his rifle, he lifted the wire. Two holes appeared at the top edge of the container and two-gun barrels slid into the open spot. Both guns started spewing bullets and had we been standing; we would have been hit.

Walter put a HELAP round in the rifle chamber. He aimed at the side of the container and fired. The container must have also been filled with explosives because when Walter's bullet hit the container, it exploded. We had no idea what was in the container, but it turned into a bomb. Luckily, we were already on the ground. If standing, we'd have been knocked down by the concussion force. Pieces of the container rained down around us, and we crawled deeper into the forest as quick and as far as we could.

I watched the back doors from the container fly and land several yards away from the smoldering ruins. The doors were still locked together, and from that we assumed there had been nobody inside. As the smoke cleared, there was little left of the container. We didn't want to have to answer a bunch of questions and we ran back the way we'd come, got in the car and left. Several police vehicles went by, lights flashing and sirens blaring heading towards the destroyed container.

We drove back to town and found a café where we ordered coffee and discussed what to do next. "We still have one more address to check out." Walter said.

"After the last encounter, I wondered what's in store."

"Let's check it out. While Talon is loose, we ain't safe." I agreed.

Following the map, we drove west and were almost out of map before I found the street we were looking for. The road was a side street and I use the word street loosely. It was a poorly oiled, single lane path with deep potholes. Since we didn't want to alert anybody we were coming, after a short distance we turned around and returned to the main highway.

We drove for a quarter of a mile when we came to an ancient, deserted gas station. All the windows were busted out and only one pump remained with all the glass in the front display was shattered and the hose missing was left. I pulled abound back and parked next to a couple of old dumped derelicts. Our car wasn't as bad off as the other two, but it was in poor enough shape it didn't stand out.

We selected items from our duffle bag; a com-unit, night vision glasses, our magic gumball hearing devices, a couple of Glock pistols, two rifles along with different ordnances and several HELAP bullets.

We started down the long winding lane, potholes getting deeper and larger as we went on. "What kind of vehicle would a person have to use on a road like this?" I wondered.

We came to a locked gate with a tall cyclone fence going off in each direction away from the gate. Razor wire was wrapped around the top of the fence, and several signs hung on the fence stating beyond the fence was private property and we were to keep out. Another sign said trespassers would be shot on sight.

Walter pointed out the insulators holding the razor wire in place indicating the fence was electrified. It was obvious whoever was inside didn't plan for any Halloween trick or treaters.

Following the fence to the left, we kept twenty feet away from it since we didn't know what kind of warning devices might be planted around the perimeter. Accidentally setting some device off would lose any element of surprise we might have.

Finally, we spotted a place where the fence should have been tight against a large rock, but a bush was growing through the fence and pushed it away from the rock. A couple of the glass insulators were broken next to the rock, and it appeared the fence wasn't electrified.

Walter used a stick to push against the side of the fence, using the rock as a fulcrum. He was able to move the fence further away from the rock and as he moved it, no sparks erupted. We thought it was a reasonable assumption it should be safe to wiggle through the gap he created. Once inside, we prodded the fence back into position.

Making sure our voice coms were working, we split up to cover more territory. There was the possibility of more sensors in the ground, but we decided to take a chance. I thought we were far enough from the front edge of the property to be reasonably safe from detection.

Walter disappeared into the forest, his ability to move undetected was one I envied and wished I could emulate. I moved forward, keeping watch for any sort of trip wires or devices which would warn of our presence.

I reached a large clearing with a small wooden building in the center. I wondered why such a large clearing had been created around the hut. I removed a slender metal object from my stash of goodies and pushed the button on the side to fire it up. It reveals invisible laser lines, a trip field, and makes a soft alert sound if a field is booby trapped. Pointing it at the ground around the hut I saw it was crisscrossed with red lines. The field around the little wood hut was a trip field. I activated my com. "Walter."

"Yes."

"Be careful. I've come across a shack in the middle of a trip field. There might be more."

"I know, I'm looking at one now and I see the field."

"Is there a small wooden structure in the middle of the field?"

"Yeah."

"I wonder what's in the huts."

"I think I can get through the field. The spaces between the laser lines are big enough for me to walk through." Walter said.

"Do you want to wait until I get there?"

"Not necessary."

I pulled the scope out of my pocket and carefully examined the area above the door of the hut and the area on the ground in front of the door. Rain and wind had exposed the smallest piece of wire lying in the dirt directly in front of the door. "Walter, stop. Now!"

"Why?"

"The door on this hut is rigged. I can see a little of the wire buried in the ground in front. I'm positive your hut is the same."

It seemed like the longest couple of minutes I'd ever spent before I heard Walter. "I'm clear."

"Stay where you are. I'm coming to you."

I knew approximately where he was, and I moved as slowly as I could through the brush. I spotted a trip wire which I avoided setting off.

Walter was standing at the edge of a similar open field with a small wooden hut centered exactly like the one I'd found. While he was waiting, Walter had dug out his scope and carefully looked over the area directly in front of the building. "Somebody does not want anybody to know what's in those buildings.

"Look directly above the door. Just under the roof." Walter said. I looked and saw what resembled a can the size of a soup can attached above the door. "What do you think?" He asked.

The can was painted so it blended with the siding and without the scope, we'd have never spotted it. I shook my head. "No idea. Let's move on and see what else is here. By the way, on my way to you, I found a trip wire. I wanted to get to you, so didn't explore where it led. Be careful."

We spread out 50 feet apart and slowly continued to move towards the center of the property. Walter stopped once and motioned for me to look at the trip wire he'd found. Carefully we stepped over the wire and moved on.

Ahead we could see the forest starting to thin until we came to another open space. In the middle of this space sat a log cabin surrounded by cyclone fencing. At one time it must have been an attractive structure, but now it needed repairs. The front porch sagged and there were several pieces of roof shingles missing with underlying tar paper exposed. A crooked smokestack had a whisp of smoke coming out and

I heard Walter whisper over the com, "Do you think somebody's in the cabin?" I shrugged my shoulders. "Did you bring any of your listening balls?"

I reached into my pack and pulled out the air pistol, checked the cartridge, and loaded one of the balls into the chamber. It was a longer distance than I thought the ball might travel safely, but I tried it anyway. Taking aim at a window, I squeezed the trigger. The pistol made a pop, followed in a few seconds by the soft sound of the ball hitting the window. The ball had made it and it wasn't a bad hit, more in the middle of the window than I would have liked, but it would work. Walter put on his earbuds and turned on the listening device.

The two of us listened for a long time without hearing any sounds inside the cabin. Walter continued to inspect the front of the cabin with his scope. When he lowered the device, he whispered. "The front door has a trip mechanism along the bottom. I can't tell if the porch, or the door is set to go off when it's tampered with. I suggest we toss a rock up close to the door and see what happens."

I wasn't comfortable with the idea. I told him, "I'd rather wait. I don't have a good feeling about this whole place. I feel like we're missing something. Something very important."

"I understand, but how long are we gonna wait?"

"Dunno. Do you have someplace you need to be?"

Walter laughed. "No!"

"Okay, then let's give it more time." Walter agreed.

Lying on the ground, we discussed various options in soft voices over our com units. We were lying in wait when Walter lifted his head and put his finger to his lips. I also heard the sound in the distance. A ragged truck engine badly in need of maintenance was moving our way.

"What are we going to do?" I heard Water's voice ask over the com unit. I shook my head.

The engine sounds grew louder. There was no need to answer Walter, we were going to stay until we knew who it was. The truck continued to labor up the trail to the old cabin. There was no reason for anyone to be here unless they owned the cabin. In addition, considering the safety precautions around the building, the situation could quickly turn violent. We kept our weapons ready and settled deeper into the woods staying well concealed.

An old beat-up camouflaged Dodge power wagon with came lurching around the bend, avoiding potholes as best it could. The truck was either late 50's or early 60's, it showed a lot of wear and badly needed a muffler.

The power wagon rolled to the edge of the clearing surrounding the cabin and stopped. Two men got out and from the latest picture I'd seen, I recognized the driver as Talon. Had I not seen his passport picture, I'd never have recognized him. His face was drawn and pasty white. Several long scars ran across his forehead and down one cheek. Because of the scaring, one of his eyes bulged and it looked like when he shut his eyes, one eye would still be partially uncovered.

Talon was carrying a Sig Sauer SP2022 Pistol 10 RD 9mm in his left hand and the way he held his right hand it appeared damaged. When he took a step, there was a pronounced limp. I took my scope and focused on the passenger. The two men looked enough alike I assume it was Talon's brother. I watched his brother reach back into the truck and pick up something from the dash and then point it at the cabin. My warning device showed the laser field turned off. Talon's brother pushed another button on the device in his hand and the gate swung open. At the same time, part of the front deck of the cabin slowly dropped, revealing steps under the cabin. The entrance to the cabin wasn't through the front door.

I looked over at Walter and pointed at Talon's brother. He nodded in understanding.

"Talon, you're surrounded." I called out. "Both of you on the ground, now, or we'll shoot."

Talon spun towards my voice, pulling the trigger on his Sig Pistol as he turned. When he turned, I fired and clipped his left thigh. He fired two more shots, and something hot struck my left leg. I'd been hit. I took another shot which hit the left front window of the truck. Talon ignored the missing window and pulled himself back in and fired up the truck. It lurched forward and towards the right as he fought the wheel.

Talon's brother, who'd hid behind the truck was now exposed. I heard a shot and his brother cried out. Walter shot him in the right shoulder. I heard another shot but had no idea who fired it. I was too busy keeping track of Talon.

When the bullet hit my thigh, it forced me to my knees. I watched Talon weaving back and forth as he tried to speed away. With only one good arm, steering the old heavy truck was more than Talon could handle. I emptied my weapon into the receding vehicle, managing to hit both rear tires and one of the front tires, as well as the gas tank. Liquid spilled from under the truck as Talon tried to navigate the last corner. He tired to make the turn too fast and lost control, hitting a tree.

"What's the condition of Talon's brother?" I called to Walter.

"He's down, and I think he's dead. I'd hit him once, but when he returned fire, I fired again and caught him in the chest."

"Are you hit?"

"No. You?"

"Yes, in the thigh."

We watched the truck as Talon climbed out the far side of the truck and headed into the woods. "He's getting away." I called to Walter.

"On it!" Walter crashed into the brush after Talon. Occasionally I'd hear gun fire and wondered what was happening. Through the com unit Walter finally told me Talon was cornered and I asked for directions, then limped off to find them. It was arduous moving through the brush with my injured leg, but I was determined to talk to Talon before he died. Eventually I found Talon on the ground. Slowly I approached him. Walter's bullet hit him high in the left side, and there was a lot of blood.

I tried to kneel beside him, but my damaged leg gave out and I ended up falling. I pushed myself up and searched him for any weapons and found none. Talon opened his eyes, looked up at me and groaned. "Who the fuck are you?"

"I know, it's been a long time. Tudor? It's me."

"Tudor, you look so different."

"So do you! I've called for medical attention."

"Too late. I know you hit something important."

"You fired first. This isn't how I wanted it to end."

"I wanted both of you dead." Talon groaned.

"Why? Why us and why go after all the remaining ghosts?" Talon moved and moaned again. It was obvious he wasn't going to last much longer. I wanted information from him before he died. "Tell me, why go after the rest of the ghosts? We didn't do anything to you."

"Shit, I might as well tell you." He coughed. "My last mission was to go in and develop a plan on how to get Choe Yong-gon out of North Korea. Once the plan was secure, I was supposed to take out Kim II sung. That would leave Pak Geumcheol to take over because he was friendly towards the US." I'd heard about Geumcheol before.

"Before I killed Mescher, he told me after I was in place, the decision to try and get Yong-gon out of North Korea changed. It was decided it wasn't a good idea. Our people were having second thoughts about Geumcheol. Too many political ramifications. Problem was, I was already in place and didn't know my mission was scrapped. I was considered collateral damage. They left me in North Korea. Mescher told me McNaulty and his crowd thought I'd undoubtedly be captured and put to death, so problem solved. The whole thing would be just swept away.

"When I was given the assignment, I had a strange feeling about it. I made McNaulty give me a written order to do what he wanted, and I made copies of the orders and mailed them to my brother with instructions under no circumstances was he to open the envelope and look at what was inside. There was a seal on the envelope. He ignored my request and copied the orders. Eventually they were put on a disk and then copied to a thumb drive. There's the thumb drive in my shirt pocket with proof of everything I told you."

"Did you get Pak and Choe Yong?"

"No. I got Yong, but I only wounded Pak. I never had a chance at Kim II. The thing about Pak was he was already under suspicion of being a traitor. Our people felt since he'd been turned, they wanted him dead before he could disclose any important information. Even after I shot him, they arrested him and sent him to a rural factory to work. The weird part, I know about him because I ended up in the same place. He never knew it was me who shot him."

Talon's breathing was shallow, and I wondered how much longer I'd be able to talk to him. He tried to take a deep breath and started to cough. His voice was a whisper, "Look in my pocket, there's the thumb drive with proof.

"Our people really wanted Yong and Kim II removed. I got caught and it took me almost forty years to escape from that hell hole. I couldn't believe McNaulty didn't send in anybody to get me. McNaulty was the one who gave the order to make the kill. When I got back to the states, I tried to find McNaulty. No luck."

"You know he didn't have the authority to give that order?"

Talon moved his head. "I know it now. When I learned Mescher took over for McNaulty I demanded he kill any remaining ghosts for not coming to get me out of that prison. I threatened to release the information I had on my mission. Mescher failed and I killed him, but I never did get McNaulty."

"McNaulty is locked up where nobody will ever be able to get him."

"Great. I just wish the bastard was dead." Talon tried to move, moaning from the effort.

"From what I hear, it won't be too long. How did you find out about Mescher?"

"My brother has connections throughout the intelligence field. He's the one who got me out of China after I escaped, and then out of Russia. Is my brother still alive?"

"I don't think so. Talon, why come after the ghosts? If I'd have known where you were I'd have tried to do something. Nobody knew where you'd gone."

"Not true. Before I went on the mission, I told Snowflake and Trey what my orders were. I wondered if the order was valid, or even legal, that's why I demanded a signed copy. I gave both of them a copy of the orders. I also mailed a copy to an old high school buddy of mine who became a lawyer. I left instructions what to do if I disappeared. My brother learned my buddy was killed one night in a hit and run accident, and then his office was burned. Snowflake told me before I shot him, McNaulty got the copies from him and Trey and then destroyed them."

"You killed Snowflake?"

Talon nodded. "Yeah, the black bastard knew where I was, and he never tried to get me out of that hell hole."

"How did you find him?"

"We knew more about one another than we were supposed to. We exchanged personal information since we both lived in Kansas City. I found his address and at first, he didn't recognize me, but I made sure he knew who I was before I shot him. He kept saying my name as he begged me not to shoot him." It dawned on me the old black woman hadn't heard Snowflake say, *tell him*, but rather *Talon*.

"Talon, neither of them ever told anybody about your mission. We just knew you went and didn't come back. Other than Snowflake and Trey, nobody had any idea, and to be fair, they were probably scared shitless to say anything. I'm sorry you got stuck over there."

Talon nodded and coughed. There was bright colored blood on his lip and his voice was a whisper, "Do me a favor." I indicated I'd try. "Get that thumb drive to somebody who can get the information out. I want it known what I was ordered to do. I want revenge and you need to help me. Tell me you will do it." Talon firmly grasped my wrist, squeezing it to the point where it hurt.

I told him, "I know who to give the thumb drive to. I'll see what I can do." I could see no reason to tell him there was no way the information was ever going to see the light of day. If it ever got out, the political ramifications would be disastrous.

Talon tried to take another deep breath and coughed. He gave a deep moan, his grip on my wrist loosened and his body gave a little shake. His eyes opened wide, and he died in my arms. I gently ran my hand over his face, closing his eyes. I don't know how long I sat there with my eyes closed holding Talon.

I felt badly. I felt as if the whole ghost team had just passed away in my arms.

Somehow Spielman stayed alive in that North Korean hell hole a long time, escaped and then worked his way across Asia and back to home only to end up dying in the Michigan woods. It wasn't fair. But was it fair what happened to the rest of the ghosts?

Now there really were only two ghosts.

I looked over at Walter and asked, "What's next?"

"I'll bet the information on that thumb drive will never be made public. Imagine the fall out?"

I nodded, "However, I think to protect ourselves, we need to make a copy of the thumb drive and set it up if something happens to us, it will be released. Also, we need for Orchard to call off Cole. I'm sure Ol' King Cole would love to make us disappear once he got his grubby hands on the thumb drive. But what are we going to do about Talon and his brother?"

"Leave them. Call Orchard, tell him what happened and where they are. Send him a copy of the stick, then we disappear for a while until he straightens everything out. Can you arrange for us to get back to my place?"

"Yeah. Help me back to the old service station. Let's get out of here. I'll try and locate Dominick."

CHAPTER SIXTEEN

Other than a lot of pain, I don't remember the trek back to the car, or how we got to the plane. Dominick picked us up and during the flight, Walter decided it would be better for me to go to Sal's for medical attention. When Dominick got us to Idaho, Sal's people were waiting at the airport. I was whisked to Sal's house where there was a doctor waiting to tend to my wound. Sal demanded we stay a few days until I was in condition to travel. I ended up with an infection and lost a couple weeks in a coma. When I could finally travel, Sal's people took us to the airport, and he rode out with us. Just before I got on the plane, Sal wrapped his arms around me and hugged. "One thing about knowing you, it never gets dull. I'll see you on your next mission."

"Sorry Sal. This is it for me. No more missions. No more helping people. It's too hard on the old body."

He laughed. "We'll see. You know you can always call me."

I was lifted into the plane and Dominick took off. We headed for the Port Townsend airport and when we got to Walter's truck, Walter had me wait several feet away.

Carefully he crawled under the truck and looked it over. He checked the bed and around the bumpers.

"It looks clean." Walter said. "The dust here is a few weeks old and nothing looks disturbed. I think the truck is safe." We got in and Walter fired it up. We didn't blow up.

We returned to the old farmhouse near Walter's place and put the truck in the old barn. Walter had a few pieces of wood nailed together, and a couple of old tires attached to the bottom. With the wood and tires in place, it looked like the barn hadn't been disturbed in years and there was no way you could even get inside.

It was still difficult to walk into his cabin. I had little energy and was still sore, so it took a long time to get to the cabin. On the way to the in he examined each of his traps. None of them were triggered. When we got to the cabin, we found the kids playing on the deck and Thien sitting the rocking chair. Thien ran to Walter, and they hugged and kissed. She turned to me and wrapped her arms around me giving me a long, hard hug. I heard her muffled voice against my chest, "Thank you for bringing him back to me. I love you."

I talked to the top of her head. "You got it wrong, he brought me back. I don't know what I'd have done without him. Now I need to make a few phone calls."

I used the phone Sal had given me and called Orchard on his special line. "Is this Alaska?" He asked.

"Yes." I proceeded to tell him where he could find what was left of Talon and his brother's bodies. "I was wounded, and I've been out of action for a while. I warn you the bodies are going to be in bad condition." I told him about the thumb drive I had with Talon's orders on them. I told Orchard a copy was on the way and other copies were made and were safely in a couple of attorneys' safes. "If anything happens to either Walter or me, those thumb-drives go to the press."

"Matt, you can't do that. I've learned a lot more about Talon's mission."

"I also know about his mission. Before Talon died, he told me what McNaulty ordered him to do. Remember, those thumb-drives are ready to be mailed."

"You can't do that. The fall out would lead to war."

"That might be true. So, now everyone's safety is in your hands. Call off Cole and anyone else who might be after us. You've heard the recording of Talon killing Mescher?"

His voice was soft, "Yes."

"Have you played it for Director Cole?"

"Yeah. He doesn't believe it's real. And he's really pissed I didn't turn you in."

"Well, now you get to tell him about the thumb-drive. He'll love that! And perhaps you might want to call Bradson and tell him what's going on."

"He already knows it was Talon who killed Mescher. I'm going to let Cole tell him about the thumb-drive."

"No John. You call Bradson and tell him. I want Bradson to call off the dogs. I'm putting this in your lap. You make nice and get the two of us out of trouble."

"Why me?" John whined.

"Because you wouldn't believe me when I tried to tell you what was happening. You pitted me against Mescher and Cole and forced me to run. I have no idea what you told Lois to turn her against me, and to make matters worse, you were part of the posse that was out to get us. I'm giving you the chance to make it right."

"It won't be easy."

"Ask me if I give a shit? You made the problem, you fix it. By the way, exactly what did you tell Lois?"

"She knows everything except about the thumb drive and Talon's mission. She wants you to call her. She says she's sorry for everything."

Mentally I said to myself, "We'll see." To Orchard I said, "Let me know when you've taken care of this. I'll be waiting."

"Where are you?"

"You don't need to know. Do what I told you. I'll call you in a few days and see if it's done."

"I don't care for your attitude."

"Guess what! I don't give a damn. You'll never know how hurt I am you didn't believe me. After all I've done for you, you were ready to throw me under the bus. Now, do what I asked!"

I made one more call to Dr. Oldman and inquired about my dogs. "I was getting worried. It's been a long time since I heard from you. The dogs are doing well, but I can tell they miss you."

"I'm sorry how things turned out. Long story that I'll tell you later. Just a few more days and things will be cleared up. Thanks for taking care of them."

"Are you kidding? They're such a joy. You've done miracles with the puppies, and I can tell Max really misses you."

For the next few days, I stayed with Walter and his family at the cabin and just relaxed. It felt good not to be on the run. Eventually, I called Orchard. I was still terse when he answered, "All I want to hear from is you've taken care of everything and it's safe to go back to Florida."

"Well…"

"No John, all I want to hear is you've taken care of everything. If not, I hang up and you get it done."

"Director Cole wants to talk to you about the thumb drive. Have you looked at it?'

"No. Have you?"

"Yes, and I wish I hadn't. It gives me nightmares to think what might have happened and still could happen if any of the information got out."

"Talon kind of told me what's on it. I have no desire to see any of it. I also don't want to chat with Cole. To be honest, I don't trust the man… even now. You can tell him that too. Whatever is on the thumb drive is safe. I won't tell you who either of the attorneys are that have copies of the drive. I trust you to tell Cole about my back up plan and to leave Walter and me alone, he has to trust me not to release the information.'

"Let me make some more calls and I'll call you right back." Orchard told me.

"You do that." I hung up.

CHAPTER SEVENTEEN

There is an adage that when you have a choice to make, the hardest one is usually the correct one. I was dreading my next call. I knew I had to call Lois, but I'd been putting it off for as long as I could. My problem was I'd no idea what I wanted to say. I was hurt and pissed about the way she had treated me, but what was my end goal? Was marriage still in the cards for us?

No! I don't think so. The trust thing is gone.

Did I even want her back?

I didn't have an answer.

Evidently, she didn't know it was me on the phone, after she answered and discovered it was me, there was a long silence before she started to talk. "Hello Matt. Where are you?"

"Walter and I are hiding out until Orchard resolves a few things."

"The Admiral told me everything. I understand now." Another long pause. "I know this doesn't help, but I'm sorry."

"Yeah! And so am I. I won't sugar coat it. I was, and still am hurt the way you treated me. You said you loved me, but you were ready to give me to Director Cole. You didn't care what my side was, you believed the worst of me."

"I didn't know your side."

"Of course not, you wouldn't even make the effort to listen to me. And the way you were acting, I didn't trust you. You put me in the position where I had to work on the problem myself. I needed your help, but I got nothing. Everybody thought I was guilty, even you."

"I didn't."

"Really. At least be honest, you're telling me you didn't think I'd done something wrong?"

"Well…"

"Yeah. Well! I don't know Lois. Besides, it wasn't like things were great before this happened and now, I just don't know."

"Can we at least see each other and talk? I'm sorry."

"Let me see what John works out. There are still a few odds and ends that need to be resolved before I feel free to move about."

"I've missed you. I want to see you."

"Let's talk when we see each other. I'll call you when I'm back in Florida. Goodbye."

"Bye. I do love you Matt."

"Bye." I wasn't gonna say that back unless I really meant it.

~ ~ ~ ~ ~

My next call was to President Albert Bradson. I had to go through a few hoops to finally get to him. "Matt, good of you to call."

"Sir. I wanted to call and clear the air. The last time we spoke it didn't go well."

He chuckled. "Yes, you hung up on me just after you told me to go fuck a rolling donut. Do you know nobody has ever told me that?"

"Well, I'm sorry. But you seemed to have forgotten who I was and had assumed the worst."

"And for that I apologize. I've heard from Admiral Orchard what happened. I see I should have trusted you."

"May I point out when you were running for office, you had me handle a few sensitive issues for you. Not to rub it in, but I'd have thought you'd have more trust in me."

"Yeah, I said I was sorry! Can me move on now?"

"Yes sir. I just wanted to make sure things were okay between us"

~ ~ ~ ~ ~

There was one more important call to make. I needed to apologize to my childhood friend. "Hello, this is Chief Davenport."

"Jeff, it's me, Matt."

"Well, I've heard all sorts of things about you. First, I hear you murdered some high-ranking person back in Washington. Next, I hear you didn't. Next there is a bounty on you, dead or alive. Now I understand you're an unofficial hero. How come you called me?"

"You called to warn me. I wanted you to know I appreciated it. I was rude and I apologize. But I was concerned for my life, and it looked like nobody was going to get to the truth about what happened."

"I understand. It means a lot you called me to straighten things out. I should have trusted you. That was my bad."

"Don't worry about it. Who loves ya' baby?"

"I know you do."

I felt good as I hung up. Nobody has enough child-hood friends.

Next, I called Orchard back and asked about Liisa Curtis. "Who's that?"

"That's a person who helped me locate Mescher, kind of like you should have done."

"When are we going to get over that?"

"I don't know John. I thought we were... well, at least I thought I was somebody you trusted. Anyway, somebody had Liisa transferred after I spoke with her, and nobody seems to know where she is. I want you to find her, have her reinstated at her old position and get her a promotion."

"I can't do that. I don't have the authority."

I raised my voice. "Bull shit John. Since this whole Talon thing broke, I've learned you have more juice than you've let me believe. I know right now you're operating Mescher's spot. You can fix it for Liisa Curtis, and you will fix it. You owe me."

"I'll see what I can do."

"No John! You will do this! I'm going to check back in a couple of days, and Liisa had better be back where she was. And I also want Mouse released."

"He never was arrested."

"Well perhaps he wasn't arrested, but I know he was detained. Release him now and instruct him to call me as soon as he can."

"Is there anything else, sir?" His tone was snarky.

"Yeah. Make sure any charges against Dominick and Henry are dismissed. They're to be exonerated and re-ceive a medal."

"Are you serious?"

"Yes!"

"I also want Zampuchini to receive a total pardon for anything you suspect him of. As of today, he's clean and there are no outstanding warrants."

"Matt, I can't do…"

"Bull shit. Don't ever say that to me. You will do what I ask. It's the least you can do for me after the crap you put me through."

"Is that all now?"

"Yeah, but if I think of anything else, I'll let you know."

Finally, I called Zampuchini. I had a direct number and I used it. "Hello Sal. This is Matt."

"Matt. Good to hear you. I take it everything is over and turned out well."

"Yes sir. I wanted to call and thank you for your help. I'm sorry I brought trouble to your place in Idaho. Were you able to take care of it?"

Sal started to laugh. "Yeah, we found a little bank in Montana, and we broke in and left the bodies and the three fellows who were still alive all shot up with tranquilizers. We made sure there was plenty of incriminating evidence on them and then alerted the police and the FBI. Bank robbery is a federal offense, and it falls under the FBI's investigation. Since the guys were already some sort of federal agents, it will make for very interesting problems they will need to solve."

"Again Sal, thank you for everything."

"You have my special number. If you ever need anything, call and it's yours."

"Oh, by the way, I've arranged things so after today you have a clean bill of health. There are no warrants on you, or charges. You're clean."

"Are you serious?"

"Yes."

"Matt, seriously, if there is anything I can ever do for you, ask. It's yours."

I thanked him again for all his help and rang off. I checked with Henry about his upcoming schedule. "Looks like I can be in Port Orchard in about a week and take you back to Florida. Will that work?"

"That's perfect. Call me the day before and we can set a time to meet."

~ ~ ~ ~ ~

The next few days were perfect. The weather was amazing. Cool breeze kept things comfortable, but the sun shone and kept us warm. By the second day, Walter and Thein seem to have forgotten I was there since they both were nude all the time. The kids never wore clothing anyway and being naked, or seeing naked people was nothing new to them. The third morning I said to hell with it and came out sans clothing. Both Walter and Thein clapped, and whistled. Now I was embarrassed.

Walter mentioned to me one morning about the problem with the bank. I apologized and he reminded me that we'd been together, and he knew how busy we were. I called my contact at the bank. I greeted her.

"Matt, wonderful to hear from you. How did you know I needed to chat with you?"

"I have psychic powers."

She laughed. "You know the money we've been transferring over to your friends account over the years?"

"Yes, funny that's what I'm calling you about. What's going on? How come the deposits stopped?"

"Because the money we used to get from the London bank stopped. We wrote the bank a letter along with a copy to you."

"I've been dealing with some other problems. I haven't seen any mail for a while now."

"We contacted the London bank for you. The funds originated from an account in Portugal. London said that a couple of months ago Portugal notified them the account was closed. No explanation."

"Don't worry, I'll take care of it. Thank you for your help."

"We miss not seeing you at the bank."

"I live in Florida now, but I miss you too."

I looked for Walter and found him working on making a new chair. "What's ya doin'?"

"Making you a chair. Just for you when you come and visit."

"Thanks. I called my bank." I proceeded to tell him what I'd just learned. I ended with, "I don't have a contact number for Jennifer with me, but when I get home, I'll see what I can do."

"I'm not worried about the money. I'm doing fine and there is a large savings account for the kids' college fund. I just wanted you to know about the change."

"Thanks. I'll let you know what I find out."

That night as I lay in bed, my thoughts drifted to Jennifer. I assumed it was because of the money and the bank stuff. But as I thought about her, I remember her wit and her charming accent. I helped her deal with a problem and part of it involved a nasty fat woman who wore the most stupid hat you'd ever seen. The hat had a fake daisy sticking up out of the top of it and every time the women moved, the daisy would flop back and forth. We were at an important meeting and laughing at the spectacle she made would have been inappropriate. Later Jennifer gave a special dinner for all of us who were involved. A large cake was brought out and the cake was in the shape of the hat and sticking out of the cake was a huge floppy plastic daisy. That evening I was blown away with Jennifer's delightful sense of humor.

Her attorney and I had been invited to come and visit her in Europe, but I never found the time. Besides she was living with a man and woman whom she said she was going to marry. I still would have liked to have seen her again. She was a special person.

Finally, I fell asleep with Jennifer thoughts in my head.

~ ~ ~ ~ ~

In the morning I called Melissa. "Hi. Remember me?"

"Yeah, you're the guy who keeps asking me to do things that could end up putting my ass in prison." She laughed.

"Yeah, that's me. Are you interested in having the dinner tonight at Hanney's Hideaway I promised you?"

"YES! Are you going to pick me up and everything?"

"What about Ralph?"

"It will be just the two of us. I'll explain about Ralph over dinner."

"Pick you up at your North Seattle place?"

"Yes. Pick me up at 7."

"Looking forward to it."

I caught the next ferry to Seattle and drove to the condo. Picking out my best suit, I prepared for my dinner with Melissa. As I was getting off the elevator in the lobby, I ran into Mouse. He rushed up and hugged me. "I was so worried about you."

"Worried about me, I was worried about you. When I heard you had been detained, I felt so bad. I had to keep moving to keep from being caught, but I knew as soon as I could, I'd make it right for you. How long have you been free?"

"Well, I was never locked up. A device was put on my front door and anytime I went somewhere there was a phone number I had to call to check out. It was an inconvenience, but it wasn't so bad. Jade was the one who was really upset. She didn't like the idea somebody was keeping track of our movements."

"Has Orchard contacted you?"

"Oh yeah, and so has Bradson. Both were very apologetic. It was fine. I was so concerned about you and any time I asked what was going on, I was told it was none of my business."

"Walter and I caught the fellow who was responsible for a couple of the ghost's deaths and also for Mescher's death."

"John Cole called me after Mescher was killed and told me you'd done it. I won't tell you what I said to him, but you can guess."

"I want you to know all your equipment worked great. Those sticky listening balls were amazing. We were even able to record Talon killing Mescher. Thanks for everything."

He hugged me again and I noticed my car had arrived. "I promise to see you before I go back to Florida. Tonight, I pay a debt."

"Looking like that. Must have been quite a debt. Good night."

"Night."

~ ~ ~ ~ ~

I understand today that one must be careful how they describe a woman. But since you all know I'm kind of a pig, I'll make my comments anyway. I've always felt Melissa possessed a killer figure and tonight the dress she wore called attention to it. It was both stunning and sexy at the same time. Things were covered but the dress also accented her attributes.

Melissa entered the room and I stood. When she stepped up to me, I gave her a peck on the cheek. She leaned back and snapped. "What the hell was that?" She took my face in her hands and kissed me with gusto. Just as she started to pull back, I slipped my arms around her, pulled her to me and returned the kiss in same. During the kiss she rubbed herself against me and this time when she leaned back, she had a big grin. "Now, that's what I call a hello kiss."

I escorted her to the car and after I got in, we headed north on the freeway. I made a comment about traffic and how bad it was, to which she agreed. Pulling under the portico at Hanney's we were met by two valets. One opened Melissa's door and the other opened my door. I pointed to the keys sitting on the dash and joined Melissa. Every time I go to Hanney's I'm totally blow away. The place has such a 50's feel, with its white table clothes, waiters in black aprons, hidden mood lighting and a piano bar at the far end playing softly. We were seated at a corner booth. Melissa leaned over and kissed my cheek. "What was that for?" I asked.

"I love this place and being here with you makes it perfect."

"Well, thank you. With me? Makes it perfect?" She nodded. "I think that brings up the subject of Ralph. What's the problem?"

She hung her head for a moment. When she looked up at me, her eyes were glistening. "This is difficult. I know he's told you about me, and how I'm built a little... ah, different and because of that, how difficult it is for me to get satisfaction from sex?" Even in the dim lighting I could see Melissa blushing. I indicated I was aware. "Due to the way he's built, in that area we have no problems. But there is so much more to a relationship than sex. He's so clueless about everything. We can't spend our entire lives in bed." I laughed. "I know he's totally into his work and a relationship with a woman isn't one of his best attributes. We've discussed his attitude about women. He views them as sexual objects."

I opened my mouth and she put her finger on my lips and shook her head. "I know you're kind of the same way. But not nearly as bad as Ralph. When we're intimate, Ralph tries to make sure I get something out of it, which is nice. But all he really wants from me as a person is sex. When I try and talk to him, he's too busy. But he's never too busy for sex and I'm tired of it. And I know it's not fair to dump this on you. But you asked."

"I'm pleased you consider me enough of a friend that you shared this with me. It's a bit much, but it's okay. Are you considering leaving him?"

"Yeah, I am." I was surprised, and a bit sad. "I've tried to talk to him, but it doesn't seem to sink in. I don't think he believes I'd leave him. Basically, he thinks because of his trouser monster I'd never leave. Well, he's wrong."

"Is there anything I can do?"

"You're doing it right now. Talking to me and letting me get this off my chest helps a lot."

Food arrived and we stopped talking.

The meal was finished, and we waddled out to the car sitting under the portico with the doors open. I helped Melissa get in the car and as she slid in, she made sure to show me she was commando. I laughed and shook my head but said nothing and drove her back to her place. I pulled into her driveway, and she reached over and turned off the motor. I asked her, "What's up?"

"I'd like for you to come in for a while."

"I don't think that's a good idea."

"Why? Not interested?"

"Wrong! That's a stupid question. Of course, I'm interested, but Ralph is a friend. You're a friend. I value both of you and I don't want to interfere. Whatever the problem is between the two of you is just that, between the two of you. You two need to work it out. Us being together isn't going to help either of you. Thanks, but no thanks. Besides, I have my own problems I need to work on. And making love with you for sure isn't going to help."

I got out of the car and walked around to her side. Opening the door, I held out my hand to help her out. She put her right foot on the ground and slid her dress up, making a point of holding her legs apart for a lot longer than I thought she needed to.

Looking up at me, she grinned. "Are you sure? I know how to make it excellent. I've always wanted you. Look."

"Melissa, knock it off. Of course, I'm interested. But I'm not going to do anything about it. Now please get out so I can walk you to the door." At the door I gave her a peck on the cheek and when she grabbed at me, I ducked out of reach and left.

On my way back to my condo I had to admit, I was horny. It was difficult to walk away. However, I wasn't going to get involved in problems between her and Ralph. The problem is walking away didn't do much for me. Somehow, I knew just a cold shower wasn't going to take care of things. Perhaps I needed to patch things up better with Lois.

On second thought, naw!

That wasn't a good idea either.

I spent the night at the condo and drove back to Walter's the next morning. Later that day Orchard called and told me he had fixed everything."

"What about Henry?"

"He's out, and I think he's in Florida checking out a new plane he found. Liisa is back at her old post. Mouse is back in Seattle," I already knew that. "Zampuchini has a clean record, and all the ruckus has been dealt with and things are as if nothing ever happened. When are you coming back to DC?" John asked

"It will be a while. Nothing I really want there."

"I'd like to see you,"

"That will be a while too. You know how I feel."

"You don't want to see Lois?"

"Not yet. I couldn't believe how quickly both of you bought into the idea of throwing me under the bus. Let's give it some time and we'll see." I hung up. I was more over the whole issue than I was letting on. But I was still hurt! With Lois more than John.

I called Lissa just to make sure she was okay. She gushed over her promotion and how pleased she was to be back at her original post. I told her it was the least I could do. She inquired if there was any way we could see each other. "I really don't think that is a good idea. But thanks for the offer." I was wondering what was wrong with me; I'd turned down two propositions in two days. I'm gonna have to turn in my horn dog medal at this rate.

It was time to leave and return to Florida. There was going to be a plane waiting at Port Angeles for me to take me home. Mouse called and said he'd heard from Director Cole. Mouse disclosed to me he had something on Cole but wouldn't tell me what it was. "Matt, you know I am the collector of information. Johnnie boy treads lightly around me. That's why I wasn't arrested but rather just detained."

I laughed and repeatedly apologized for any difficulty I'd caused.

"Stop Matt! I knew what I was getting into when I helped you. I knew from the start something was wrong, and I trusted you to fix things. You owe me no apologies. Now stop!"

"Okay, to make this right, I demand you take Jade to Haney's Hideaway. Will you do that?"

"Yes." As soon as we were off the phone, I called Haney's and told them who I was. I arranged for the dinner to be taken care of courtesy of me. I thanked them again for the great evening I'd had the night before with Melissa. I wanted to make sure they knew who I was. I was assured they would take good care of Mouse. Even though he's a silent partner, I wanted to be sure he got the royal treatment.

~ ~ ~ ~ ~

The trip back to Florida went without a hitch. It felt good to be home again.

I picked up Max and the puppies from Dr. Oldman and spent lots of time with them. All were pleased to have me back and they bickered on who was going to get to sit in my lap. All three of them wanted up and to be petted at the same time. I wasn't complaining.

Lois called several times asking when she could come and visit. I tried to tell her as nicely as I could something had died because of the Talon debacle. She didn't pick up on what I was feeling which just reinforced the way I felt.

Eventually, I had to relent and invited her to come visit. We discussed the possibility of getting back together, well, to be honest, she was the one talking about it. I knew how I felt and getting back together wasn't something that interested me. We'd talked through a lot of the issues we'd been facing before the Talon incident, and somehow, they all seemed to be my fault. Since I had no desire to change things, getting back to the way things were wasn't realistic. We also covered a lot of how things had gone down during the incident. She disclosed she was under pressure from Orchard, Mescher and Cole to tell them where I was, or for her to come and visit so they could pick me up. She admitted she was aware of what might happen once I was picked up. What upset me was she was still willing to go along with it. That wasn't something I could forgive or forget.

There was a lot left unsaid. Things were not as comfortable as they used to be and my feelings of abandonment didn't abate, even with her being in Florida. Not to beat a dead horse, but when I needed her most, she sided with Director Cole's group which included Orchard who at the time I considered the enemy. It didn't seem to matter that neither of us knew at the time who the enemy was, Lois should have supported me. I knew we were growing apart before the Talon incident. The magic was missing, and

I take the blame, it was mostly on my part. I've said it before, perhaps there's something wrong with my DNA when it comes to relationships. I just can't seem to stay the course. Eventually my feelings change and grow distant. And at my age, I wonder if it's possible to change. More to the point, at my age do I want to change?

I still needed to find out about Jennifer and why the bank account closed. I called my old attorney friend back in Seattle who'd represented her when she was dealing with her father's estate. I asked him if he could find any information on her.

He called back later that afternoon. "Matt, I just happened to have information for you."

"What's ya got?"

He gave me a name and phone number of the bank in Portugal she'd been using. I called the bank and was informed that they could not give me any information on the account since I wasn't listed as a signer. I was told I needed to talk to Jennifer.

I thought about Jennifer for a couple of days, and I wondered if I should go to Portugal and see what was going on. I was worried. Lois kept asking me why I was so quiet. "For as much as you talk to me, I might as well go back to D.C. What's going on with you anyway."

"I have a lot on my mind." I told her. I wanted to tell her I wish she would go back to D.C.

"Like what?"

"Like things. Come on, I'm still trying to get over why all the ghosts are gone."

It was later in the week, and I was sitting in my chair brooding over how difficult it was to get information on either Jennifer's location, or her bank account when I felt my cell vibrate. I looked at the number. The number on the screen had several more digits than normal and the listing said Faro, Portugal. Who's calling me from Portugal? A spam call? Naw!

I answered.

The voice was soft, feminine, frightened and she sounded like she'd been crying. "Hello Matt. This is Jennifer, Jennifer Rockingham." Her voice was so soft I barely heard her.

I recognized the accent. It was a voice from the past. I was pleased to hear from her from her on so many levels. "Jennifer, what a wonderful surprise. How did you know I was trying to get a hold of you?"

There was a long pause before she started to speak. "My bank told me you called. Matt," She stopped talking, then whispered, "Please".

"Please what? What's wrong?"

"Help me. Help me, Matt!" Her words a whispered plea.

"Do you need me to come there?"

"Yes, please. I'm sorry, I don't have anybody else. Please. Help me."

"The number on my phone says Portugal, is that correct?"

"Yes. I'm in a town called Faro. It's close to Lisbon."

"I'll go to Lisbon and rent a car. I'll call you when I'm on my way and get directions."

"It's not necessary to go to Lisbon, there's an international airport in Faro, but I have no idea what airline services it."

"Not to worry, I can go anyplace. I'm on my way."

Another pause and she asked, "Aren't you going to ask me what's wrong?"

"No Jennifer, if it's important enough for you to call and ask for help, that makes it important."

I heard a sob before she whispered. "Thank you. Let me know when you're coming. I'll pick you up."

"No, stay where you are. I'm coming. Are you safe?"

"I don't know. I think so."

"I'll be there as quickly as I can."

I hung up and Lois asked, "Who was that?"

"An old friend and she needs help. I'll be gone for a while."

"What?" Her voice rose in volume.

"I said I'm going to be gone for a while."

"Where? What's going on? I want to know what's happening. Some woman calls you and you tell me you're leaving. And you don't know for how long?"

"Sorry."

"Sorry! What the hell is that supposed to mean? Where are you going?"

"Faro, Portugal. I'll call you when I know more."

"I don't want you to leave. I want you to stay."

"Sorry. I have to do this."

"What? Faro wherever?"

"Portugal."

"Whatever! And you'll tell me when you know more? Is this for John?"

"No. This is for me."

"I want you to stay. We need to work on us. You don't need to go see some strange woman."

"Sorry, Jennifer is in trouble, and she called me and begged for help. I have to go."

"I forbid you to go."

I didn't recognize the strange woman in front of me. This was a new attitude for her. "Forbid! You forbid me? Are you serious? Forbid me? You don't want to take that road Lois. Jennifer is an old friend, and she seems to be in trouble. I'm asking you to trust me. I need to go see what the problem is."

"Well fine, just don't be surprised if I'm gone when you return."

I stared at her and shook my head. "It's not the way I would have ended things, but if that's the way you want it… sorry Lois. Make sure you lock the door when you leave."

As I turned to leave, I heard a scream and I felt something hit my back and bounce off. It hurt! Lois had thrown something, but I didn't look back. I called over my shoulder, "Goodbye." And kept walking out the door. I felt she was the one who just permanently ended our relationship.

My first call from the car was to my vet friend, Dr. Oldman. "Matt, what a pleasure to hear from you."

"I need a favor. Can you go to my place right now and pick up the dogs and take care of them for a few days? I must leave the country unexpectedly."

"Does it have something to do with the strange things you do?"

"Yes and no, this is a favor for a friend. I'll warn you; Lois is there and she's angry. But she also needs to get back to D.C. If you can watch them, I'd really appreciate it."

"I'll go pick them up as soon as I can.'

"Thanks."

My next call was to Henry. "Hello Matt. Let me guess, you need to go somewhere?" Was his greeting.

"Yeah. Like Portugal."

Henry was laughing. "You're so lucky. I have a plane in the hanger they're servicing, and it's capable of going from Florida to Portugal. I think Dominick is in Florida and he'll take you."

I was pulling into the parking lot, and I saw Dominick. He came over and opened my car door. "I just got a text from Henry. You want to go to Portugal?"

"Yes."

"Let's go. I have a friend I want to see in Portugal. Get in the plane." I was still laughing when we took off. I wondered what place in the world Dominick didn't have a friend. After I was settled in the righthand seat, Dominick informed me, "Because of the umm, ah, the weird stuff we do for some government agencies I'll make a call once we're airborne, and our flight plan will be taken care of. Do you have a destination in mind?

"Yeah, I wanna to go to Faro."

"Faro is an international airport. We can use it."

"I know. Let's go."

"Did you know I have a friend in Faro?" I started to laugh so hard I was afraid I was going to wet my pants.

CHAPTER EIGHTEEN

During the flight to Portugal, I closed my eyes and reminisced. I remembered Jenifer and how we met because of the houseboat I'd won from her father in a poker game. And then his subsequent murder when she'd asked me to help with the estate and find out who killed her father.

There's a restaurant downtown Seattle located on the end of a wharf where I first met her. When she entered the room every man in the place watched her walk past. She looked like she'd stepped out of a 1940's movie. Tall, beautiful, elegant, dressed to compliment her figure, she was a knockout. After her estate problem was resolved, she generously set up a large amount of money to be deposited in my bank account every month. I said it wasn't necessary, but she insisted. Most of the money goes to Walter and Thein to help with their kids, and the rest goes to satisfy dear old greedy Uncle Sam. We kept in touch through emails and Christmas cards, but eventually we stopped communicating. It's been some time since I'd heard from Jennifer.

The trip over was fast and uneventful. I asked Dominick if he had something to do while I looked into Jennifer's problem. I made arrangements to contact him once I knew how long I'd be here. He looked at me and grinned. "Remember, I have a friend in Faro I want to visit."

I considered commenting that he had friends everywhere, but wisely kept my mouth shut.

I rented a car in Faro which is the southernmost town in Portugal. I was leaving the airport and I called Jennifer. "Matt?" Her voice was soft and timid. I was worried, this wasn't the confident self-assured Jennifer I remembered.

"Yeah, where do you live?" She told me how to find her. Her home was outside of town on a three-mile strip of sand along the ocean. I found it and pulled into a courtyard. I was amazed at the grandeur of the place. The home was white stucco with soft yellow trim. I could hear the ocean on the other side of the home. The weather was warm with a slight breeze. It was a beautiful day.

I'd barely gotten out of the car when Jennifer came running out the front door, and threw her arms around my chest. I slipped my arms around her and gathered her tight against me and she immediately broke into deep sobs. We stood there for a long time while I held her as she cried. I gently patted her back and with my arms wrapped around her I felt how thin she'd become and I was concerned. Her dark hair was lank and lay on her head and had lost its luster. Her face was thin and drawn, her cheek bones very prominent. The more I felt her body, the more concerned I became. She wasn't healthy.

Eventually she looked up with a sheepish grin, "I'm sorry. You've come halfway around the world and all I can do is cry all over you. But I'm glad to see you."

I kissed her cheek, "I think you and I need to have a chat."

Jennifer took my hand and led me into the house. She was wearing shorts and a short sleeved shirt; her legs looked like pale sticks and her arms were in the same condition. When we entered the house, we were greeted by a middle-aged woman dressed in a peasant blouse and full flowered skirt. She introduced the woman as Val, her housekeeper. They exchange something in Portuguese, and She led me through the house out to a covered patio looking over at a stunning view of the ocean. We sat down in comfortable chairs and Val came out with a tray holding a pitcher full of ice filled with a red liquid and two glasses. She poured us each a glass and left. I took a sip and was pleased. There were so many different flavors it was difficult to describe exactly what the drink tasted like.

I took a second sip, set the glass on the table, leaned back in my chair and looked at Jennifer. "What's going on."

Tears came to her eyes again which she quickly wiped away. "I don't know where to start."

"Start anywhere, if I don't understand I'll ask questions. Just start."

"You know when I returned from Seattle it was to live with a man and another woman?" I nodded. "His name is Miguel. I met him through Sara. Sara and I were lovers, and I knew she also had a man friend. I had no problem with that." I'd known that Jennifer was either a lesbian or bi and I really didn't care then or now. It was her life.

"After I met Miguel, the three of us were inseparable. As I told you in Seattle, we were making plans to live together as a family before I received word father died." I indicated I remembered. "You know how that turned out. I know I've thanked you many times, but you were a God send. Thank you again."

I must have made a face because Jennifer said, "Stop that. You need to accept the fact you're a very special man."

I shook my head. "Go on with your story."

"I returned and the three of us lived as man and wife and wife. We all took turns cooking and whenever we had sex, Miguel was very careful not to spend too much time with either one of us. He always made sure we were both satisfied. I thought we were all very happy. Happy until..."

Tears started to flow again, and I reached over and took her hand. "It's okay. Just tell me what you can."

Jennifer had the hiccups, and it was hard for to her to continue her story. "About six months ago I overheard the two of them talking. Sara said something about getting rid of me. Miguel said that was easy and Sara said she didn't want me killed. She just wanted me to go away. Miguel told her they couldn't live as well as they did with me gone since I was the one with money.

"Sara said something about how she'd think about it. Miguel told me once his business provided him with money, but not same amount I could provide. The conversation frightened me. Because now I knew how they felt, I was afraid of what he might do to my bank accounts, so I froze everything and moved to a new bank. When I did it, I forgot about the monthly checks you were getting." She looked up.

"I notice you'd stopped the checks, but I had no way to contact you. I didn't care about the money; I was concerned why it stopped. I was worried about you."

She continued. "I had no idea what Miguel might do to me after I overheard that conversation. I knew I had to get away."

"Were you three living here?"

"No, I own a villa east of here in Monte Gordo. They're living there now. I didn't say anything, I started looking for a new place. A few weeks ago, I found this place and I snuck away and moved here. One day I got a call from Miguel telling me to move back, if I didn't, he'd find me and kill me. I hung up.

"A couple days later he called again and said if I didn't want to live with them, I had to send money every month. I hung up again. The next morning somebody shot at me from the beach and that's when I called you.

"Later that day I got another call from Miguel. He told me he missed on purpose, and he wasn't kidding. I had ten days to get money into his bank account, or the next bullet wouldn't miss."

"Are they still living at your villa?"

"I really don't know. I stay away from them."

"You want me to make Miguel leave you alone?" Jennifer nodded. "I need the address for the villa. I want to see if they still live there. Also, I need to find a place to stay while I'm here."

"NO! You will stay here, with me. I have lots of room and I feel safer with you here. I'd like to go with you to the Monte Gordo villa. Besides you don't know what they look like." She had a point.

"Since the two of them don't know my car, get a hat and some sunglasses and you can come with me. We're going for a ride. I want to see the other villa."

Fifteen minutes later we were headed south-east on the freeway towards Spain. Jennifer gave me the directions to her villa which was almost on the Spanish border. The day was brilliant, the water to my right was a deep blue and the skies had large fluffy clouds. It was a wonderful day to be alive.

Jennifer's old place hung out over the sea, and it was spectacular. I thought her current place was a knockout, however this villa was something out of a dream. I drove past it as slow as I dared and when I got a chance I pulled over to the side. We turned around and passed by the house a second time and I noticed a new, bright red Jaguar XKR sitting in the courtyard. There was a man behind the wheel and a woman was walking across the courtyard towards the car. "Is that them?" I asked. She scrunched down in her seat and nodded.

I made another U turn and pulled over. We watched the woman climb into the car and then the car pulled out and turned towards us. I told Jennifer to keep down and waited for the Jag to pass. Once they were well ahead of us, I started to follow.

"Who bought that car?" I asked.

"I don't know. We didn't have it when we were together."

"It would seem Miguel has more money than he lets on." I quipped.

The bright red sports car was easy to follow, and I tailed them to the next town where they pulled into a parking lot and stopped. I told Jennifer to stay in the car; I'd be right back.

There was a street fair going on, but it was easy to follow them. They entered a restaurant and from the amount of time the waiter spent with them, I assumed they were ordering lunch and it was going to be a while before they moved on. I returned to the car.

When we got back to the villa, Val served lunch. We finished and the two of them led me upstairs and showed me my room. The door was open with a gentle breeze flowing through the room. The view from my balcony was a post card picture, or calendar picture. I wanted to stay forever in that room. "Will this do?" Jennifer asked.

"It's a little cramped." I said with a smile. "No really, this is amazing. Thank you for putting me up." Jennifer leaned forward and kissed my cheek. "What are you going to do?"

"Let's go downstairs and chat some more."

We sat on a lanai overlooking the sea with a light beverage of unknown origin. I could tell it had a little liquor in it, but it was very refreshing. After a couple of sips, I put the glass down and looked at Jennifer. "I'm not accusing you of anything, right now I'm trying to understand why things changed for your friends." Jennifer indicated she understood. "Did you do anything to upset either one?"

"Not that I know of. We had stupid little arguments occasionally, but three people can't live together and not have disagreements."

"Mainly, you want me to get Miguel to leave you alone?" She gave me an affirmative nod. "How far do you want me to take it… to get him to leave you alone I mean?"

"I'm hurt and angry and I know I'm in no position to make a rationale call." A long pause ensued before she continued. "But I want you to do whatever it takes."

"And if I have to seriously hurt him?"

Jennifer looked me in the eyes. "Do whatever it takes."

"Consider it done."

"When are you going to start?"

"Remember, it's best if you don't ask any questions. The less you know, the better off you will be in the long run. Trust me."

"I do Matt."

We spent the afternoon swimming in the pool. Her appearance shocked me. Her bikini top had nothing to hold, and the bottom of he suit showed her hip bones protrude. Whatever was going on was affecting her health.

Val served an herb crusted fish for dinner which was excellent. I watched Jennifer pick at it, eating just a couple bites. We watched the sun sink into the sea and sat having an after-dinner drink while a gentle breeze kept the lanai comfortable.

I wanted to ask what she planned to do after I dealt with Miguel, but thought it was better not to make her plan so far ahead. There was plenty of time to discuss what would happen after the issue with Miguel was finished. Finally, it was time for bed and Jennifer walked me to my room. I took her in my arms in the hall and I kissed her forehead and hugged her tightly. "Are you feeling better?"

"A little. I'm not so scared now you're here."

"Don't worry. It will work out."

"Thanks Matt. Once I again I owe you."

"No! We're friends and friends do things for each other because they're friends. You owe me nothing."

She lifted her head, leaned back and whispered, "Thanks anyway." I shook my head and went into my room. It took a long time for me to finally go to sleep. I thought a little about Lois, but the way she had acted when I left only made me angry. I thought about Jennifer and how frightened she was. She wasn't at all the woman I'd met a few years ago. Whatever Miguel did to her robbed her of her confidence and self-worth. I really wanted to chat with the boy.

~ ~ ~ ~ ~

I woke, got up, did my morning business, and then went off in search of Jennifer. I found her on the lanai sipping a cup of coffee. I'd no sooner stepped onto the lanai when Val handed me coffee, exactly how I like it, with a goodly dollop of cream. I smiled my thanks and went and sat down next to Jennifer. "Good morning. How do you feel?"

She smiled. "Now you're here, I'm good. Should I ask what you're gonna do?"

"Remember? No questions. And I really don't have a plan yet."

We finished our coffee and Val brought us a warmup and some breakfast. Jennifer said she had errands to run.

"I'm going back and scope out your old villa. I have an idea, and I need to make a couple of calls. I'll see you later today." Jennifer stood and came over to me, leaned over and kissed me softly on the lips. "What was that for?" I asked.

"Because you're such a special person. I've never met anyone quite like you. I call and say help and within twenty-four hours you're here. No questions, you just show up. Thanks."

I reached up and pulled her onto my lap. "And you too are special." I kissed her and gave her a big hug.

~ ~ ~ ~ ~

I was headed for Jennifer's old villa when I saw Miguel's red Jaguar speeding in the other direction. I made a U turn and was given a few nasty honks by drivers expressing their displeasure. Keeping the red car in sight, I followed him to the next town. Miguel parked in a lot in front of a tall office building and entered. I parked on a side street and walked back to the office building. I entered the lobby and read the directory, noticing the building was made up of a mixed assortment of firms. There was no way to know which office Miguel was visiting. I returned to my car and drove home. I needed to have him followed to see what kind of routine he had. But who could follow him?

On that way to the villa, I had an idea. I pulled my cell out and called the emergency number Salvatore gave me. The voice answered and I gave him my code. "Give me a number where you can be reached." I gave him my cell number and we hung up.

Within 10 minutes my phone rang. "Sal?" I answered.

"Matt, great to hear from you. Why didn't you use the special direct number I gave you, and where the hell are you?"

"I need a favor and I'm in Portugal."

"I'm dying to hear the story, but I'm sure that's not why you called. What do you need?"

"Do you have contacts here in Portugal? I need someone who can follow a person for a few days without being spotted. I need to establish this person's routine."

"My boy, anybody I send you can do a tailing job without being spotted! You should be ashamed to say something like that." I heard a chuckle. "Now, do you need somebody to remove this person?"

"I hope it's not necessary. I just need to establish the guy's routine so I can figure out a way to let him know I know where he is, and I can change things for him if he doesn't alter his course."

"I have a cousin who lives in Barcelona and does what I do. Do you understand what I'm telling you?"

"I do." Also, I didn't want to ask more questions.

"I'll have him hook up with you in a couple of days. Depending on your needs he can provide as many people as you need to assist you."

"Give him this number and have him call me when he's here."

"Done. Take care of yourself."

"Thanks for your help."

"Remember, I want to hear this story. You do keep life interesting." Sal laughed as he hung up.

~ ~ ~ ~ ~

Val served us dinner on the lanai, and we watched the sun set with the sea spread out before us. I could get really used to this life. The view was stunning, and dinner was magnificent. The dish tonight had chicken, clams, chorizo sausage, rice and other great stuff in it and I was pleased to see Jennifer take a few more bites than last night. Val said she had cooked it and I joked with Jennifer that if she wasn't careful, I would steal Val and take her back to Florida.

"What did you do today? I mean about Miguel?"

"I contacted an old... ah, I guess I'd call him a friend. We have a strange relationship anyway I've done him a couple of favors."

"Sounds interesting. I know I'm not supposed to ask questions. Right?"

"Correct. When the time is right, I'll let you know what's happening."

When it was time for bed, Jennifer walked me again to my room and I hugged her. She hugged me tightly and spoke against my chest. "Good night. I just wish there was some way to let you know how much it means to me that you came halfway around the world to help me. All I had to do was ask for help." She leaned back and smiled. "I feel so much better. The first time we met I thought you were a very special man, now I know you are."

"Well, I don't do this kind of thing for just anybody."

She reached up and softly kissed me on the lips. I had to remind myself I was here to help her, not seduce.

I was asleep when I woke to the feeling of a warm soft body cuddling up next to me. It took a moment to realize it was nude. Jennifer had her head on my shoulder and one leg was thrown over my legs. My shoulder was wet, and I knew she'd been crying. "Do you think this is a good idea?" I asked.

She whispered, "Shut up and hold me. Sorry about the sleeping attire, I always sleep naked. Just hold me, please. I don't want anything else."

And I always do what a naked woman asks.

Especially when her body is curled around mine.

~ ~ ~ ~ ~

I woke the next morning to an empty bed. I laid there for a moment and wondered what was going on. At my age, naked beautiful women don't crawl into my bed. I wasn't feeling guilt since Lois decided to end our relationship. Basically, it made me a free man. I knew last night wasn't about sex. No, it was more than that. Why did Jennifer come to my bed last night? Frightened? Probably. Anyway, it was too early in the morning for such deep pondering. 'Sides, I needed coffee.

I found Jennifer and Val together in the kitchen and before I was at the table, I had a cup of coffee in my hand the exact color I liked. "Are you feeling alright?" I asked Jennifer.

"Yes. I woke in the night, and I was frightened. Thank you for not throwing me out."

"Anytime." She picked up my hand and kissed the palm. "Feeling better now?" She smiled.

We breakfasted and she and Val went off together. She told me the situation with the bank was straightened out. I called my bank and reestablished the monthly checks going to Walter and his family.

I called Dominick. "Good morning. Ready to head out?" He asked.

"No, and I don't know how long everything is gonna take. I just wanted to let you know you can go. When my business is resolved, I'll call Henry and let him know I'm ready. But thanks for waiting."

I heard him chuckle. "You have no idea how much fun I'm having."

"And I don't want to know!"

"If you don't mind, don't let Henry what's going on. I'm in no rush to go anywhere. You do what you need and then call me."

"Tell your friend to treat you well. You're important to me."

He snickered. "And you take care of your Jennifer."

CHAPTER NINETEEN

The next day I got a call from Sal's cousin. "Good afternoon. Is this Matt Preston?"

"Yes, it is."

"My name is Donato, Donato Zampuchini. My cousin Salvatore called me and asked me to assist you. Salvatore says you have a problem and that you're a man to be respected. I understand you have done a lot of kind things for Salvatore. What can I do for you Mr. Preston?"

"To start with, please call me Matt?"

"Ahhhh, that'll be difficult after all of the things Salvatore told me about you, but I will try."

"Thanks." I proceed to tell him about Miguel and why I needed to know his schedule. Arrangements were made for us to meet in town. I was already at our meeting place when he arrived with two other men. I watched them walk in and I recognized the identification sign. I didn't need any sign to recognize Donato. Salvatore and Donato looked more like brothers rather than cousins. The olives didn't fall far from the tree in that family.

Donato wore a bespoke light blue suit with a white shirt worn with a couple of buttons undone and several gold chains showing around his neck. His shoes were blue leather and matched the suit. His black hair was combed straight back and was silvered at the temples. He cut quite a handsome figure.

One of the two men with him was short and his suit had seen better days. The discolored collar had a greasy sheen and the pants bagged at the knees. His yellowed white shirt and the tie showed repeated handling.

His partner was right out of central casting. If I was doing a remake of *The Godfather*, this person would fit right in. His dark grey pinstriped double-breasted suit was tailored to fit his tall slender frame and hide the gun under his left arm. He sported an immaculate white shirt with a tie tied in full Windsor. A light grey felt fedora capped his head and well-polished black Italian leather shoes graced his feet.

Extending my hand to Donato I introduced myself. As we shook hands, he said, "I think it best if you don't know the names of my friends here. You can call that person Uno," Donato pointed towards the well-dressed fellow, "And let's call this person Due." He pointed at the fellow in the baggy suit. I knew the word 'uno' in Italian meant one and "due" was two.

Over a glass of red wine, I outlined what was required in detail. "Salvatore said you don't want us to remove this guy?" Donato asked. I nodded. "What if he spots us. What then?"

"Sal told me you had top talent. He told me there was no need to worry. He assured me they wouldn't be seen." I laid it on thick.

"Of course," Donato pointed at the two men who were with him, "They aren't expecting to be spotted, but what happens if they are?"

"Break it off and report to me. Does either of them speak English?"

The well-dressed one spoke up, "I speak English Mr. Preston."

"Please call me Matt."

"No sir, I don't know you well enough. I know Americans are less formal than we are, and I respect that, but it will be a long time before I can call you by your first name."

"What's your name?"

"Like Signori Donato said, I think for now, it's best if we go by the names Uno and Due."

Even though Uno had an accent, his English was outstanding. I asked, "Your English is excellent. How come?"

"I moved to the US when I was 12. As I got older, I tried to be Cuginegot, and got into trouble..."

I held up my hand. "What's a Cuginegot?"

"It's a young punk who wants to be inducted into the family. I had a problem and got caught. Don Zampuchini sent me back to Italy where I was accepted into Signori Donato's family. I was lucky because there was an opening in Barcelona. I speak Spanish. English, Italian, Portuguese and French. I was a perfect fit for the position. By the way, my friend here doesn't speak any English."

"Okay. Hope you didn't mind me asking."

"No problem."

"Where do we find this person?" Donato asked. "You didn't tell us where to find him."

"Meet me back here tomorrow morning and I'll show you where he lives and where he works."

"I'm only going to send Uno and Due back to help you. I've business back in Spain. They will help you."

"Sounds good. By the way, how much is this will cost me."

Donato put his hands up in the air. "Please! Do not to ask that kind of question. When Don Zampuchini asks a favor, I'm only too glad to do it. My people will see you to-morrow morning.

~ ~ ~ ~ ~

That night when I went to get in bed, I found Jennifer waiting in my bed. When she flipped the cover back to let me in, I noticed she was again sans clothing. Being the pig I am, I stared for a moment. This was the first time I'd seen her nude and she was beautiful. It looked to me like she had gained a little weight and I was pleased. After a moment, I realized it wasn't a good idea and pulled the covers back over her. I sat down on the edge. "Do you think this is wise?"

Putting her hand on my arm. "Yes. I'm grateful you're here helping me."

"I understand how you feel. But don't thank me this way." I waved my hand over her covered body. "I didn't come here to make love with you."

"I know." The way she said it sounded like she was explaining something to a child. "But because you came to help with no idea what was the problem, that excites me."

"I think you need to go back to your bed."

"If I put something on, may I stay? I don't like sleeping alone and you don't have to make love to me."

"Why do you want to stay?"

"I slept better last night than I have in a long time. I feel safe with you."

I went to the closet and took out a shirt and tossed it to her. "Please put this on." Jennifer slipped it on and got back in bed. She curled up against me and was asleep before me.

~ ~ ~ ~ ~

The next morning, I found my shirt on the chair next to my bed and Jennifer was gone. I didn't know what the day would bring, but I wanted a cup of Val's wonderful coffee.

After coffee I checked the courtyard and found Uno and Due waiting for me in a 4-door Peugeot which looked like dozens of other cars on the road. Uno was driving and Due moved to the back seat. Both were wearing dark grey long-sleeved shirts with dark grey slacks. Their black shoes had rubber soles, and both were wearing black beret's. If I didn't know them and they were standing in a group, there was nothing that would make them stand out.

I direct them to the villa where Miguel stayed. After we arrived, Uno drove around the neighborhood for a while. The two of them were chatting about something while I just sat there. Finally, Uno asked me where Miguel worked, and I directed him back to his office. We drove around the block and as we were turning the corner, Miguel came towards us in his red Jaguar. "That's Miguel right now."

"Damn, he sure is making it easy to follow him driving that car." Uno remarked."

"Yeah, I thought that too when I saw his car." I responded.

We parked and Uno got out and followed Miguel. When he returned, he smiled and told me. "I know where Miguel works. I found his office. Now we know where he lives and where he works. Working out his schedule should be easy."

The two of them took me back to Jennifer's and dropped me off. Just as they were leaving, Uno said to me, "Give us some time. You have a number to reach us if necessary. I'll call you when we have his routine established. Will that do?"

"Yes. Thanks. I'll wait for your call."

~ ~ ~ ~ ~

When I got ready to go to bed, I found Jennifer waiting for me, wearing the shirt she'd worn last night. She flipped back the cover and looked up at me. "Please, can I stay?" I slid into bed, pulled her to me, and held her as we fell asleep.

Mother nature woke me in the night, I slipped from bed and headed to the bathroom. Returning to bed I passed by an open window and glanced out across the villa's grounds. Movement caught my eye and I stopped in the shadow next to the window. I watched a shadow slip across the lawn and disappeared behind the house. I felt I was back at Sal's home. I slipped on my shorts, and retrieved a pistol from my travel bag.

Moving into the hallway, I descended the stairs and heard the soft tinkle of breaking glass. I stopped momentarily, whoever was outside was now inside. Silently I moved into the room where the intruder entered. Flicking on a light and pulling the hammer back on my pistol, I startled the intruder who turned toward me. "Do you speak English?" I asked.

"A little."

"Down on the floor now and I won't shoot you. If you make any other movement, I'll shoot." I watched him lie down. Reaching over and flicking on one of the table lamps I told him. "Put your hands over your head." He obeyed. Now the question was what to do with the intruder. I called out for Jennifer. She came to the top of the stairs. "What's it?"

"We have a visitor. Please get dressed and bring down my cell phone."

I'd decided to call Donato. After a few rings he answered.

"Donato?" I asked.

"Si."

"I'm sorry about the lateness of the hour."

"Not to worry Mr. Preston. What do you need?"

"I have a person lying on my floor who just broke into our house. I don't really know what to do with him."

'Either Uno or Due will be there in a few minutes. Keep him there. I can't come now, but I'll be there as soon as I can."

"Okay. Tell them to just come in when they get here." The call ended.

I told Jennifer, "Go and unlock the front door."

When she came back in the room she asked. "Who's that?"

"I don't know yet. One of Donato's people is on his way."

Uno was there in less than 15 minutes. He knocked once on the door and opened it. When he stepped into the room, he spoke to the person lying of the floor. They conversed for a minute, and Uno turned to me. "Is there a place we can lock him up until Signori Donato gets here?"

"There is a wine cellar downstairs that has a lock on the outside. It's a little cramped, but he can't get out." Jennifer said.

"Lead the way." Uno replied.

We took the man downstairs and place him in the wine cellar. Jennifer was correct, it was small. I made sure the lock was secure and we went back upstairs. "I'm going now. I will return when Signori Donato comes." Uno told us.

We went back upstairs and got into bed. "I'm not sleepy anymore." Jennifer told me. We began kissing, but eventually we fell back to sleep.

The next morning, we were having coffee when Donato arrived. He joined us for a cup of coffee, and I explain what had happened the previous evening. A short time later Uno and Due arrived and we all went down to the wine cellar. Uno opened the door and our night visitor stepped out.

When he saw Donato, he dropped fearfully to his knees. Speaking so rapidly I couldn't understand a thing, he kept repeating, "Signori Donato. Mi dispiace. Come si dice she non lo sapevo."

Donato turned to me. "I know this man. He's a hired assassin. He's Romanian and his name is Bogdan. He's saying he's sorry, he didn't know you and Jennifer were under my protection. Even though I've never used him, he knows who I am. I also know people who have used him. Now he knows who I am, he also knows because of our relationship, he's a dead man."

"Do you have to kill him?"

"He was hired by Miguel to frighten your lady friend, or worse. What do you want me to do with him?"

Bogdan started to talk. I didn't understand the words, but I realized he was begging Donato to spare his life. The conversation between the two men continued until Bogdan kept repeating, "Grazie, grazie."

Donato told me. "Bogdan said Miguel doesn't know you're here. He thinks only Jennifer is living here. Bogdan says Miguel claims Jennifer has stolen a lot of money from him and won't pay it back. He was supposed to break in and frighten Jennifer into paying the money. He claims he wasn't going to kill her, just scare her into paying the debt."

"So, what are you gonna to do with him?" I asked.

"Like I said, Bogdan knows who I am. He's convinced I'm going to kill him. With your permission, I would like to make a deal with him. Since you asked for his life to be spared, as a favor to you, he won't be killed, but instead be taken to the Hungarian border and released. He will agree not to contact Miguel and he will return to Romania and never come back. If he does come back, I'll have him killed. What do you think?"

"I agree. He seems to be frightened of you. I don't think he'll return."

Donato proceeded to explain the arrangement. Bogdan reached up and kept kissing the back of Donato's hand. "He's thanking me for letting him live."

Bogdan crawled over to my feet and started kissing them, while continuing to repeat. "Grazie, grazie."

"Make sure Mr. Bogdan understands that if he ever returns, if you don't kill him, I will. And you know I can and would."

Donato nodded and explained what I'd just told him and some of the things I'd done over the years. The look on Bogdan's face told me he was as afraid of me as he was Donato. Donato told Bogdan to get up and Uno and Due took him out to the car. Bogdan kept bowing to me and Donato, repeating. "Grazie, grazie!"

~ ~ ~ ~ ~

For the next couple of days, I lived the good life. Val cooked us amazing meals and I went swimming several times a day in the pool. Since it was totally private, the best part was I didn't have to wear a suit.

The next two days we went down to the beach to a private place Jennifer knew. After we dropped our gear, I watched in awe as she walked naked to the water. Jennifer was filling out very nicely. We swam for a while, and she swam to me and wrapped her legs around my waist. We kissed and in a short time things woke up. I pulled away. I kept reminding myself the reason I was here wasn't to seduce her; but it was difficult.

A little less than a week after Bogdan broke into the house, Jennifer received a call from Miguel. I told her to string him along; tell him she was frightened because of Bogdan, and he'd the get money, but she needed to arrange it. Nervously she did her best putting him off while I listened on another phone.

"I'm getting tired of waiting Jenny." Miguel groused. I know she hates that name. "There had better be something coming soon, or you'll be sorry. I know where you're living. Pay the money or else." And he hung up.

That evening I held a very frightened Jennifer. It took a long time before she was able to sleep. I kept promising myself this clown was going to pay.

The next morning Donato called. "I'm coming over tomorrow morning, we need to talk, we have a slight... ah, problem."

"What?"

"Tomorrow. See you then." He hung up. I wondered.

Next morning, standing in Jennifer's courtyard I watched a black S class Mercedes pull in. Uno was behind the wheel. I got in the back seat with Donato, and we headed towards town. On the way, Donato explained. "I need to give you a little history lesson. There are five or six prominent families like mine in greater Europe and a few lesser ones. One of the most prominent families happens to be Miguel's father. Yes, Miguel has an import/export business all right, but their main import is drugs. They also deal in human trafficking and anything else that makes money. Your Jennifer is lucky she got out when she did."

"How so."

"Miguel might have decided to have his people kidnap her and ship her to the Middle East and sell her. But then he couldn't get to her money. However, he doesn't need her money. Miguel's business makes as much, if not more than mine. Additionally, there is what his papa earns."

"Okay. I understand his family has power, and a lot of money. Why is that a problem for you?"

"Miguel's father is Zeno Fibrine. Don Fibrine's family is much larger than mine. A few years ago, our two families struck a deal and we've lived in peace since then. If Zeno ever found out my people were following his son... well, I hate to think of what might happen. I want to help you as much as I can, but I also have to protect my family."

"What's going to happen now?"

"To start with, your boy is a very busy little fellow."

"What do you mean?" I asked.

"Just watch." Uno had pulled into a two-level parking garage and on the top level, there sat Miguel's car. We parked at the opposite end of the garage and waited. About ten minutes later, Miguel came through the stairwell opening and walked to his car, got in and drove away. We followed him to his office where Uno parked across the street and Donato turned to face me.

"Miguel has three mistresses plus, the woman with whom he shares the house. He uses the parking garage we just left when he visits one of his paramours in the morning. She lives across the alley. He visits the lady twice a week. I told you what his business is, and it's owned by Zeno. Miguel spends three hours a day, tops at the office.

"The garage is the best place to corner him. When he comes to get his car, we'll pick him up. I know a place north of here and it's totally deserted. My associates will take you there and then you can have your long serious talk." Signoria Donato said.

"It appears you're washing your hands of this whole thing. I also understand why you don't want to get involved." I asked.

"No, but I need to be careful. Very few people know Uno and Due work for me."

Uno turned around and looked back at me. "If you want, Due and I will help you. The three of us can capture Miguel and you can talk.

"When it's done, Signori Donato is sending us back to Italy where we can hide for a while. Will that do?"

"Yes. Thank you. When do you think we can pick him up?"

"He won't be back to see this woman until Friday. When he visits, he always comes out to his car approximately the same time."

"Okay. You two pick me up and we'll do this."

Donato looked at me. "Say the word Mr. Preston and Miguel will be history."

"Thanks, I really hope it won't be necessary. From what you tell me about his family, if we take him out, the Fibrine family will be out for blood."

Donato nodded. "I appreciate that you understand what's at stake."

I said nothing to Jennifer about my scheme. The evening before we planned to pick Miguel up, he called, and I listened in while Jennifer talked to him. "I tried to be reasonable. You walked out on me. You totally disrespected me. I was willing to let it go for some sort of payment, but you wouldn't listen. You didn't believe I'd do anything. I thought sending my man to visit you would make you understand I meant business. Now, you're going to find out the price for not cooperating. You're dead bitch!"

Miguel hung up and Jennifer was shaking and crying as I held her in my arms. I told her not to worry, I had the situation under control, and I promised he'd never bother her again."

Jennifer looked up with tears streaming down her face. "Are you going to kill him?" She asked.

"I'm not planning on it, but if I did, would it bother you?"

She was silent for a while and then slowly shook her head. "No! He hurt me so much and threatened me and expected me to support him, I've lost all feelings for him. If that's what it takes to make him leave me alone, no, it wouldn't bother me if you killed him."

I gave her a strong hug. "Let's hope it doesn't come down to that. I don't want to kill him, but one way or another, he's going to leave you alone."

She hugged me back and I heard a muffled, "Thank you." Spoken against my chest.

Lying in bed later that evening, Jennifer asked. "What are you going to do once this situation with Miguel is done?"

"I don't know. I have nothing happening back stateside, so I'm in no rush to get back."

"What about Lois."

"I think when I came to help you, that ended."

"Oh Matt, I'm sorry. I was frightened and I didn't even think what my request might do to your life. I didn't mean to upset things."

"It's okay. The relationship was in trouble before you called." I proceeded to tell her about the trouble with the ghosts being murdered. I explained when I needed Lois what happened. "I was hurt when I realized she didn't believe me. When it was all over, we had a talk, but it just wasn't the same. The trust is missing on both our parts, so even though we didn't say goodbye, when I left it was understood we were done."

Jennifer was still for a while. In a soft voice I heard her ask, "Would you consider staying for a while?"

"Is that what you want?"

"Yes." She timidly replied.

"I assume since you're asking me to stay, you also want to make love?" She said I was correct. "I thought you were lesbian or possibly bi-sexual? I don't feel comfortable with either in a relationship."

"Let me explain. You know I basically grew up in boarding schools?"

"Yes."

"There are not a lot of boys at an all-girl school." I snickered and Jennifer slapped my arm, "Be nice! However, a lot of sexual experimentation went on at school, so all my first activities were with women. I was in my early 20's before I had sex with a man, and it was a disaster. Neither of us knew what we were doing, and when he tried to push it in, it really hurt. The best part of the ordeal was it only lasted a few seconds.

"Since it was more pleasurable with women, I looked for female lovers. Miguel was the first male lover since my bad experience and the experience of being with Sara and him turned out to be a good one.

"To answer your question, I guess I'm considered bi-sexual. I enjoyed Miguel and I enjoyed Sarah, but I'm curious what it might be like with you. You would be my second. For a lot of reasons, I'd like to make love with you."

"I'd enjoy spending time with you after the situation with Miguel is over. However, I have three dogs I need to get back to and I really miss, two are puppies. They're all properly vaccinated and stuff so it shouldn't be a problem bringing them here. How would you feel about having my dogs here?"

"I'd like that."

"But then there's the problem where would I stay?" Jennifer softly bit my nipple. I kissed her. "Let's see how it turns out with Miguel before any decisions are made."

Jennifer put her arms around me and pulled me to her chest. "Thanks. I couldn't ask for more."

CHAPTER TWENTY

Uno and Due showed up on Friday in a Mercedes Sprinter van, Due driving this time. Uno explained, "You see vans like this all the time around town. Nobody is going to notice another one."

"Where did you get this one?" I asked.

"Mr. Preston, please don't ask questions you really don't want, or need answered." I'd been put in my place.

At the parking garage we found Miguel's red Jaguar parked in the same place as before. The space next to it was empty which made parking easy for us. He came out on schedule and just as he was getting into the Jag, Uno opened the van door and pointed a gun at Miguel. Uno spoke in Portuguese, but I understood what he said. "Get in the van and lie down on the floor. It makes no difference what you do. I'll just leave your dead body, and your four lovers can fight over your remains. Now get in."

"Do you know who my father is?"

"Yes, and we don't give a shit. Get in the van now or I shoot." Uno cocked his pistol.

Miguel crawled into the van and laid on the floor. Uno reached out and patted him down for any weapons. He was clean. I put a blindfold over his eyes and put two Zip ties on his hands and feet. In a half hour we arrived at the spot my two accomplices knew about.

Due pulled off the main road and drove down a dirt road for a couple of miles. The silence was palpable when Due shut off the motor. Uno opened the side door, reached in and grabbed one of Miguel's feet, pulling him out of the van. Miguel hit the ground, grunted and lay in the dirt. Uno removed the blindfold and Miguel looked up snarling. "You're going to be sorry when my father hears about this. You're all dead meat."

Uno reached down slapped his face as hard as he could, then grabbed Miguel's nose, squeezed it and twisted it as Miguel roared in pain. "What makes you think you're going to be able to tell daddy anything. You didn't think we're going to let you just walk away, did you?" He growled.

I could see by the look on Miguel's face it dawned on him how much difficulty he was in. "What do you want? I'll do anything." His voice quavered.

Now it was my turn. I knelt beside him. "Miguel, we know all about you." He tried to turn his face away and I took his sore nose and moved his face to look him in the eye. "Look at me when I talk to you. Didn't you wonder why Bogdan never contacted you again?" Miguel moved his head.

"Bogdan doesn't exist anymore." There was fear in his eyes. "I know all about you." I proceeded to tell him what I knew about his four lady friends and where they were located. I also told him what we knew about his business.

"Now, do you see I can reach out and touch you any time I want. There is nothing I don't know about you. I know your parents address in Barcelona. I even know the addresses of your father's mistresses. Both of them!" Miguel's eyes got big. "If you don't do exactly what I tell you, I'll find you and kill you. Do you understand?"

"No. What's so damn important you have to bring me out here and threaten me?"

"What you're doing to Jennifer? That will end."

"Oh, that stupid bitch." I lost it and reached down and slapped him across his face open handed. His head snapped to one side and when he looked up at me, I back handed the other side of his face even harder. There was a little trickle of blood running down one side of his chin.

I grabbed his nose again and twisted it as far as I could. Tears were running down his face and his body bucked as he screamed. "Don't ever call her that again. Understand? If you do, I will kill you."

Miguel looked at me, his eyes filled with anger. I twisted his nose the other way and shook it. He moaned in pain. "Do you understand what I told you?"

"Yes" He screamed. "What do you want?" His words were slurred due to his fat lip.

"I just told you. Leave Jennifer alone. You and Sara are to leave that villa and move somewhere else outside of Portugal. Leave Portugal at once and never return. You're not to contact Jennifer again. If she tells me she has seen you anywhere, or you called her, I'll find you and kill you. If something happens to me, my two associates will find you, screw your women and make you watch before they kill them and then kill you. Is that clear?"

Miguel lay on the ground staring up at the three of us. Due pulled out his pistol and cocked it and placed it against Miguel's forehead. "I believe you were asked a question. What's your answer?" Uno asked Miguel.

"All right, all right. I agree. I'll leave Jennifer alone."

"And you're going to move."

"Yes."

"At once?"

"What's going to happen to my business?"

"I don't really care. Besides, daddy can find another flunkey to do your job." I remarked.

Uno snarled at him. "Besides, you don't do a damn thing except pinch the women on the ass and screw one of them from time to time."

Due had a knife in his hand as he knelt beside Miguel. He poked the point of the knife against Miguel's chest making his body jump. "All right. I agree to everything. Please don't kill me. Please loosen the ties on my hands. My fingers are going numb." Uno motioned to Due to cut the tie on his wrists but leave his ankles bound. Miguel put his hands to his face and carefully touched his red and swollen nose and swiped a hand across his bloody chin.

Uno motioned for us to step away. We moved behind the van, looking inside to see what we could use to tie him up and still leave him a way to get loose after a while. We discussed what to do. "You want to tie him up, but leave the rope loose enough so that he can eventually free himself?" Uno asked. He then said something to Due and they chatted for a while.

"Yes, I agree." I told Uno. "Let's tie him up and get out of here."

Returning from behind the van, we saw Miguel managed to free his feet and run off through the scrub brush. We could hear him moving through the brush, we split up to give chase. It was obvious he wasn't used to moving through the woods and it was easy to follow his trail of broken bushes and noise. Stopping occasionally to listen for sounds of his retreat, I'd change my direction. The sounds stopped and I heard Uno call out, "Be careful, he's hiding."

I heard Due call out, and I assumed he was letting Uno know he'd found Miguel. I headed in that direction. Again, I heard Due shout then he was silent. I continued to make my way towards the last sound I'd heard. I could still hear somebody moving through the brush and I was making my way towards the sound when I heard Uno call out, "Look out. Due is down. It appears he's been struck on the head. He needs medical attention now."

"I'm coming." I shouted.

As I was getting closer to the sound of Uno's voice, I heard a shot, a pause and then more shots. I moved towards the sound.

When I entered a clearing, I found both Uno and Due lying on the ground. Miguel was gone. Uno looked like he was dead from the way he was crumpled on the ground, and I moved over to Uno and put my fingers on his neck. There was still a pulse, but weak. I pulled Uno's pistol from his waist band and stepped into the protection of some trees.

My mind moved back to a forest in Michigan where I'd been in a similar situation. That time I was lucky, and I'd killed somebody. Was this going to be the time when my luck ran out? I heard a noise off to my left and carefully started towards the noise. Ahead I heard a twig snap and quietly moved towards the sound.

Stepping into a clearing, I heard a voice behind me. "Stop! First, I'm gonna kill you and then find that bitch Jennifer and kill her. But I'm going to take a long time with her. I'm going to tie her up and make her suffer before I let her die. Nobody moves out on me. Now turn around."

I turned. Miguel stood in the middle of the clearing with Due's pistol aimed at my head. I watched him pull back the hammer and I could see he was ready to pull the trigger. My luck had run out!

In that moment, I thought of Jennifer. I felt bad that I wouldn't be able to protect her anymore. I heard a shot and waited for the hot searing pain I knew would come.

There was no pain, I watched the pistol fall from Miguel's hand. A red spot was growing on his chest, and he looked down in disbelief. He put his hands over this chest, and I saw his lips move but I didn't understand his words as he pitched forward.

Looking over at the edge of the clearing, Bogdan stepped out of the woods with a pistol in hand. "Sorry," he said, "I come back. I see. Follow many days. I not like what he did. He lied." He pointed his pistol at Miguel and pulled the trigger again, hitting Miguel in the back of the head. I was pretty sure he was dead from the bullet to his chest, but the second bullet left no doubt.

Note to self, don't piss off Bogdan! He carries a grudge.

"Your friends need doctor.'"

I thought for a minute. "Yes, both of them need immediate medical attention."

"We need go, now."

I told Bogdan, "Let me look around the area and make sure we're not leaving any evidence." I pointed at Miguel. "Can we take his body back to where we picked him up and leave the body for somebody to discover."

With a lot of difficulty, we got all three of them into the van and Bogdan drove. I called Donato while we were on the way and told him what had happened. He said his people would meet the van when we dropped off Miguel's body. I also told him what Bogdan had done. "Tell Bogdan I wish to see him. He's not in trouble. I'll meet you back at the villa, bring Bogdan with you."

We returned to the garage where several of Donato's people were waiting to help move bodies. After we laid Miguel's body behind the Jag, Donato's people carefully loaded Uno and Due into another van. One of the men pointed to a car parked in one of the slots, handed me the keys and told me to use that car and go back to my villa.

Bogdan and I got in the car and headed for the villa. I stopped and parked a couple of blocks away and Bogdan and I started to walk. We'd only gone half way down the block when Donato's car pulled up. Donato got out of the car and spoke to Bogdan. He must have told Bogdan to get in the car. Bogdan extended his hand toward me, "Graze." We shook hands and he climbed into the back.

Donato turned to me "Don't worry. To be honest, I have no idea if Miguel would have stuck to any agreement that was made. I know his father wouldn't. This way the problem is solved. You're off the hook and didn't have to kill anybody. This isn't what I'd have chosen, but it's resolved, and I'll deal with the outcome."

"What's going to happen to Bogdan?"

"Good things. That's all you need to know. Very good things, now go home and I'll contact you in a few days."

"I wouldn't mind keeping Bogdan as our bodyguard if he's interested."

"We'll see."

When I got to the villa, I entered and went to the kitchen. Taking down a bottle of Scotch, I poured myself a small, but nourishing. Actually, it was a rather large shot of Scotch. I was still trying to get over how close I'd come to dying in some forest in Portugal. I was taking the last sip when Jennifer came into the room. She looked at me and then at the open bottle of Scotch. She took down a glass and poured herself a shot.

She drank it in one swallow and looked at me. "Okay, what happened?" she asked.

I explained what happened out in the forest and how we'd left Miguel's body in the garage. "I'm sorry, Miguel is dead."

Jenifer stared at me and then shrugged her shoulders, "It wasn't how I wanted it to end, but now I don't have to worry. I'm glad you weren't the one to kill him. I don't know why, for me it's better that somebody else did it."

"I think I understand. I'm glad too. I've had enough death to last me for a very long time."

I held out my arms, she came to me and wrapped her arms around me. Her head was against my chest. I held her tightly.

We stood that way for a long time.

CHAPTER TWENTY - ONE

That night I found Jennifer waiting for me in bed. Flipping back the covers, tonight she wasn't wearing one of my shirts. Jennifer was nude. We'd gone swimming naked together but tonight I noticed since my arrival she was filling out and looked pretty good. She looked more like the woman I'd knew in Seattle. She patted the side of the bed for me.

After I sat on the edge of the bed, I asked. "Is this a good idea?"

"Yes. I have nothing holding me back, do you?" She was right. I had nothing holding me back. "But…"

She reached up and put her hand on my mouth. "Stop, because you came to help, that makes me want to make love with you so much. When we met in Seattle and you helped me, I wondered what you would be like as a lover. But you had someone, and I was looking forward to returning to my two lovers. I knew having sex at that time would make things complicated for both of us. Now you tell me your relationship is over and I have no one. I want us to make love. I've dreamed about it and now I want to make the dream a reality."

I reached down and took her hand from my face and kissed her palm. "You make it difficult to say no! I still think you're doing this for wrong reasons. I'll admit when I met you, I was captivated. You reminded me of a movie star from the '40's. When you walked to my table, every man in the house watched you. And when you sat down next to me, every face showed disappointment. I wanted you then, but as you said, you didn't need complications in your life, you needed help and I was happy to provide it."

"So, why are you so reluctant now?"

"I'm afraid it might ruin things. You have this illusion about me, and I like that. I don't want to destroy it."

"How about let me deal with my illusions? Get in bed and let's see if you're better than I thought you'd be."

"My God Jennifer, talk about how to put pressure on a guy." She giggled and pushed me to stand up. When I was off the bed, she pulled the covers off and motioned for me to get into bed. I undressed and moved to the bed. Taking her in my arms, I kissed her and murmured, "I just hope I can measure up to your expectations."

The rest of the night doesn't need to be covered…

Except to say all expectations were met.

On both sides.

~ ~ ~ ~ ~

The next morning, we lay wrapped in each other's arms as Jennifer looked at me. "Are you okay?" she asked. I thought about it and realized I was pleased with the way things turned out. I didn't have to shoot Miguel, but he was gone and there was nothing to fear anymore.

"Yeah, I'm good. However, are you okay?" I asked and I felt her head move on my chest as she nodded.

"Can we go somewhere, together?" She asked.

"Like where?"

"London, I love London. Can we go?" It had been a long time since I'd been there, and it sounded like a great idea. I called Henry, since I knew Dominick had been pulled to take care of an issue. "How's it looken' for a flight from Portugal to London?"

"We just finished the mission and don't ask questions. Dominick is landing in Germany as we speak. He was supposed to come back to D.C., but we have nothing planned. I'll dispatch him to pick you up and he'll call you when he's landing. He'll be there within twenty-four hours. Is that acceptable?"

"Thanks Henry." I turned to Jennifer, "The plane will be here within twenty-four hours to take us to London."

"What? You have your own plane?"

"Well, in a way I have several planes, but none that are actually mine. I own part of an air charter company. Pack what you want, but not too much. We're shopping in London. You have about twenty-four hours to get ready."

I called Donato. "Have you spoken with your guys?"

"Yes. Both will recover and they're on their way to a couple of secret places. Lucky for you Bogdan returned, even after we told him not to come back. He was angry with the way Miguel played him and he wanted to punish him. If he'd known the truth, he'd never have taken the contract. I have a place for him in my family, but he's free to come and spend time with you as well. He can be very useful.

"In addition, I was able to plant a pistol in the garage and the make and model will point to a family I've been having problems with over in the East. Even if they do a ballistics test, there is so much false evidence left around it will never be totally resolved. My people are clean, and I know you're safe. However, I'd advise you go someplace for a while."

"I've already taken care of that. We're headed for..."

"Stop, I don't want to know. Just go. Ciao."

"Ciao."

That night as Jennifer and I lay in bed, she asked me if I'd been thinking about staying for awhile with her. "I told you about the dogs. When we get back, I'll return to the states and get them. I'll see what I can do about a long-term renter for my house. After that, I'm yours."

I felt her head move and I pulled her close to me. She was obviously tired since she was asleep before I was even comfortable.

Dominick called the next morning. "I hear you want to go to London?"

"Yeah. When can you take us?"

"London! That's great. I have a…"

I interrupted, "You have a friend in London you want to see. Right?"

"How did you know that?"

"Lucky guess. When do you want us at the airport?"

He set a time, we met and were off. The weeks in London were fantastic. We stayed at the Mandarin Oriental Hyde Park and every day we walked someplace new and found a new place every evening for dinner. Jennifer made me go to the bespoke tailors Gieves & Hawkes, on No.1 Savile Row, to be honest, I didn't put up much of a fight. They were founded in 1771 and I ordered several suits. Next door I went to another shop and ordered shirts to go with the new suits. As a special favor, the shop did a rush job on one of the suits and by the third evening I had a brand-new suit complete with vest. Not to brag, I looked pretty good.

After we returned to Jennifer's villa, I told her I was going to go back to Florida and get my dogs.

"While you're gone, I'm moving back to my original villa. It's empty, I own it and I like it better than this one." I failed to see how any villa could be nicer than where we were now, but I held my tongue.

I called Henry and asked him when a plane might be available to fly me back to the states. "Can't do a thing for a couple of days. Day after tomorrow perhaps. I'll text you the time when I'm on the way."

This time it was Henry who flew me back to Florida. The dogs were overjoyed to see me, and I was just as excited to see them. I made arrangements with an agency to take care of renting my house and rented a storage space to keep what I wanted to save. I bid farewell to my poker buddies who were sad to see me leave. I think they were just sad to see my quarters leaving.

Jennifer was blown away with the puppies. All three dogs were just as pleased to meet her. We settled into her original villa and the dogs loved it. I had to admit, even though the first villa we'd stayed at was nice, this place was a step up. A major step up! The dogs had full run of the place and Val fell in love with the three of them. I had to keep re-minding her to cut back on the treats. I was afraid they were going to get fat.

One night as we lay in bed, I took Jennifer in my arms, and I felt her crying. "What's wrong?"

"I'm so happy. I'm afraid."

"What? That doesn't make sense."

"I'm afraid one day you'll leave. I've never felt so com-fortable in a relationship before. This is wonderful."

"And that makes you cry/" I said with a chuckle.

"NO! I just don't know what I'll do when you leave."

"And who said I was leaving?"

"Well, you know, you still have a life back in the states and there really is no reason to stay here. And you told me your relationships tend to fall apart after a while."

"Well, I know what I said, but there are many reasons to stay here. My dogs are here, and then there's the oth-er reason."

"What?"

"You!"

"Me?"

"Yes, I stay because I care for you, I love you and I want to be with you. You said you've never been so comfortable in a relationship before this one?" I felt her move her head. "Well, I feel the same way. There isn't much left in the states. I've sold most of my stuff and my house is rented. I like it here and if you want me to stay, I will."

"Really?"

"Yes. And if you wish, we can get married."

Jennifer quickly sat up. "Are you kidding?"

"No. I've been thinking about asking you if you'd like to make our relationship more permanent. Would you marry me?"

"Are you sure?"

"Yes, I'm sure." And as funny as that seems, I knew it was true.

"Yes, I'll marry you." She kissed me. "Yes, yes, yes!"

Jennifer wrapped her arms around my head and held me against her chest. "I heard her whisper, "I love you." Lying between her lovely breasts, I did what any man would do, I started to get aroused, and then I started to play.

And now we need to pull the curtain and leave.

Use your imagination.

~ ~ ~ ~ ~

It took about a month to get all the paperwork arranged and various regulations straightened out. We were married by the town mayor followed by a big celebration. Henry and Dominick came for the wedding in our largest plane, bringing John Orchard along with Walter and his family, Mouse and Jade, and also brought Jeff Davenport and his wife Dee. Even Don Salvatore and his cousin Signori Donato

Zampuchini came to the celebration. I was impressed. I doubted if either went to many weddings and for both to be together for a wedding was a first. I felt honored.

I was surprised to see Bogdan at the wedding. He was with a very lovely woman and when the two of them stepped up to congratulate the two of us, I made a comment about his lovely companion and asked who she was.

"You already know me Mr. Preston." She smiled and held up one hand to display one finger was missing.

"Mrs. Addams?" She nodded. "Should I be alarmed?" I was concerned. At our last encounter she had been hired to kill me.

"No. That was a long time ago. I got in trouble over here and Bogdan and Signori Donato stepped in and saved me. Bogdan is such a darling man. Signori Donato has found several things for us to do together. I'm glad to be able to tell you all is forgiven. To be honest, Dave was kind a of ass anyway."

After the ceremony Donato cornered me. "Congratulations and I wanted to thank you."

"For what?"

"Because of what happened to Miguel, there is a small war between some of the families. A rival family is suspected of killing Miguel and Zeno Fibrine has sworn vengeance. The Don Fibrine war has brought on a lot of hardship for his family, and he has lost a lot of his people. As it turns out, my family is now in a much stronger position. Actually, because of what's happened, we're the major family in Europe now."

"I don't know if congratulations are in order or not?"

Donato laughed. "I just wanted you to know how everything turned out. We suffered no fall out from Miguel and I see things have worked out for you."

"When I came to help Jennifer, I didn't see it ending this way. But yes, things have turned out great. I'm very happy. Nobody here knows about my past, so I'm not asked to do favors for people and ending up in untenable situations. I'm very happy."

Donato hugged me and kissed both my cheeks. "I'm pleased, this is good for both of us." Don Salvatore entered the room and expressed his greetings and good wishes for our marriage.

At one point in the day John cornered me. "Are you planning on returning to the states soon?"

"No, I think I'm pretty much done with the states. I like it here. Why?"

"Well, I kind of need you to do a favor for me."

I looked at him in disbelief. "You've got to be fucking kidding me! John, I'm gonna pretend you never said that. I'm done doing favors for you. I'm retired."

"Okay. I'll try Walter."

"John, my advice is to stay away. Don't ask Walter to do anything for you. If he doesn't kick your ass, Thien will. Trust me."

John walked off dejectedly. I really didn't care. I'd done enough things for him, and I didn't feel I owed him a thing.

Our villa was huge and Walter and his family, and Mouse and Jade all stayed with us for a few weeks. It was one of the best times of my life. Almost every evening we sat on the lanai and watched the sun slip into the ocean drinking wonderful drinks served to us by Val.

By the time everyone was ready to head back to the states, Little Matt had learned enough Portuguese that he could chat with Val. Every morning when I went down to the kitchen for a cup of coffee, I found Little Matt and Val chattering away. I also noticed his meals were always a little nicer than the rest of ours. Not that ours were bad, but his were always perfect. Val doted on the lad and the dogs. It was a happy time for all.

Before Walter, his family, and Mouse and Jade headed back Jade and Thein cornered me. Both wrapped their arms around me, and Jade looked up. "You've done so much for Thein and me and we always wanted to do something for you. We're so happy to see you with Jennifer. You deserve it. We love you so much and are happy to see you're finally happy." I got a kiss on each cheek.

Marrying Jennifer had a lot of perks, but I thought getting kissed by the two of them rated right up near the top. I was touched by their words.

CHAPTER TWENTY-TWO

After everybody was gone, life finally settled down and to my surprise, I discovered I enjoyed married life this time around. Far more than I expected. I don't know if was because we were living in a foreign country or if I'd finally met the person who could put up with me, or perhaps I'd finally grown up. I had no idea what tomorrow might bring, but I was happy.

We started taking ballroom dancing lessons and every Friday evening we went to a party with a live band and danced. Time passed and the two of us were happy and content. Every summer Walter and his family came to visit for a couple of months, and I never knew when Mouse and Jade might show up. Whenever Henry or Dominick was in town, they'd spend a few days with us. Even The Admiral came and visited a couple of times with a woman he'd met at work. He seemed happy with her. Life was good.

~ ~ ~ ~ ~

One day Jennifer came home, and I could see she was sad. I asked her what was the problem, and she told me she'd gone to see a doctor. I didn't know anything was wrong and I could tell it hadn't been a good visit. "What's the problem?"

Tears streamed down her face, "I've been getting horrible headaches, so I went and saw a doctor. They've found a growth inside my head, and they want to do exploratory surgery."

I was devastated. "What do they say your chances are?"

"They won't know until they operate. I wanted to talk to you before I scheduled it."

Over the next few days, we talked it over and decided the operation needed to take place. We needed to know what we were dealing with and what might be done to fix it.

I met the two doctors and they explained what they would do and the various outcomes. Depending on what they found it would affect everything. I didn't say anything to Jennifer, but I wasn't pleased with what I heard.

After she left the room, I said to the doctors, "I don't mean to cast any negativity on your skills, but is there another doctor we can see who might have a better outcome?"

"My friend is the leading specialist in Europe. Your wife can't be in better hands." One of the doctors commented."

Arrangements were made and finally the day arrived. I wore a path in the rug waiting to hear how the operation went. Finally, both doctors took me into an office. We all sat down, and I knew at once they didn't have good news.

"I wish I had better news." The doctor told me. "The lump is growing and there is really nothing we can do. It has attached itself to parts of the brain that if we tried to remove it, we'd be removing important parts of her brain. We can keep her comfortable and basically pain free for the remainder of her time."

"How long does she have?"

The doctors looked at each other before either answered. "Sorry Mr. Preston, we give her four to six months."

I stood and walked to the window. Tears were streaming down my face. I thought of all the women I'd cared for and the number of times I'd almost married. And the woman I'd finally married would be taken from me and there was nothing I could do to stop it. Somehow it just didn't seem fair. "Have you told her this?"

"No. We wanted to tell you first and then have you present when we explain what's going to happen."

"You're sure there's nothing you can do? Some sort of new experimental surgery or something?"

"No. If there was, we'd tell you. We considered sending you to a specialist in New York but after we sent her information to them, they told us there was nothing they could do either. They concur on our diagnosis. There is nothing we can do in a case like your wife's. We're sorry to have to tell you this."

The conversation with Jennifer went better than I thought it would. After the doctors left the two of us, she reached out for my hand. "I'm so sorry."

I was stunned. "Sorry for what? I'm the one who's sorry you must go through all of this."

"No! I'm sorry when this is over, you will be alone, and I won't be there to hold you and comfort you. I love you. I'm so sorry things turned out like this."

"Just being with you for the time we've had has been wonderful. I wouldn't give that up for anything."

When we got back to the villa, I found Walter and his family were there waiting for us. "What's this?" I asked.

Thein stepped up and put her arms around my neck. "Jennifer called us and told us what was happening. You've done so much for us, now it's our turn to help."

Little Matt, who wasn't that little any more came into the room chattering away with Val in Portuguese followed by the two puppies and Max. Seeing that lifted my spirits. I gave Thein a big kiss. "Thanks. I think this is going to work out."

I wish I could tell you it all turned out well. But the doctors knew what they were doing. Jennifer lasted just over five months. We were still at the villa; I was holding her in my arms when she passed away. Her last words were, "I love you. Thank you for making my life so wonderful. My darling, I'm sorry to leave you. Please find another woman and give her your love."

I held her head against my chest. "You're one of a kind. There were a lot of women I almost married, but you had the something special I needed. There is no one else out there. I love you." I kissed her forehead and I felt her give a little shiver and she was gone. I ran my hand over her eyes and held her as I cried.

The next few days were a blur. At her instance we'd taken care of any legal paperwork and the legal part of her passing went as planned. The villa was to be sold and all of her holdings were put into a huge trust fund with some money going to me, which I didn't need and the majority going to Walter and his family. His two kids were set as far as schooling and life was concerned.

I notified my renters back in Florida I was coming back, and they would need to vacate. As much as I loved the villa where Jennifer and I had lived, there was no way I could stay. Too many memories.

Back at the Florida house I became a hermit. Val came with me, so I had a full-time housekeeper. The grocery store was less than a mile away and she did all our shopping. There was no need for me to do a thing. I took the dogs for long walks, and we sat on the lanai, and I stared across the river while enjoying a small, but nourishing.

I noticed Max was starting to move slower and seemed to be out of breath a lot. I took him to Dr. Oldman and X-rays showed a lump growing on his lungs and it was slowly cutting off his air passage. He was seventeen which is a good age for that breed of dog. She told me to watch him and when he could no longer sleep the whole night, it was time to do something.

The other two dogs were no longer puppies and they started to watch out for Max instead of the other way around. When we walked, they walked with Max and seemed to sense when he needed to sit and rest. Max had raised them and now they were taking care of him in his old age. It was touching to witness.

A couple of weeks later Max coughed all night and I took him to Dr. Oldman the next morning. She took another series of X-rays and when she returned, there were tears in her eyes. "The lump has grown and now it almost restricts his ability to breath. It's time to do something. He's in a lot of discomfort."

I held him as she gave him the injection that put him to sleep. I swear he looked up at me and his eyes said, "Thank you. It's time." Dr. Oldman arranged to have him cremated and I went home. I went out on the lanai and sat looking down the river. Both dogs came and jumped up in my lap. Usually they would bicker a little, each trying to find the best spot. Thunder stood on my lap once and licked at the tears on my face. Then they both settled down and fell asleep. Val brought out a glass of Scotch and leaned over and kissed my cheek. That was something she'd never done. I was touched.

A few days later John Orchard came down to visit along with Henry and Dominick. They all came onto the lanai and sat down without letting me know there were coming. Henry spoke first. "Matt, this isn't healthy. You need to start doing something."

Dominick added, "We're worried about you. You need do something. Just sitting here brooding isn't good."

"I'm fine. I just want to be left alone." I was serious. I wanted to be left alone.

John spoke. "If I set up a fishing trip back at that place in Alaska, would you go with me?"

I thought about it. It was true, I hadn't done a thing. I didn't care, I didn't want to care. But a fishing trip with John? I remembered a trip I took a long time ago with him and sitting on the dock one evening watching the sun go down. I remembered how long twilight lasts up there. In Florida the sun goes down and it's dark. There is very little twilight in the south.

"Yeah. I'll go with you. Set it up."

~ ~ ~ ~ ~

Sunsets were just as spectacular as they were the last time we were there. We sat every evening on the docks nursing a small, but nourishing. To tell the truth, they were a bit bigger than small. One evening John held up his glass and tipped it towards me. "I owe you an apology."

"How so?"

"Back in Portugal, I had no right to mention I had something I wanted you to do for me."

"I just hope you didn't say a thing to Walter."

John laughed. "No, I thought it over and realized it wasn't a good idea."

"Did your problem get resolved?"

"Yeah, Henry, Dominick and Lois took care of it."

"How is Lois doing?" I asked.

"Why, are you thinking of talking to her?"

"No! That's over. I was just curious how she was doing. If you're using her to take care of problems for you, I wanted to know she's safe."

"She's safe and so are the other two. Henry feels you don't call him anymore."

"Why? I used him to come up here."

"You know what I mean. We're all concerned about your well-being. We're all so sorry about Jennifer."

"Well, this trip is helping. Thanks John. I'm having a great time. You have been a butthead at times, but all in all, you're a good friend."

We clinked glasses and we watched the Pacific Ocean swallow the sun. Eventually we made our way back to our cabin. A couple of days later we had to head back to civilization. Orchard could only stay away from work for so long and then he couldn't stand it, he had to go back.

A month later I got a call from Lois early one morning. "Matt, this is Lois."

"Hello. What a nice surprise."

"Well, when you hear what I have to tell you, I don't think you will be so happy to hear from me."

Right then I knew I didn't want to hear what she had to say. "John had a massive stroke during the night, and he passed away. He never regained consciousness."

I understand death is another part of life's adventure, but it's getting more difficult for me to deal with. First Jennifer, then Max and now John. For the rest of the day, I sat on the lanai looking off down the river. I was aware when Val took the dogs out because my lap was empty for a while.

"Do you want dinner Mr. Matt?"

"No. I'm not hungry."

"Not good. You need to eat."

"Not tonight. Thanks."

I flew up to D. C. for John's funeral and for the first time Lois and I talked since our fall out over Portugal. The talk went well, and we parted friends. I was so pleased John, and I had our last fishing trip. It had provided perfect closure for me.

I returned to Florida late in the afternoon and I took an extra-long walk with the dogs. When we returned, it was time for bed. In the past I'd never let the dogs spend the whole night with me. They could be with me for a while and then it was off to their beds. Tonight, they both curled up against me and I let them stay. They knew I was hurting, and I knew they wanted to help me. Besides, I wanted their companionship.

I tried to stay busy. I had my poker night and my dogs. I'd found another 1932 Ford that needed restoration. It had a lot of dents, and the top was rotted away. The frame was bent but since the body was all steel, that could be repaired. I bought a new custom frame and a new crate motor for it, and then set about having it turned into a hot rod. Between poker with the guys and my hot rod, life was as full as I could hope for.

However, to be honest, I was still lonely.

I missed my Jennifer.

CHAPTER TWENTY-THREE
Present Day

There were several reasons for my visit to Seattle and I didn't want anyone to know. I took a regular airline flight and even if Henry had known about my visit, I'm sure he'd never tell, but still, I wanted to do it on my own.

Dad was in WWII as a combat pilot in the Pacific Theater and had lots of stories. Every few years the members of his squadron would get together and talk over old times. At their last reunion they were down to four members, and they decided it was time to end the reunions. The members kept track of each other, and until a month ago there was still one member alive. A couple of days ago I received a phone call from his widow telling me the last member had passed less than a month short of his 100th birthday. I wanted to see the widow and visit dad's grave, and mom's too, but most important was visiting Jennifer's resting place.

Since there isn't a lot to do on a commercial flight, I settled back in my seat and wandered through my memories of Pop's stories about the reunions and all the men who gave up their youth to go and fight for what they thought was right and to keep America free. So many didn't come back, but I was lucky, my father returned. Lucky because without his return, there wouldn't be any me or any of my tales.

I wondered how all those brave men and women would feel if they knew what our country was like today. Would they be unhappy they gave up their youth to defend our country for the way things are today?

The intercom told us to put tray tables and seats in an upright position and get ready to land. I was still mulling over the state of things today, and I was beginning to wonder if coming to visit was such a great idea, but I did want one last visit. I wished Jennifer was still alive and could have come with me and that seemed to set the mood for this visit even more.

The plane landed and as we taxied to the gate, looking out the window I could see rain falling. Yep, I was back in good old November Seattle. Dark, damp, dismal and dreary.

I located my rental and headed for the freeway. One reason for my visit was to see Jennifer's grave. I wanted to put her in my family's location, but she asked me to put her next to her father. There is a huge cemetery in North Seattle where her father Slim had purchased a triple site. This was going to be my last visit to Seattle, and I would stop to visit one last time.

At the last minute before I pulled onto the freeway, I remembered my previous visit and how crappy freeway traffic had become. I cut over at the US 99 exit deciding to take it through town. After sitting stuck in the middle of a traffic jam, I realized it really didn't matter which way I went, traffic was just as screwed up either way through town.

I parked in front of Jennifer's and Slim's graves and walked over to the granite bench I installed in front of them. Somebody had tagged the bench with graffiti. WTF, is nothing sacred? I sat for a time missing my Jennifer. Even though I dated a couple of women since her passing, it just wasn't time same. I missed her so much. Eventually I had enough and returned to the car.

~ ~ ~ ~ ~

I pulled into the parking lot at the Seattle Police department. There was just one place left to park, the Chief of Police's spot. My childhood friend Jeff Davenport's spot. I pulled in and parked. Walking away from the stall one of the officers hollered at me. "Hey, you can't park there. That's the chief's spot."

"I'm here to turn myself in, they're going to arrest me." I called back.

The officer looked strangely as I walked away. Jeff was in his office, but his secretary told me he was busy. I asked her to tell him he had public enemy number one waiting to surrender. She asked me to repeat what I said, and I did. She picked up her phone. "Chief, there is some crazy out here who wants to see you. Do you want me to have somebody come deal with him?"

"I'm coming out." I hear him say.

When he saw who it was, he rushed over and wrapped his arms around me. "I had no idea you were in town. Why are you here?"

"Well, I parked in your space. I came to turn myself in! And since you never come and see me anymore, I came to shame you." He laughed.

We went into his office and just before he shut the door, he said to his secretary, "Linda, make sure I'm not disturbed."

I could see the confusion on her face. "Okay chief."

We had a nice long talk. He told me he was going to retire in two months and his home over on the peninsula was about done being remodeled. I congratulated him on his retirement. He told me about Sakol and his passing. We both agreed how much we missed hearing his broken English. Jeff promised me he and his wife would come and visit, soon. By the end of my visit, we were back to the way we'd been when we were kids, best friends. One purpose of my trip was satisfied.

Another reason for the visit was to attend my 60th high school reunion. I texted Walter about the reunion and that I was in town. I told him where I was staying for the reunion and asked him if he could come over and see me for a day.

The next day as I headed out, I thought I had enough time to make it on time to the reunion, but I misjudged how bad traffic had become. The drive north took longer than expected and I arrived a half hour late, but everyone seemed happy to see me. The next couple of hours were spent reliving old school memories. I was surprised to see Digger's wife, Heather, but she knew a lot of Digger's friends and was invited to attend. The two of us shared a few small, but nourishing together remembering Digger and how much we both missed him. I had a room rented in the hotel, so I wasn't worried about trying to drive anywhere that evening.

It was wonderful seeing so many old friends. But along with that was the sorrow of remembering how many friends were no longer with us. The Viet Nam war claimed a lot of the guys in our class, and I felt a bit guilty because I made it back in one piece. I also saw a couple of my loves from school. Of course, they had no idea, their click then had nothing to do with my group, but privately I'd still lusted after them.

The next morning there was a knock on my door, when I opened it I was stunned to see the whole McLaughlin clan. Thein wrapped her arms around me and hugged me. "I've missed you."

Walter and I hugged. It was great to see the family. Standing just behind him was a tall familiar young man and a very lovely young woman. The young man stepped forward, extend his hand. "You look good Uncle Matt. It has been too long."

"Little Matt?" He nodded and I was stunned. "Oh my God, you are as tall as me and you've grown into quite a handsome man. What are you doing with your life?"

"I went to the University of Washington when I was 15, I petitioned for entrance. Since I'd been home schooled, I didn't have a high school diploma. I passed all their exams and was accepted. I completed my undergraduate studies in three years, and I just finished with med school. The problem is I'm just 22 and nobody takes me seriously. I'm supposed to start residency at a hospital on Pill Hill, but I think I want to look around for a while first. I'd like to spend some time chatting with you and hear more about some of the things you've done in your life."

"What! Are you serious? You want to know some of the things I've done?" He nodded. I looked at Walter, "What do you think of all this?"

"Later. We all want to spend some time with you."

I turned to the young woman. "You must be Tuyet?" She nodded. "You are just as lovely as your mother. What are you doing?"

She stepped froward and gave me a big hug. "I speak several languages and I'm thinking about living in New York and working at the United Nations. I took a battery of tests and passed them all and they have offered me a very attractive contract."

"Sounds good, but isn't there a special man in your life?"

"Yes, and I just hugged him." I laughed. "If I take the job in New York, will you come up and visit me from time to time?"

"Only if you will come to Florida and visit me."

"Deal." The five of us spent the day together and for dinner I took them to Hanney's Hideaway. It was perhaps one of the best meals I've ever had there. Being with the four of them was perfect. They took me back to my hotel and we all agreed they must come and visit me in Florida. I gave them Henry's private number and told them anytime they wanted to visit; a plane would be waiting for them at the airport.

The next day I wanted to satisfy a longing to revisit a part of my youth. I hadn't been back to the old neighborhood in a long time, and I wished to see it one final time. The years are piling up and time's running short. Chances are this would be my last visit. I waited for rush hour traffic to subside and then headed back toward Seattle.

In the middle of my old neighborhood is a park surrounding an old brick building which over the years has seen several uses. When I was in first grade, schools were being built as quickly as possible to accommodate Baby Boomers, and this is where I started first grade. I don't remember a thing about the teacher, but my parents were appalled I had to go to a park's clubhouse for school and switched me to a private boarding school. The school was southeast of Seattle and at night I could hear a train going through the valley. When you're homesick, hearing the lonesome whistle of a locomotive in the middle of the night doesn't help. I'd rather have stayed at the clubhouse, but who cares what a six-year-old wants?

One of the streets paralleling the park comes to a five-way intersection a block later. In the old days, you were just careful when you drove through the intersection. No big deal! Now, there's a traffic circle with signs warning you about the upcoming circle and who must yield and who has the right of way. I was amused that somebody felt the need for a traffic circle and even more amused there had to be signs instructing motorists on how to use the damn thing.

Have I turned into an old curmudgeon?

I parked in the clubhouse parking lot, took my cane from the car and started my walk through the old neighborhood. The weather matched my mood, rain let up slightly and was now a gentle mist, and the walk wasn't bad.

Each step brought back a flood of memories and I let myself float down the stream of sweet nostalgia. Most of the houses in the old neighborhood were in pretty good condition and as I passed them, I remembered childhood friends who'd lived there. After a couple of blocks, it dawned on me how many of my friends were no longer with us. Fond memories of them were still there, but now were tempered with the realities of what happened to so many.

Walking down the alley behind the old family home, I passed by another friend's house from childhood who passed away many years ago from the big C. Over the years we grew apart, but still, I missed not being able to talk to him. I stopped and looked up at his old house. The little tree out front we covered in Christmas lights when we were kids was huge now. I don't think we could afford to purchase enough lights to cover the tree. Ya' know, the house seemed so much smaller than I remembered.

The two vacant lots next to our old house now had houses built on them and the huge orchard where my dad grew fruit trees was gone. Dad's hobby was fruit trees, and as I recalled a couple of his trees were one of a kind. At one point, the orchard contained over fifty fruit trees. Now, the orchard was just a memory, except for the lone pear tree along the side the garage. I so wished I'd listened to Dad so I could remember the variety of that pear tree.

Our old home was re-roofed since my last visit with a lower grade of singles than Pop used, and it made the house look shabby. The old swimming pool was gone, long since filled in because it cost too much to fix it and digging it out and replacing it with a new one would cost even more. Remembering the old pool put a grin on my face. If only that old pool could talk. The tales it would tell.

Come to think of it, perhaps it's best the pool can't tell tales. I think I'm too old to be grounded, but I don't care to find out.

I passed by Digger's old home. It was nice to see the plantings around the house were kept up and the house had a new coat of paint. It looked great. Because I went to the 60th reunion, looking at Diggers house made me sad. I wish Digger was still with us, it would have been nice to see him. Judging by how I felt, I wondered how smart I'd been by going to the reunion. Did I really need to deal with this?

Thinking back to old school days, I fondly remembered Cheryl Quinn, who was one of the women who arranged the reunion. Cheryl was my secret crush back in junior high. I could still close my eyes and remember the first day of my seventh-grade math class and seeing her sitting by the window. Yeah, I had it bad, but in the junior high social strata, she was on a totally different level than me. At the time I doubt if she knew I existed. Also, there was Sherrell whom I admired from afar, but was too timid to even approach. She also was out of my league in my mind. At times I wish I could go back and redo so many things, but all in all, things turned out okay; they made for fond memories.

I continued my wanderings down familiar streets. The neighborhood looked the same, but not the same, if that made sense. In my head I could see so much of how it was, and I chose to overlook the changes.

The old white colonial Dad built, then moved up the hill behind us and sold to a vice-president at a bank which no longer exists, was still there. I remembered going with my parents up to his place on his 50th birthday. A portly man answered the door with his suit jacket off, his vest unbuttoned, shirt collar unbuttoned, his tie loosened and a drink in hand. I always thought that was what being fifty would look like. Since I've never looked like that, it must mean I haven't made fifty yet.

I wish!

Walking down the next block, I noticed a woman coming out of her house and walking to her mailbox. When I walked by, she turned to look at me. Surprise on her face as she asked, "Matt? Matt Preston? Is that you?"

"Yes." She looked familiar, but I couldn't put a name to the face.

"You don't recognize me, do you?"

Hearing her voice helped the coin drop. "Valery, Valery Lockwood." Her hair was a lovely shade of white and she still retained her alluring figure. "You look great! My God, Valery how are you?" We hugged.

In my mind it was now a warm summer night, and I slipped out of the house. We met and then ended up swimming together in our pool. Since neither of us had swimming suits with us, we went skinny dipping. At first Valery had a lot of body image issues. It was true there was a little baby fat, but I was so stoked that I was skinny dipping with a girl it didn't matter. I don't know where she learned to kiss, but she was incredible. I concentrated on telling her how sexy she looked and every time she brought up her weight, I assured her she was perfect. By the end of the summer, she'd lost some of her roundness and she was breathtaking in the moonlight. Seeing her now brought back a flood of memories. Wonderful memories.

"Considering my age, I can't complain. What are you doing back in the old neighborhood?" She asked.

"Takin' a trip down memory lane. I was in town, so I stopped to look over the old neighborhood." I frowned. "I'm starting to think it might have been a mistake. Too many changes. Do you still live here?" Pointing at her house.

"Yeah. My parents never sold the place. Mom died six years ago, and I came back and took care of Dad until he passed last year and left me the house. My husband died in a freak industrial accident many years ago, and with the insurance money and all, it has worked out well. Where do you live?"

"I have a place in North Fort Myers, Florida and I have a condo downtown. But I'm going to give up the condo since it's so far to travel, and the way Seattle is now, I don't want to be part of it. It isn't the city we grew up in!"

"I know. I feel the same way. But this house is paid for and living here works the best for me. I guess I'm stuck here. Did you ever get married?"

"Yeah, I tried it a few times and my last wife just recently passed."

"I'm so sorry."

I wanted to tell her more about Jennifer, but I didn't know how to start.

We both found, at the same time, we'd nothing left to say, and we were uncomfortable. I think she was remembering the nights we snuck out and went swimming and the rest of what happened. She turned and headed for her house. After a few steps she turned and smiled back at me. "It's been nice seeing you again Matt. Take care of yourself."

"You are still a very lovely woman. And you take care of yourself as well." I started to turn to walk away, but I stopped and looking back and watching her go into her house. A lot of happy memories floated around in my mind as I headed back to the car. Reminiscing about the nights I'd spent with Valery in our pool, the memoires were happy and fun, and I know I there was a smile on my face.

The day was turning cold which caused more pain in my legs, and hips. I leaned on the cane more. My time in Nam, and all the crazy stuff I did over the years was catching up with me. Ignoring it I push on, but I hurt.

The light mist turned back to rain, and I wasn't really dressed to be out wandering around, I needed to return to the rental car. Besides, it was getting late, and I needed food.

I still had the condo I leased from Mouse. Over the years he tried many times to gift it to me, but I always refused. Something told me this visit would be my last. I needed to clean out the condo and return the key to Mouse. As I climbed into my car, I remembered the old saying about how you can never go home again. I realized it was true. This was my neighborhood in my childhood, but not now.

Turning the key, the motor caught, and I sat for a moment waiting for the car to warm up. I looked out over the playfield and remembered being a child playing on the grounds. I was no longer a child; and the sandbox was long gone. It was time to leave, in so many ways. Backing the car out of the space I headed towards my condo downtown.

My face was wet, and it wasn't from the rain. I didn't know if it was from the realization of my age, or sadness over a spent youth, but I was feeling blue. What I thought might be an interesting trip to visit the old haunts wasn't turning out like I'd thought it would. I needed to finish my business and get back to Florida. Seattle was no longer home.

Driving to the condo building I was shocked at the number of empty buildings all boarded up downtown. It resembled a war zone. I heard things were bad, but I had no idea it was this bad. When I pulled into the condo portico, a person I never saw before greeted me. "Can I help you?"

"I have a condo here."

"How come I ain't seen you before?"

"I also have a place in Florida. I'm here for a few days. I don't know when I'll be leaving so, please keep the car available."

His uniform was dirty, and he needed a shave. Things sure had changed since my last visit. Walking towards the entrance I noticed the driveway was strewn with litter and when I stepped into the lobby there was nobody behind the main desk. The lobby was as filthy as the driveway and all the furniture that had been in the lobby was missing.

Stepping into a waiting elevator, I inserted my key for my floor and rode up to one floor from the top. The door opened and I was greeted with more trash. There are two condos on this floor, mine and someone I'd never met. I noticed the door was open to the other condo, so I peeked around the door. The condo was vacant, but the floor covered with trash. I took out the two keys needed to open my condo door, wondering what I would find.

Other than a layer of dust, my unit appeared untouched. Picking up the house phone I wanted to call Mouse; but the phone didn't work. I had a key to Mouse's level, and I took the elevator up one floor. His is the only unit on that floor so the elevator door opens into his front hallway. I stepped out and called his name. A heavy-set Hispanic woman came bustling out of the back. "What you doin' here? What you want?" She snapped at me.

"Is Mouse here?"

"Who you?"

"My name is Matt Preston and I'm a friend of Steve's. I have the unit just below this one."

"You stay there. I bring him." The woman turned and walked away.

Shortly Mouse came out. It had been a couple of years since I saw him at Jade's funeral. His hair was snow white, and he needed a cane. When he saw me, he grinned, came to me, and wrapped his arms around my waist. I heard his muffled voice, "Matt, oh Matt it's so good to see you."

I stood there with my arms wrapped around him for a long time. Finally, he stepped back, wiping tears from his eyes. I asked, "How are you?"

"Not so good. Things ache and the doctors keep telling me for a person my age I'm doing well. The horse's ass! Telling me that still doesn't make the aches any less." I nodded in agreement. "You know about Jade?"

"Remember I was at her funeral?"

"Oh yeah." Looking up at me with tears in his eyes, "I seem to have forgotten things. Sorry! Matt, I miss her so much. It just isn't the same without her. Part of me is missing and I find it difficult to go on." I understood since that's how I felt about Jennifer. I missed Jade as well; both were such special ladies.

Leading me to the living room he sat in one chair, and I sat in one across from him. He asked the maid to bring two cups of coffee. Frowning at both of us, she eventually turned and left.

"What's going on downstairs. The place is filthy and there's nobody in the lobby." I asked.

"Seattle is so bad nowadays. I can't find anybody who'll work. Between drugs and the homeless, it's dangerous under the portico, and besides, nobody wants to work anyway. Going into the basement is unsafe too. There have been a couple of people killed down there and on one floor is a homeless camp and the police tell me I can't interfere.

"I've lost count of how many units are vacant due to the crime on the streets around us. So many people have either sold, or if they can't sell, they just move away and leave their units. I'm looking for a new place. The city council won't do anything to clean up the city and one third of the police force has either quit or been laid off. This isn't the city I knew and loved."

"I understand. I just came back to clean out my unit, but I guess I'll just leave it as is. Mouse, if you want, I have room for you down in Florida."

"Thanks. I think I want to stick around. I go and visit Jade's grave every day. The area behind the cemetery is filled with homeless tents and I know it's dangerous to go there, but I can't leave her. I have a driver who is also my bodyguard."

"I understand. Remember, Jennifer's grave is out there too. My offer stands. Anytime you want, come and live with me. I have plenty of enough room for both of us."

We sat and looked at each other. There was really nothing more to say. We both felt we'd lived too long. I stood, "I'm going back to Florida. You know how to get a hold of the air service. Call them and they will bring you to me." Mouse stood and we embraced again. As I held him, I felt his sob. I gave him a hug, turned to leave.

I stood in the vestibule and thought about in my condo. Was there anything I wanted to take with me? I couldn't come up with a thing, so I didn't even bother to return. I rode the elevator down, got in my car and drove away. On the way to the airport, I called Henry. "Hey Matt, great to hear from you. What's happening?"

"I'm in Seattle and I'm going to Boeing Field. I want to go back to Florida, and I'll wait there until a plane can come and get me. Not to worry, there's no rush."

"What the hell are you doing in Seattle? How did you get there?"

"I came on my own, you know on a commercial airline. I wanted to see the old neighborhood, my old home and go to a class reunion. And you know something?"

"What?"

"It's true, you can't go home. Please call me when somebody can come and get me."

"I'm so sorry, Matt. I'll have somebody on the way to get you as soon as possible. The plane is in San Fran and it'll be there in less than two hours. They'll call on final approach."

I turned in my rental at Seattle/Tacoma Airport and called Uber to take me to Boeing Field. On my way to Boeing, I thought about taxis and Ubers.

What the hell is an Uber anyways?

I was ready, I was going home.

EPILOGUE

Henry was right on; just under two hours they called and told me the plane was on final approach. I watched it land and taxi up to me. The door opened and a lovely young lady got out, along with a pilot I'd never seen. The pilot was the color of coffee with cream and looked physically fit; I believe the term now days is *buff*. He smiled and extending his hand. As I took it, I felt the power in his grip. "Good afternoon, sir. My name is Darrell. We're supposed to take you to Florida."

"Hello Darrell, where are your two brothers, Darrell and Larry." Giving him a grin.

He looked at me for a moment and then shook his head. "Mr. Preston, do you have any idea how many times I've heard that joke?"

"Let me guess, I'm not the first?"

He continued shaking his head. "Not by a long shot. I hate that old television show."

I wondered how many people would understand the reference to the old show. "Sorry, I was trying to break the ice."

"Thanks anyway." He smiled. Darrell was handsome and the way he carried himself exuded confidence. It was plain to see why Henry hired him.

"Let's go." The two of them helped me into the cabin and once aboard I heard Henry holler out, "Come and sit up here with me."

With Darrell's help, I made my way to the right seat and sat down. I declined the young woman's offer of something to drink. By the time I was buckled in we were under way.

"I see we have a new pilot." I remarked to Henry.

"Yeah, and damn lucky to have him. He was drummed out of the navy."

"What! And you hired him?" My voice rose.

"There's a story behind what happened. Darrell was a top gun pilot. He was on patrol with his squadron off a carrier over in the middle East when his squadron was attacked. Their squadron leader chickened out and beat feet leaving the group to defend themselves. Darrell took over and shot down four enemy planes, saving the squadron. When he got back, in order to save his ass, the squadron leader filed trumped up charges against Darrell. The squadron commander was a navy academy grad and his buddies pulled strings to make sure the charges against Darrell would stick. He was offered the choice of leaving the service or facing a court martial."

"How come that never made the news?"

"Matt, there are a lot of things going on over there that never make the news. Anyway, when I heard about Darrell, I hired him at once. There are people who know the true story about him, and they use our service just because of him. He is amazing."

"He sure looks buff."

"I know!" Henry grinned at me, and I laughed. "Yeah, but that's not the reason I hired him." Henry winked and I shook my head. "He's usually working in either Europe or the Middle East and is very valuable to us."

I was pleased to know we were still growing, and we had pilots like Darrell working for us.

The trip back to Florida was fast and I napped for part of it. Even still, there was time to just stare out the window and brood. The trip had been a lot like all of our lives. There were the sad parts but seeing Walter and his family and how well they all turned out were the happy parts. They made the trip totally worth it.

Henry reached over once and patted my leg expressing how sad he was about my visit back home. I acknowledged his condolences.

"Are you okay?" He asked.

"Yeah, I guess."

"I hate to see you so blue. Wish there was something I could say."

"I was expecting something else from my trip. I don't know exactly what I was looking for, but it wasn't there. Anyways, it was my fault for having expectations." I snorted. "I just wasn't ready to grow up yet."

Henry chuckled. "Matt, you'll never grow up."

We landed at Fort Myers and Darrell and Henry helped me out of the plane. I shook Darrell's hand and thanked him for joining our little group.

"Sir, I'm the one who should thank you. Henry and the rest of the group have made me feel welcome. And if I might add, you pay me a shit ton better than the navy ever did." That I knew was true.

Since my car was still over at the other airport, I asked Henry if he had somebody who could drive me home. Darrell spoke up. "Sir, I'd love to drive you home." Darrell walked me over to a restored 1962 Corvette parked in the pilot's lot.

"This is yours?" Stunned by the condition of the old car.

"It's my baby. Get in and I'll take you home. I purchased it with my bonus from my last mission for the company." I didn't know what the mission was, but if it paid well enough for him to purchase this classic, it must have been one hell of a mission. I got in and the smile on my face never left for the ride home.

My new housekeeper Betty was pleased to see me, and Thunder was even more overjoyed. I had to put Lightning down last year, but considering they came from a puppy mill, it turned out well and both lived a long and healthy life.

Betty helped me to my favorite chair on the lanai. Thunder put her paws on my legs begging to be picked up. Betty picked her up and sat her on my lap. After she gave a happy grunt, she promptly settled in. "Bring you coffee Mr. Matt?"

"Would you bring me a Scotch? You know how I like it."

"Doctor say…"

"Betty, please forget what the doctor said." She looked down at me shaking her head as if to scold me. "Please, just bring me a Scotch."

Betty held up her hands. "Okay Mr. Matt. Not good for you, but I do."

"Thank you, mom." She smiled at me and shook her finger.

Betty brought me my drink and from the size it looked like a double. What a wonderful woman. She placed it next to my chair and asked if I needed anything else. "No, I'm good"

As I sat there looking out over the river, I felt my cell phone vibrate in my pocket. It was Mouse. "Hey you, what's up?" I asked.

"Were you serious about me coming and living with you?"

"Of course. I'd love to have you here. I have a lot of room. What's going on?"

"I was just visiting Jade's grave and a couple of home-less bums tried to hit me up for a handout. When I wouldn't give them anything, things got violent. One of them was no problem, but lucky for me I had my driver with me, and he ran the other one off. Matt, I don't want to live here anymore. This is no longer Seattle. This is not home. If you'll have me, I'd like to come down and stay with you."

"I have plenty of room for you. I'll call Henry and he'll arrange for somebody to come and pick you up. Watch for his call letting you know when someone will arrive."

There was a long silence. When he spoke, I heard a sob in his voice. "Matt, you've been an amazing friend. Thank you."

"Hurry and get down here." I was getting choked up myself.

We hung up. I called Henry and set up a ride for Mouse. I tried to get over it, but I was still bummed about Seattle. I'd felt not one good thing had come out of it, except for my visits with Jeff and the McLaughlin clan. But now I'd be able to take care of Mouse. That made me feel good.

Being in Seattle also made me more appreciative of my little nest in Florida. I continued petting Thunder, listening to her grunts of happiness. That was comforting and Mouse was coming, Walter and his clan were all doing well and that made me very happy. The thought that Tuyet and Little Matt might come to visit put a smile on my face. I was coming out of my funk.

It was a long time before I took a big sip of my drink. It was sometime since I had a drink and it hit me fast and hard. I wasn't fall down drunk, but after a couple of sips I could feel effects of the Scotch.

Yeah, Seattle turned ugly. Not my problem. I weighed how I felt about Seattle's problems with the rest of my life. I did a lot of interesting things and been to a lot of amazing places. I did things most men never even dream about. I'd bedded a lot of lovely women and even married three of them. I found the love of my life. I was on first name basis with a past president of the United States. If I was still interested, I had access to several top levels of our national security. I have more than enough money to take care of myself.

True, it's lonely being alone, but after Jennifer, I'm not interested in another woman. And now I would have a roommate. In addition to all of that, I have a network of friends who live in the complex around me, and I know they care. All the McLaughlin clan promised to come and visit too. I took another sip of my drink and petted Thunder. My eyes started to close.

I was back home in Florida, and I was at peace.

Reflecting, I have to say my life has been great and I'm happy and content.

Very content!

When my time arrives and I get to join Jennifer and my dogs, I'm ready…

My hope for you cherished reader is that you are as content with your life when your time comes.

And now dear friends, this will be ……..

THE END

PS: And so, another Matt Preston adventure is completed. Matt and I would like to thank you for your interest in all our stories. This probably will be the last in the Matt Preston series, I feel I've taken Matt as far as I can, and Matt has requested I retire him. It seems his body can't take another adventure.

Right now, I'll have to see if any new characters come to mind. Presently, I don't know if I'll write another story.

As always, thank you for your previous interest. Remember, without you there would have been no Matt Preston.

Good night …

ABOUT THE AUTHOR

Paul lives in North Fort Myers, Florida with his wife and biggest fan, Sandy. Along with their two beautiful American Cocker Spaniels, Bijou and Boots, better known as "The Kids".

Born and raised in Seattle, and now transplanted to Florida, in addition to writing, Paul keeps busy learning ballroom dance, and working on an HO scale train layout. Another interest is his 1932 Ford Tudor which is in the process of being re-built, for the second time.

A graduate of Western Washington University in Education, Paul taught for four and a half years and became self-employed when he left teaching. Over the years, Paul has owned and operated many businesses where he met many interesting people who always seem to confide the most astonishingly personal information to him, hence the varied knowledge of people, parts of which he uses to create his fictional characters.

To contact Paul Shadinger, please email him at pshadingerauthor@outlook.com. He enjoys hearing from his fans.

ACKNOWLEGEMENTS

As always, I dedicate this novel to everyone who has read any of my novels and continues to encourage me to keep writing. I don't know if it was because they enjoyed reading about Matt Preston, or they figured if I wrote enough, I just might improve. Without a doubt, none of my novels would exist without your words of inspiration, encouragement, and support. Positive words are truly food to any author, and I cannot begin to describe the number of banquets so many of you have provided. Thank you all for your wonderful comments and inspiration. I've said in the past I would love to make a list of everyone who has encouraged me, but for fear I might forget someone which would be inexcusable, so I will refrain. Thanks to all of YOU for your kind words. They mean a great deal.

I'd like to thank my editor, Ellen Campbell. I was very lucky to find her. She has put up with me and has taught me to be a much better writer. I'm beholden to her for everything she has done for me over the years. Ellen, you're one of a kind.

I'd like to thank Kevin G. Summers. Kevin helped design my covers and changed my words into the bits and bytes and whatnots which allows this novel to be printed and sent out in Kindle and print form. It's said you can't judge a book by its cover. True! But if the cover isn't attractive, people will not pick it up and look at it. Kevin has created great covers for my series, and I'm grateful for his efforts.

All my novels are dedicated to my wife, Sandy. The book you have in your hands is a testament to her faith in me. She saw something in my writing I never saw. Without her encouragement, I'd never have started, or continued to write. Without her, Matt Preston would have never seen the light of day. Thank you dear.

Thank you to my youngest daughter, Robyn who also happened to be one of my biggest fans. Without her constant "Is it done yet? Is it done yet?", this novel would have taken longer than it has. Okay Robyn, here it as, now give me a break!

I'd also like to thank the real Digger, Burt Fraley. Almost every conversation we have Burt would ask when the next novel was coming out. I'd also like to thank him for all the PR he has done for me over the years as he spread the word about my books. Thank you Burt.

And finally, I dedicate my books to all my faithful Cocker Spaniels. First to Buttons who was my inspiration for BJ in *Houseboat* and to the others: Pepper who we lost way too soon, Max, Brenna and Samantha who are waiting for me at the rainbow bridge. All of them are greatly missed.

During the last novel we took on two new puppies: Bijou, which means jewel in French, and Boots because she's all black with four white feet. I'm grateful to Bijou for keeping track of how long I work at my desk and notifying me when it's time to stop and take her outside by putting her paw on my hip. Without her, I'd keep working for who knows how long. Thanks little one. And to my precious little Miss Wiggle Butt, Bootsie you really are one of a kind. When she sees you, her tail starts to wiggle and then her whole-body quivers in joy and the anticipation of being petted. How can you beat that kind of love?

Animals enrich our lives so much, and yet cause so much pain when we must send them over the rainbow bridge. They give so much more than they ask of us. Regardless of how our day went, when we come home, they act like the best thing that will ever happen to them, just happened. They're always overjoyed to see us return. How do you beat that? I know all my dogs are waiting for me over the rainbow bridge.

Thank you for reading my novel. I hope you enjoy it.
Regards,
Paul Shadinger
NFM 2022

THANK YOU

Thank you for reading *Seven Ghosts*. If you enjoyed this novel, I would appreciate it if you would help others enjoy this book too. Some ways to share it are:

Recommend it: Please share this book by recommending it to friends, reader groups and discussions boards which help readers find books. It can also be found in Kindle Unlimited at Amazon.

Review It: Please post a review on one or more of the websites or pages listed below. Even a short review will do, tell others what you liked about this book. Also please tell your friends! (If you didn't like it, let Matt know… Just kidding. An author lives for feedback of all kinds)

AMAZON:
https://www.amazon.com/author/paulshadinger

Or call up the purchase page for this novel and click on the book cover. From there scroll down the page and find the 'Review this Product' button to leave a review.

Goodreads:
https://www.goodreads.com/book-review/pshadingerauthor

Readers Favorites

https://www.readersfavorites.com/book-reviewSevenG-hosts

Follow Paul on:
https://www.facebook.com/pshadingersuthor

TWITTER: @paulshadinger

AND

Paul's Website
https://www.paulshadingerauthor.com